STUPID FAST

GEOFF HERBACH

sourcebooks
fire

Published by Sourcebooks Fire, an imprint of Sourcebooks, Inc.

P.O. Box 4410, Naperville, Illinois 60567-4410

(630) 961-3900

Fax: (630) 961-2168

teenfire.sourcebooks.com

Library of Congress Cataloging-in-Publication data is on file with the publisher.

Printed and bound in the United States of America.

VP 10 9

For Leo and Mira, the best kids ever

CHAPTER 1:
NOW

This could be a dark tale!

It's not.

I don't think so.

Maybe.

I can't sleep. It's 1:03 a.m. Almost September. The weather is warm, even though it's football season. There's this huge moon in the sky, but I can't see it from the basement, where my bedroom is. I saw it plenty.

Tonight.

Dark tale? My dad did commit suicide.

Not so dark? I'm me. I hop up and down.

Where to start?

Not in the '70s, when Jerri was a little girl. Not ten years ago, when I was five and found Dad dead in the garage. How about last November?

I should really be exhausted. But I'm not.

I, Felton Reinstein, stand on my bed because I can't sleep.

Go.

CHAPTER 2:
MY BODY GREW HAIR

I am not stupid funny. I am stupid fast.

My last name is Reinstein, which is not a fast name. But last November, while I was a sophomore, my voice finally dropped, and I grew all this hair on my legs (and other places) and then I got stupid fast. I'm serious.

Before my voice dropped in the fall, when my class was outside for gym, I played flag football and felt like trying for some reason. I was pretty good because even though I hadn't yet fully gone through puberty like all the chuckleheads in my grade, and never tried before and wasn't even interested in the slightest, I've always been good at sports (a fact I hid by not trying) but not ridiculously good.

Then Thanksgiving came, and I couldn't stop eating and I couldn't wake up before like noon, which drove Jerri nuts, and I grew taller and got all this crazy hair.

The hair was like corn coming up in June. You look one day and there are sprouts in the dirt, but mostly, you see dirt, and then like a week later, those sprouts aren't sprouts but corn and are already knee-high and you can't see the dirt at all.

I ate too much at Thanksgiving, about a thousand pounds, and I couldn't wake up in the morning, and I sprouted hair. A week later, I had a thousand pounds of hair everywhere.

Then because my voice dropped, I got moved to baritone for the Christmas concert, which was bad news because I didn't know the parts at all, so I sang the tenor parts except an octave below, which you could totally hear.

And it went on. I kept sleeping and eating, and Jerri yelled at me to get out of bed, and I yelled at Andrew to stop playing the piano so I could sleep. So Jerri yelled at me for yelling at Andrew and I'd get pissed and get out of bed and go to the refrigerator and stuff bread in my mouth because I was so hungry. Then Jerri would yell at me for eating too fast, and Andrew would shout "Felton's a pig!" and on and on all winter—my pants getting too short and my shirts looking shrunken, not covering my belly button, which is gross (Jess Withrow and Abby Sauter told me it was gross), and Jerri and Andrew shouting at me and me shouting back.

Jerri never yelled before November.

And then in the spring, my gym class had to go outside to run the 600 yard dash for some physical fitness test thing (apparently the last one we ever have to do), and I was just mad, all wound up from all the yelling and my clothes not fitting right, and when Coach Knautz, the gym teacher, yelled go, I took off. I ran like an angry donkey, a very fast one, even though I didn't care about winning. I just needed a release. I sprinted all 600 yards. And I beat everybody, even the other fast kids, by about 150 yards. People were screaming, "Look at Rein Stone go!" Peter Yang, my second best friend, whispered, "What happened to you?"

"Hee-haw!" I shouted and pumped my fist.

Peter Yang rolled his eyeballs and walked away.

• • •

Jerri—who happens to be my mom but also a big hippy who doesn't like hierarchy, so she's always had me and Andrew call her by her first name—was all puffy and weird during dinner that night. She was a crossing guard at the middle school at the time. The middle school is right next to the high school but lets out a little earlier so the high school kids don't scare and beat the pee out of the middle school kids. She was out there on the corner when I ran the 600. She saw it. I could hear her screaming from the corner. "Run, Felton! Go! Oh my God!"

"Felton," she said, serving me and Andrew whole grain, organic macaroni and cheese, "Listen. You need to do something about that speed of yours."

"Oh," I said, digging in.

"Are you listening to me? Really, Felton. That speed is a gift… from the Universe…and I know you need to be who…need to be who…" She sat down at the table and stared up at the ceiling.

"Who, Jerri?" I asked.

"I heard you're fast, Felton," Andrew nodded at me.

"I'm eating macaroni here," I said. "Mind your own business."

"You're super fast, Felton Reinstein," Jerri nodded. She spoke really quietly. "It's like you're Jamaican instead of…the son of a small, sad Jewish dude."

She was referring to me and Andrew's father, who was already long dead but was in life—so we were to believe—not built for speed.

I thought for a moment before sticking more macaroni in my face.

"Were you fast, Jerri?"

"No. Not fast. I played guitar and read poetry. You've got a gift from the...from your...from the Universe, Felton."

"I'm not fast either," said Andrew. "Of course, I wouldn't want to be. Athletic prowess is a curse, I think."

"What the hell do you know?" I glared at him. He stared back at me through his big, plastic nerd glasses. "You're a punk middle schooler."

"It's just the way I feel," he said.

"No, Andrew. Wrong," Jerri said.

"I simply think sports are bad for a young man," Andrew said.

"No, goddamn it," Jerri said all hot and red-faced, "We...We have to support...what the Universe provides. Do you understand me?"

"You shouldn't swear, Jerri," Andrew said.

"Just shut up, Andrew," Jerri said.

"Don't say shut up," Andrew shouted back.

"I'm sorry," Jerri said, looking down.

"Dad wasn't a Jamaican Jew, was he?" I asked.

"No," Jerri frowned. "Your father was a sweet, fat American Jew." Then she stood up from the table, walked to the sink, and dropped her bowl of whole grain, organic macaroni into it. I didn't even see her take a bite.

Jerri was acting a little freaky. This might have been a sign to me, but I didn't really pay attention because she was standard issue weird forever (big hippy sandals, organic turnip soup, drumming circles, making us call her Jerri). But freaky? Not really. Well, maybe a little. Sometimes. Off and on.

• • •

Jerri wasn't the only one acting weird. Coach Knautz pulled me out of biology the next day. He knocked on Mr. Willard's door, pointed at me while the whole class stared, and then said he had to have a word in private. Private? That's a gross word. It reminds me of bathrooms and people's privates all hanging out. Gross.

I was scared. I hadn't gotten in trouble since eighth grade, when I took a bathroom stall apart with a screwdriver (totally grounded from TV and suspended for three days, which ended my life of crime and vandalism), and I couldn't imagine why a coach would pull me out of class. He walked me down the hall without saying a word. He took me into the gym offices in total silence. He sat me down across the desk from him and then stared at me and shook his head and breathed through his big nose.

"Yes…uh…sir?" I asked.

"Listen, Reinstein, I have never seen anything like it." (Nose breath.)

"Like what?" I said meekly. I was completely shaking in my shoes because I thought I must've done something horribly terrible.

"I have never seen a kid run so damn fast in the fitness test," he said.

"Ohhhhh," I breathed easier. "Yeah. Jerri is pretty excited."

"Who?"

"My mom."

"Right. Jerri. And she's right to be excited, Reinstein. I've been

6

doing this for twelve years, and I have never seen anything like it. Ken Johnson wasn't even close to as fast as you, and he took two firsts at State last year."

"I know," I said, without any enthusiasm, I might add. Why? Ken Johnson has always been a jerk. The summer after eighth grade, Ken Johnson shoved me off my Schwinn Varsity, which he called a stupid bike because he said my brake lever scratched his car, which maybe it did, but only because he parked like a jerk so I couldn't get my bike past him. Ken Johnson.

"I'm guessing you're a sprinter," Coach Knautz nodded, "just by the way you run. I'm guessing you're really built for 100 meters or maybe 200."

"Maybe," I said, still not knowing what he was getting at.

Mr. Knautz's eyes were watery. He nodded more. He was sweaty.

"You have to do something with your God-given speed. You have to go out for track," he said.

"Oh," I said. I squinted and thought, those locker room lights beating down on my head, *Hmm. Am I going to say yes to this silliness? Hmmmm.* I wouldn't have said yes, but I had Jerri's voice echoing in my head from the macaroni dinner *(the Universe…the Universe…the Universe)*, and I thought about Andrew all arrogant and superior, even though he's just a punk kid, and there was this poster hanging on the wall behind Coach Knautz (I was squinting at it) with this dude running in the desert with the word ACHIEVE underneath him, and I was emotionally moved by it, which is ridiculous, I know, but whatever. And, yes, I wanted Jerri to be proud of me. Andrew has his thing, his piano, which everyone loves him for. Jerri's so proud of Andrew. Jerri has never seemed proud of me. I mean, man, what young son doesn't want his mom to be proud of him even if he has to call her Jerri? *(The Universe, Felton…the Universe…)*

So I said, "Uh, okay, sounds good," which caused Coach Knautz to punch his fist in the air, shout yes, and then try to high-five me.

• • •

So even though track season was half done by that time, and even though I had no intention before to do anything but eat and sleep and grow hair on my body and practice my completely lame and humorless standup routine (I'll get to this later), and even though I've always thought that track is dumb because you just run like you're a scared buffalo getting chased by hyenas on Animal Planet, I joined the team.

It was right to do so.

I was totally nervous about it. The juniors and seniors have always been jerks.

But seriously, I did pretty well.

In fact, right away, it became obvious, even though my last name is Reinstein and not something Jamaican like Bolt or Lightning or Nitro or Napalm, that I'm sincerely fast. Actually, it turned out that I am so fast that I made varsity in the 100 meters, which pissed off a couple of seniors, *boohoo*, but it wasn't my fault. (Coach Knautz kept me off the relays for political reasons, he said.) It turned out I could already run almost as fast as that jerk Ken Johnson.

All the rest of the spring, a growing crowd of sweaty dudes who looked like Coach Knautz—balding, wearing those elastic coach shorts pulled halfway up their fat bellies because they're also coaches, albeit football coaches—kept coming up to me, saying, "I've never seen anything like it. You're what, fifteen?"

All the rest of the spring, Jerri kept yelling from her crossing guard position out on the corner or from the stands at other schools or from next to Andrew at big invitational meets, where I always placed a closer and closer second right behind Ken Johnson. "Run, Felton! Go!" (Even as she got freakier at home.) And all spring long, all the jocks in my grade, especially Cody Frederick, who I always thought smelled like an old urinal cake in a locker room (sorry), kept saying, "Can't wait for football. You're going out, right, Reinstein? We're going to kick some ass in the fall."

"I guess," I'd tell them.

I did not enjoy the jock bus rides. I missed Gus, my first best friend, who sometimes sat on the hill watching track practice, shaking his head in disapproval. But I loved to run. *Loved it.*

Fast like donkey. Very fast. Zing!

• • •

But then at Regionals, the qualifier for the State meet, because I was filled with donkey adrenaline that made me shake, because I knew—seriously understood—that I'd gotten as fast as that jerk Ken Johnson and I had a good shot at beating him and making him feel like the jerk he is, I false-started twice—yes, two times— and was disqualified and then—oh, I'm not proud—I cried and blew chunks right there by the track. I did. Vomited. And then... drum roll...it was all over.

Ken Johnson whispered "Head case."

A couple other seniors whispered "Squirrel Nuts," for that was my nickname with the upper classes.

Coach Knautz said, "Another year of experience and that won't happen to you, my boy."

Gus showed up outside the locker room and said, "You should quit stupid track because it's foolish and dumb," because track made it so I didn't have time to drive around with him and Peter Yang. He didn't have to say that, by the way. Track was done for me for the year.

And Cody Frederick said, "We'll kick ass come fall, Reinstein."

For the next five days, I stayed home. I didn't go to school because I was wrecked by the false starts. I didn't barf anymore, but I felt sick. I felt sweaty. I couldn't eat. I couldn't rest. Moist sheets. Disgusting. Didn't smell good. Jerri paced around the house all day while I lay there. She only stopped pacing to stare at me (or to go be a crossing guard for an hour). By day six, I was pretty hungry, so I ate a couple of bagels.

And that was that. No more track. Sophomore year was almost over. Summer was almost here.

While track was going, I felt I had a reason for getting out of my bed: Beat Ken Johnson. Without track, I was back to lying in bed wondering if I'm funny. (I really wanted to be a comedian…maybe I still do.)

CHAPTER 3:
PROOF IN MAY I
SHOULDN'T BE A COMEDIAN

A.

Nobody laughed at my jokes except for Gus, who is my best friend. He thinks I'm hilarious, of course, but he's been my best friend forever, so he's biased. My so-called second best friend, Peter Yang? He never laughed at anything. What funny man would hang out with a dude who never laughs?

B.

In seventh grade, I did the school talent show, and I ripped a routine right square out of my *Jerry Seinfeld Live on Broadway: I'm Telling You for the Last Time* DVD and nobody laughed. Jerry Seinfeld is hilarious. He's a comic genius. Everybody laughs at him. I did his shtick, and I got nothing except for Ben Schilling shouting at me to get off the stage (yes, he got detention) and also a couple of other kids booing. That means the bearer of the jokes wasn't funny (I was the bearer, if you didn't get that).

C.

When I talked, I often talked way too fast, sometimes so fast I even annoyed myself (not to mention others), especially when I talked too fast in my head, which, for most of my life, I have done

24/7, which is not funny. This can still be a problem. *Shut up, voice in head*. Not funny! Not funny! Seriously, not funny.

• • •

Let us address some larger issues, shall we?

My dad must be part of this discussion:

I used to think about my dad a lot. I used to think he was with me wherever I went, and that made me feel good. I used to ask him for help and ask him to keep me safe, which is weird. He's dead. I thought a ghost was keeping an eye on me.

Aha! When I was eleven, it occurred to me that he killed himself (I found him when I was five), so he obviously didn't want to be with me at all because he made sure he'd never see me again no matter what, so I stopped kidding myself that my dad's ghost was hanging around taking care of me. Hanging around is a bad way to put it.

Ha ha.

See? None of that's funny.

• • •

Let's address the bonfire.

There really aren't any pictures of Dad left because when I was seven, Jerri had this giant bonfire to help me and Andrew "let go of the past." We listened to Celtic music and burned Dad's books and shirts and photo albums, etc. Just about everything. (Not totally everything.)

You can't burn memories, Jerri. I guess you know that now.

I have some memories.

Here's a memory:

One time, when I was maybe four, Dad put me in our old Volvo station wagon (a car Jerri got rid of around the time of the bonfire, even though I screamed "Noooo!") and drove us out to the big Mound east of town (an important Mound). I sat down at the bottom while Dad jogged up and down it, which doesn't make a lot of sense given what I knew about Dad from Jerri (a short, fat dad). He jogged, and I played in the dirt or whatever, and he jogged, and I remember shouting at him, "Daddy! Daddy!" etc., and he jogged. When he stopped, he was all sweaty, and he walked over to me and whispered, "That's better. That's better." Then he said, "What the hell are you doing, Felton?" I believe I was eating a rock. I remember the Volvo smelled funny on the drive back because he was so sweaty. Not exactly like Cody Frederick funny but sort of. When we got home, Dad said, "Thanks for accompanying me, buddy." That was nice.

I really loved that car—it was freaking huge—but Jerri said it had bad vibes. So it went away like all Dad's pictures.

I do have some memories though. Not funny ones.

• • •

Let's delve into Jerri a bit!

While I was home from school sweating and not eating after my Regionals screw-up, Jerri, between her crossing guard shifts, often stood at the landing of the stairs that lead into the basement, where my room is and where I watch TV. She would stand there and watch me sleeping. Except, I wasn't asleep. I was watching Comedy Central. I would pretend to sleep when I'd hear her creep down the stairs so I wouldn't have to talk to her (as she had taken to saying very weird things, very incomprehensible things that my brain did not understand). I'd squint my eyes so they looked closed, but they were open just enough to continue watching Comedy Central. Sometimes, she'd stand there looking at me for a whole episode of *MADtv*, and I'd get uncomfortable and want to move, but I didn't because her freakiness was freaking me out. Sometimes, I could hear her swallowing, like she was crying or something, which was totally weird. I got disqualified from a stupid track meet, for God's sake. I was pretty upset, but it wasn't so tragic that my mom should've been crying about it.

You know what? Of course she wasn't crying about the track meet. I was just a dumb kid back in May.

One day, she stood there for like an hour, swallowing and staring, and it just got to be too much. I had an itch on my leg and couldn't hold on anymore, so I said, "Can I help you, Jerri?"

She flinched and said, "No…just checking on you."

"Okay!" I said.

"I don't think it's bad to be in sports, Felton."

Why the hell would it be? Incomprehensible!

Then she went upstairs.

Incomprehensible jokes aren't funny, by the way.

* * *

And, finally, let's address Bluffton.

Disclaimer: Jerri says I shouldn't say "retard" all the time because it's disrespectful to people who have really low IQs, but that's not what I'm talking about, you know? I sincerely apologize to anyone I offend by saying "retard." Okay: There have been times when I truly feel like

I'm a retard and that everybody thinks I'm retarded, and because they think I'm retarded, I get nervous and I act like a retard, which simply fulfills their expectations. It's a big circle. The retarded circle of my life.

Am I retarded? Well...

I am a Reinstein. I live on the outskirts of a small town in southwestern Wisconsin on ten acres from which I can see the town's little country club and golf course—which I've called ugly. From my home, I can also see all the alcoholic, blithering golf dads who swear and scream.

I blamed my dad for this situation, for abandoning us here by hanging himself in the garage. And I also blamed Jerri because she's from here and should've known better. I believe Bluffton, Wisconsin, is a terrible place.

On good days, this is what I've thought: I'm not retarded. Bluffton is retarded. It has a dumb little college, which is why my dad came here (to teach). Mostly all the students at the dumb little college are dumb, and they think they're king shit or whatever because they're drunk and walking around shouting and in college. Other than the college, Bluffton has a dumb main street, where kids my age stand around staring at each other, or, if they're old enough and have access to a car, they drive up and down the street, staring at the dumb kids staring at each other. Sometimes, they drive to Walmart, which is really big. Bluffton also has a McDonald's and a Subway and a Pizza Hut and a combo KFC–Taco Bell. (KenTacoFrickinBell—retarded.) And there are lots of hills and lots of farms outside the city limits and lots of farmers who drive their pickup trucks and smell like poop and lots of black and white cows standing on the hills staring at you like you're a retard or like you're a kid on main street.

And listen to this: I never even minded cows. I never minded poop-smelling farmers, even though they can be mean and gross (they blow snot out of their noses onto the snow). Farmers and their poop-smelling kids are not why Bluffton has seemed retarded and why me and my friends have called it Suckville.

Me, Peter, and Gus (my only friends forever) figured the facts out in eighth grade. The reason we wanted to rename Bluffton *Suckville* is because of the town kids: the public school teachers' kids and the lawyers' kids and the doctors' kids and the cops' kids and the insurance salespeople's and the bankers' kids and the orthodontist's daughter, Abby Sauter, who has been very mean.

"They're all dumb and annoying!" we shouted. "They're the retarded ones!" we said. They honestly do think they're the special children of God. Gus calls these kids honkies. I don't know why, but it makes me laugh. Even now. Honkies.

We aren't honkies (maybe I am). Me, Peter, and Gus are college kids (that is, kids of college professors).

At least, I used to be.

We are a minority! We are oppressed!

At least, I used to be. I'm crazy.

Gus and I tried to write a horror movie script last year titled *The Retarded Honkies of Suckville!* We wrote two pages actually. Gus wrote some good jokes.

I didn't write any jokes because I wasn't funny.

Gus is hilarious. Gus could be a great standup comic right now, even though he doesn't want to be. He's really small, and he's got this wad of black hair that's always sort of long, and he ducks his head so his bangs cover his eyes so he can hide the fact that he thinks everybody is just dumb. I know he's under his hair rolling his eyes and making faces. Everybody else knows too. He used to drive the junior and senior honkies crazy because they knew he was making fun of them, but they couldn't catch him because his hair wad was in front of his eyes. He's so dang funny, hugely hilarious, which is the greatest compliment I can give anybody.

He also left for the summer, which threatened to make Bluffton double Suckville, maybe triple Suckville, as I wasn't exactly in love with Peter Yang, who was my remaining friend.

Not funny. Not funny. Not funny.

A comedian? I don't think so.

• • •

It's 1:20 a.m. I am not sleepy.

CHAPTER 4:
THE TERRIBLE PHONE CALL
OF LATE MAY!

This is how the summer began.

Imagine this:

It's the Saturday before the last week of school. I'm lying downstairs on the couch outside my bedroom, down in the basement, lights out, resting with my thoughts and the TV, and sweating hugely because of my disqualification at Regionals. Andrew's upstairs in the living room playing about ten annoying notes on the piano, over and over, singing along with them, totally off-key and very loud, which he does a lot, which I find excessively annoying. The phone rings. Jerri answers, her voice echoing throughout the house.

"Oh, no. I'm so sorry, Teresa." Jerri says *Teresa* in her best Spanish accent, *Tayraysa*, even rolling the *r*.

Jerri thinks she knows Spanish because she took hippy drumming lessons from a dude named Tito a few years ago. *Tayraysaaa.* Teresa happens to be Gus's Venezuelan mom.

I sit up, which isn't easy as I'm weak from not eating. *Is something wrong with Gus?*

"Of course, *Tayraysa*. Felton can do Gus's paper route. He really needs to re-engage."

Paper route? Re-engage? Oh, no. Jerri said re-engage, which is code for torture Felton.

Gus's ridiculous paper route? Torture!

My stomach is rumbling, churning, burning, almost ready to upchuck, except there's no food inside of me.

What if something is wrong with Gus?

"I'll have Felton call later this morning, *Tayraysa*," Jerri says.

I leap from the couch and run upstairs just as Jerri is hanging up the phone.

"What the hell, Jerri? What's wrong?"

"Felton, Gus is leaving."

"What do you mean? When?"

"Next weekend. *Tayraysa's* mother is gravely ill. "

"Yeah? She's been sick since third grade. So freaking what?"

"The doctors don't think she'll make it through the summer, so the Alfonsos are going to Venezuela to be with her."

"Aw, hell! What am I supposed to do all summer?"

"You can help Gus out. He needs a friend."

"Who am I gonna chill with, Jerri?"

"Gus needs help with that route."

"Paper route? Come on! He doesn't give a crap."

"Well, *Tayraysa* does. And I do."

"You?"

"Yes. So you're going to help Gus out, do you understand?"

"Aw, man! Jesus Christ! Come on!"

Meanwhile, Andrew's plinking the piano behind me, still singing along with those ten notes.

Blah la la blah. Plink plink plink.

"Shut your freaking piano, Andrew. We're in crisis here," I shout.

Andrew turns. Looks at me. Says "What?" but stops, which is lucky for him because I'm about to take him down with some serious karate-chopping to the nose, throat, and mouth if he doesn't stop.

• • •

MY F-BOMB SUMMER by Felton Reinstein:

Kick off with a serious sweat fest. Add the absence of best friend. Stick in a damn morning paper route. Make sure it all goes down in Suckville. Fantastic!

"Damn, Jerri!" I shout.

• • •

By the way.

Every time in my life that Jerri has said "Felton needs to re-engage," I've ended up with a new freak tale to add to my squirrel nut history. For example, I had these scary anxiety attacks back in fourth grade. I kept thinking my heart wasn't pumping right, which seriously terrified me, of course, and me being scared would make it pump faster. So because it pumped faster, I got more scared, so it pumped faster and faster and faster, which was complete proof to me that my heart was completely malfunctioning and was about to explode, and I'd get dizzy, and squeaky-voiced, and sick, and not be able to breathe, sucking for air while Mrs. Derrell, my teacher, went on and on about Wisconsin's first settlers, who I can't remember because my heart was killing me. I think they wore straw hats and suspenders.

Jerri took me to a doctor, who said my heart was fine, but I seemed to be anxious (no crap!). Jerri was so relieved. But the doctor's opinion didn't help me because it kept happening, my heart attacks, so I stopped wanting to go to school because the heart attacks always happened at school.

After me refusing to go to school for a week, Jerri said I needed to learn to re-engage, so she took me to a cognitive behavioral therapist. The cognitive behavioral therapist suggested that when I start to have a freak-out and think my seriously healthy heart isn't working right, I should look at somebody I know well in my class, a person I like a lot, and repeat his or her name three times to remember I have good friends and I'm not alone and everything will be okay. The therapist also said that I should breathe deep to calm down my heart, all of which I sincerely tried to do, except I was probably supposed to say Gus's name in my head, not out loud, because when I did it during Mrs. Derrell's lecture on immigrants making sausages in Milwaukee, the world fell silent and the whole class turned and stared at me, their eyeballs popping out of their heads like they were looking at the famous nose-picking gorilla at the Milwaukee Zoo—completely gross and weird—which made my heart bang in my chest, completely proving I was dying.

Imagine all of them staring at me with their mouths open wide.

For years after that, my classmates would whisper softly to me, "Gus, Gus, Gus," and look at me sweetly but not sweet at all.

That's not funny either, by the way.

If Gus weren't my best friend and also sort of lacking in friends himself, he would probably have stopped being my friend because he caught so much crap too.

That wasn't the only time Jerri suggested I re-engage. There are probably ten more incidents I could report through the years. But it's late (1:23 a.m.).

And after I'd re-engage and freak out because of re-engaging, Jerri always ended up having to keep me home from school for weeks at a time and had to hug me a lot and cook me grilled cheese sandwiches and say sorry over and over.

All that stopped.

I made myself stop freaking out so much starting a couple of years ago. I got tired of being the center of attention. I don't like attention—did not anyway—and I got tired of being hugged, and I got tired of Jerri saying sorry to me. It's not like Jerri murdered Dad. Dad murdered Dad, right?

But I suppose my post-Regional dry-heaving put Jerri back in the mood.

Re-engage. Re-engage, donkey. I sure didn't like Jerri saying the word re-engage.

• • •

Two days after *Tayraysa's* call, I ate those bagels and regained some of my strength and sanity. I went back to school in time to turn in my English research report about what I want to be when I grow up (titled "Standup Comedy: Take My Wife...Please") and to take my stupid finals and to bid fare thee well to the senior class full of honkies and poop-stinkers and, of course, to Gus, who was leaving.

"I'm sorry, Felton," Gus said as we exited Bluffton High on the last day of school, the sun beating down on our heads, our eyes squinty.

"You should be," I said as we walked toward the bike rack.

"I don't have any friends in Caracas, man," he grimaced, unlocking his bike.

"I don't have any friends in Suckville," I said as we pedaled away.

"What about Peter Yang?" he asked, now a block from the school.

"Something's gone amiss," I told him, a look of resignation on my face.

"At least Peter Yang has a driver's license," he said, nearing his turnoff.

"That's true," I agreed as he turned.

"We can Skype, dude," he shouted, biking away.

"Chapter over," I mumbled, heading toward home.

• • •

Bleak. Bleak. Bleak.

Summer. Summer. Summer.

CHAPTER 5:
I MEAN, MAN! I USED TO
LOVE SUMMER!

I have very fond memories actually.

Every summer before this summer, we'd go camping at least once. For example, the summer after freshman year, Jerri took me and Andrew camping at Wyalusing State Park, right where the Wisconsin River cuts the state and hits the Mississippi. Where there are really high bluffs and huge trees and watery sand bars and little streams that look like mountain streams on TV flowing down the bluffs and ravines that cut through the forest and hiking trails right through it all. We spent two full days exploring.

Even though I hadn't hit my growth spurt and hadn't become stupid fast, I was already a jumper. I'd leap across ravines and Jerri would shout "Felton's a bobcat!" and Andrew, who apparently didn't think athletic prowess was bad for a young man at that time, would ask me to do it again because I looked so cool in flight.

At night, Jerri made campfires, and we roasted marshmallows, and we sat around and sang while she played guitar. She sang me "You Are My Sunshine" like twenty times, which I really liked, and all three of us sang "Rocky Mountain High" and "Country Road."

Jerri is a great singer. She sounds professional. "Love me some John Denver," she'd say. She's a good mom too. She's really been a good mom. Really. She took us camping every summer before this summer. And I've loved summer.

CHAPTER 6:
BUT THIS SUMMER?

It surely didn't start out so well.

So, I was down at the nursing home the other day, minding my own business, when... That might be a good way to begin a comedy routine, but it's total crap if it's an actual description of what you do every morning. Oh, yeah. I know a thing or two about nursing homes.

For example, you know what isn't pretty? Old ladies in their underwear. You know what I got to see lots of? Old ladies in their underwear.

In fact, this summer, I saw no fewer than ten thousand old ladies in their underwear. That's because one of my big stops on Gus's ridiculous paper route was a nursing home. Ridiculous. Lots of times when I ran through there, delivering the *State Journal*, the old ladies would shout "Get me out of here!" Oftentimes, the old ladies were wearing old lady robes or morning dresses or whatever, and the clothing wasn't tied right or it had slid down wrong, and I got to see their Old Lady Underwear with an Old Lady in it, which made me very sad.

What also made me sad was the very fact that nursing homes even exist because they're hot, stinky prisons for innocent old ladies who have lived too long (like that's a crime).

Not that all of them were old. One lady was actually sort of young. Whenever she saw me, her eyeballs popped out of her head, and she screamed and waved her arms and freaked out, apparently for good reason (more on that later if I can stay awake).

Through email, Gus told me to never look the inmates in the eyes, which was easy for him because of his hair wad. Not for me. My hair is curly and can't cover my eyes no matter how much I grow it and comb it down. (*Boing*—the sound of my hair springing upward.)

I biked so damn fast when I got out of that place. I would just want to run away and never go back but totally knew I'd be back the next day. *Paper route!* Jesus. Looked like a banner summer.

Poor Gus was unhappy too. He wrote that hanging with his grandma was like hanging at the nursing home all day, all summer long. Then he said it smelled like tacos in Caracas, but he hadn't yet found any tacos to eat. I answered back that I was bored and hot and tired, and I couldn't stop eating, and Jerri was being weird, and Andrew hadn't taken a shower since school got out.

We're losers was his reply. He also said, *Tell Andrew he must clean himself.*

CHAPTER 7:
THEN SOMEONE MOVED
INTO GUS'S HOUSE

Like ten days after Gus left for Venezuela, the lights went back on, and someone in there ordered the newspaper, which meant I had to deliver a paper to Gus's house every day.

Aleah. But I didn't know that yet.

So I wasn't happy at all with this development. See, there's nothing fun about visiting your friend's house when he's not home because he's in Venezuela with his dying grandma and he sends emails about taco smells and says we're losers and his house just reminds you of how great it would be to go down to the rec room and sit down on one of the giant bean bag chairs they have down there and watch some movies and eat chips and shoot the bull and exchange some serious laughs instead of having to visit that house at the butt crack of dawn just to dump a newspaper in the screen door and then bike away to another fifteen houses that don't contain your friend, including a big house full of crazy old ladies who are really prison inmates.

Peter Yang's house is on the route too, but it was clear things weren't going well between us (although we hadn't talked—I mean, that's really it, we hadn't talked). Plus, his house smells like fish, so I don't like going in anyway.

The people who moved into Gus's house for the summer redecorated it immediately, which I felt was a gesture meant to rub my nose in the fact of Gus's absence.

The second morning I delivered the paper there, the curtains on the picture window were open, and I could see that all the photos that are usually above the couch had been replaced by a bunch of scary wood masks. Boo! I mean scary. *Booo!* So I stood out there gawking and terrified, thinking about all the pictures of the Venezuelan mountains that used to be there and what Gus must be seeing, which I wouldn't know because he couldn't get Skype to work on the computer he had in Caracas, and I already mentioned that his emails were so short at that time (they got longer by the time I didn't want to read them)—when all of a sudden, the front door swung open and this black girl about my age was standing there in her white nightie or whatever, staring at me.

My jaw dropped. My eyeballs popped out of my head in total cartoon style. (*Boing-oing-oing*—that's the sound of my eyeballs popping.)

Okay, all over town, there are a lot of people who aren't exactly appropriately dressed when you're opening doors at the butt crack of dawn. "Oh, good morning, Mr. Schroeder. I can see your wang." Yeek. This girl, though, was much better to look at.

So when she opened the door? She and me, me and the black girl, we stared at each other, open-mouthed, silent: she at the door, me in the bushes in front of the picture window where I'd had my nose pressed to the glass; both of us poised to flee because I probably looked like a criminal and she was beautiful and not

Gus. I couldn't breathe. Finally, she said, all out of breath, "What do you want?"

"Paperboy," I said.

"What?" she asked, standing straight, her fear receding.

"Paper," I said, tossing the newspaper I had in my hand onto the step in front of her. I nodded at her. She looked down at the paper, then back up at me. I couldn't breathe.

So I totally kicked it, quick twitch. I leapt to my bike and got the holy hell out of there. I looked over my shoulder as I pedaled away. She stood there staring at me, her mouth open.

God. Dork. And, oh, yes, I'd sprung like a hunted, retarded, highly athletic gazelle. Or donkey. *Hee-haw!* Idiot.

To show that I was not, even then, completely lacking an understanding of social appropriateness, I'll say this: Immediately (*immediately*), my escape caused in me a feeling of deep humiliation and remorse. The humiliation was so deep, I felt sick—sick of myself. I kept repeating *Idiot. Idiot. Idiot.* in my head. "Why are you such an idiot?"

Have you ever noticed you can't get away from yourself? There is no way to get away from oneself. You're always there with you. And remember, I have a voice in my head that never shuts up. I delivered the papers to the rest of the houses hearing myself calling me an idiot in my head the whole way. Then I biked up to the nursing home hearing my own jerky voice say *"Idiot. Idiot. Idiot."* And by the time I got to the nursing home, I was so sick of being me that it was a relief to enter into it, into the prison, where I could hide from the shame of the real world. The inmates don't know or care.

Maybe I could stay? Maybe I could get a room, watch TV, get fed Jell-O and oatmeal? Get sponge baths? Disappear?

Wrong. Not disappear because I would know where I am and be with me. And my voice would call me idiot, and I couldn't enjoy watching game shows and soap operas while lying in my robe because my voice would be talking to me. Plus, I am not an old lady in my underpants. I am me, and the rest of my terrible life would still be in front of me. I delivered papers still hearing the voice in my head talking. *Why are you such an idiot?*

There is no getting away from yourself, so it's highly important to get one's brain under control. That's a fact.

When I pulled up the drive to our house after the route, Jerri was out in the garden digging up weeds. I threw down my Schwinn Varsity, a bike I inherited from my dad (one of only a couple things Jerri let me keep—this almost makes me cry, even now, because of what I did to it later), a bike he loved and I loved, tossed my paperboy bag aside, and then stomped over to her.

"Did you know some Africans moved into Gus's house?" I said.

"You shouldn't treat your bike like that, Felton."

"I said Africans!"

"Literally from Africa or do you mean African Americans?"

"I don't know. They have masks. I don't care. People, Jerri, people moved into Gus's house."

"*Tayraysa* said a poetry professor rented from them," Jerri told me, digging. "He's a summer appointment at the college."

"Oh, Jesus. They're gonna be there all summer?"

"During summer term surely."

"I don't feel good, Jerri."

Jerri continued to dig and work the soil like a peasant.

"Could you go and get me the compost pail, Felton?"

"Oh, man, I'm a fool."

I turned, walked, and entered the garage and then went into the house and into the basement, where I turned on the TV and went to sleep. Jerri woke me up some time later.

"Felton. Did you say you're a fool?"

"What? Go away."

"Gosh dang it. You are beginning to really frustrate me, you know that?"

"I'm sleeping here, Jerri."

"Stop it. Go do something. Get out into the world, Felton. You can't just lie around all—"

"I'm doing the ridiculous paper route, aren't I?"

"Ridiculous? Why can't you take a little pride in your work, Felton?"

"You take pride in being a crossing guard? Oh, that's dignified work, Jerri."

"I don't need to work. You know that, Felton. I don't work for money. I choose to work because you don't own your life unless you work for it," Jerri said, folding her arms across her chest.

"Well, I don't choose to work. But I do work. Isn't that slavery? Do slaves own their lives?"

Oops. Jerri didn't like that. She threw her arms out to the side and shook her head, mouth open, rolling her eyes around.

"I've heard this kind of crap before!" she shouted. "Look at you."

"What?" I'm telling you, incomprehensible!

"Look at you." Her eyes were all whacked out and red. "You are turning into such a little Gosh. Dang. Jerk!"

"No. I'm not."

"Yessss."

"Noooo."

"Oh, God. Look at you."

"Stop it, Jerri!" I was scared because as a peace-loving hippy, Jerri had never been a name caller (although she would shout at times).

She spat: "You are helping out a friend, you little jerk. You are not a slave."

I was scared, yeah, but she was also making me mad.

"Yes, I am. I'm a slave."

"No, you're…you're acting like an…effing jerk."

"Effing, Jerri? Effing?" I shouted.

Jerri breathed. "Oh, Jesus. Oh, Jesus."

She did a little instant Buddha meditation. (I could hear it when she breathed out—*om shanti shanti shanti shanti*—which means peace or heaven or maybe, in this circumstance, don't let me kill my kid.) Then she looked at me and said really quietly, "Felton. Please."

I stared at her. Then I said really quietly, "What is going on, Jerri?"

She breathed deeply. She said quietly, "You have to get off your butt, Felton."

I said louder, "My butt's got no place to go."

She said louder, "Please, Felton. Why don't you give Peter a call?"

I said pretty dang loud, "Peter Yang? Please no. I'm tired, Jerri."

Jerri exhaled, then sat down next to me on the couch and said really quietly, "Felton, I'm working really hard."

I shouted, "On what? What the hell?"

She tilted her head and scrunched her eyebrows and rubbed her eyes and took a big breath.

"I honestly appreciate you doing this paper route. I sincerely do. And I appreciate that you went out for track this spring. But now you've got to take these gains, this engagement, and continue to grow. You can't…recoil from life, you know?"

"Why do you treat me like a retard?" I shouted.

"I told you not to use retard like that, Felton."

"Aw, man, Jerri. Come on. I'm trying to sleep here," I groaned.

"Felton, please," Jerri said.

"Let me sleep!" I shouted.

Jerri exhaled hard, shook her head at me, and then stood.

"I don't know what to do with you," she said.

Then she left, and I shouted thank you. But I couldn't sleep. Why? Because I was totally awake and really hungry, and Jerri was crazy, and I could feel that my pants had grown too short because— I could feel it—I was growing again and probably ready to sprout another mound of man-hair from someplace. It was humid, and the doorbell was ringing, which meant Andrew had invited his dipshit friends over to play music, most likely. Chamber music. What thirteen-year-old crew of friends plays chamber music? Not me. I surely didn't do that at thirteen.

Of course, I didn't really have any skills back in June, so I couldn't have done anything. I really couldn't do crap.

That thought hit me hard. *You can't do crap.*

And then I thought, I'm almost sixteen. I'm very nearly a track superstar. This is no way to live. I've got to do something.

So I got up and emailed Gus, Jerri is crazy.

He was online, so we messaged.

what you mean crazy?
she calls me jerk then meditates then calls me jerk
grandma doesn't like my hair
don't lose hair wad, man
sucker crack ass taco poop hate this

And with that, he signed off. Gus didn't have time for my problems. He had his own. I sat back on the couch and wished me, him, and Peter Yang were driving to the pool for some relaxation instead of being off in separate worlds of pain. Peter Yang?

I listened while Andrew and his dork music friends set up their instruments upstairs. Jerri was right. I had to do something

So I thought about being almost sixteen.

• • •

Peter Yang has a driver's license.

Almost sixteen! Do you know what that means?

Of course. A driver's license. A car. If I had a car, everything would be okay. If I didn't use it to escape to Mexico or Venezuela (can you drive to Venezuela?), I could use it to gain acceptance. Oh, yes, I could be a Suckville Standard Jackwad driving around the town, tearing it up, racing the poop-stinkers over at the quarter-mile. Oh, I'll engage, Jerri! I got up and climbed the steps to find her.

Jerri wasn't upstairs where Andrew's geek friends were gathering to play their weenie music. I looked out the window in the kitchen while I stuffed a piece of bread in my mouth (growing boy). Jerri was walking out to the garden. I opened the window and shouted, "Jerri, I have to get my driver's license."

"What?"

"I need a driver's license so I can engage with the world, Jerri," I cried.

"Well, that's a good sign, I guess."

"What do you mean, sign?"

"Sign up for your permit, Felton. Okay?"

"How's that?"

"Figure it out," she called back.

"What?" I shouted.

Then she started walking back toward the house, shaking her head, looking a little mad.

"Listen," she said when she got under the window, "I'll teach you to drive if you sign up for your permit."

"Okay," I said, then closed the window. Jerri stayed right down there below the window. She wasn't looking up at me. She was seriously staring at the wall, which was like a foot in front of her face (*Jeez, what's the problem?*), so I went back to the refrigerator to look for some food. Oh, man. I wasn't sure how to get a permit. I supposed I could ask Peter Yang because he did that—got a permit and learned to drive.

I opened the refrigerator door, and my thoughts began to drift. Drive. Drive. *Drive!*

Here's an early summer fantasy:

I am *the* Standard Suckville Jackwad: Look at me: I'm sixteen, and I've got a license, and I'm driving up and down Main Street, picking up dirty girls in the Pizza Hut parking lot (You wanna make out? Okay!), driving out to the cornfields or the quarry to smoke weed (yeek) and get smashed (yeek), then I'll drive back to town to go to Kwik Trip to see if anyone's there (probably not) and then to McDonald's to see if anyone's there (probably not) and then around and around the college to see if anyone's there (drunk nineteen-year-olds! Heyo!), then I'll fight the honkies in fast-food bathrooms and race the poop-stinkers in their pickups. Oh, glorious driver's license.

Get a license. Drive around. That's what I thought.

Or be another geek in the basement watching movies and playing video games.

Or be another geek in the living room playing chamber music.

Or sit around listening to my body grow hair.

• • •

We didn't have a lot of food I could instantly jam into my mouth without preparation, so I shut the refrigerator door.

In the living room, five dorks began to play stringed instruments while Andrew tap-tapped on the piano what I think was some kind of Johann Sebastian Bach bullcrap. Andrew loves Bach. I, like my father, love the Beatles (me and Andrew do have his music). I leaned my head into the living room and listened. A couple of dorks looked at me. I shouted "Hi!" and waved at them. Then I went back into the kitchen, where I stuffed a banana in my mouth, then two more pieces of bread, then I ate half a brick of Jerri's favorite musty goat cheese, then I drank a half gallon of milk, then I ate an English muffin while listening to the dorks play their music.

Here's this: The dorks aren't retarded. They're good. Andrew is good.

I stopped chewing so I could hear them play better. Andrew is really, really good. Then I went downstairs to try to get some rest. It was so humid though.

CHAPTER 8:
I HAVE NO TALENT FOR DRUMMING—ANDREW DOES (I CARRIED AROUND A BAG OF ROCKS)

Andrew started playing piano when he was seven because Jerri's drumming teacher, Tito, said he had musical talent.

It was August, and I'd just turned nine. Jerri had invited all these musty, woodchip-smelling people out to our house to drum in this big circle around our fire pit. At one point, the sun going down, the sky orange, Tito put a drum in front of me and said I should drum along, "Let it all out, little man," but I'd had heart attacks at school all spring, and all those people drumming around the circle caused a vibration in my chest that scared the holy crap out of me, so I wouldn't touch the drum. So Tito moved the drum in front of Andrew, and Andrew just started bobbing his little mop head and pounding along and all the woodchip-smelling people oooohed and ahhhhed, and Jerri clapped her hands over her mouth, she was so happy. The next week, he was in piano lessons.

That night, Tito gave me a leather pouch full of polished rocks and crystals. He told me the rocks had special powers and I should hold them in my hands if I got scared, so I carried the leather pouch around and took the rocks out a couple of times at school that fall, but everybody made crap out of me for carrying around a "jewelry collection," so the rocks didn't work right.

It wasn't very long before Andrew's piano teacher said that Andrew was his best student ever.

Even though I couldn't pull the rocks out at school, I carried them around in my pocket. I actually carried them with me almost every day through the last school year. After my Regionals disqualification, I held a crystal in my left hand for two days.

Believing rocks have power is a lot like thinking your dad's ghost is watching out for you.

I carried them for years!

Not anymore. They're gone.

Andrew got piano, and I got a bag of rocks? That didn't work out.

I don't know. What do I know? Maybe Dad is watching?

Yikes. That actually just scared me.

• • •

Holy crap. It's 1:51 a.m.

Go!

CHAPTER 9:
THINGS BEGAN TO
SERIOUSLY CHANGE
AT THE POOL

After an hour of sweating in the dark basement, I figured I'd better really do something with my day or else the summer would begin to seriously kill me. We don't have air conditioning. Have I mentioned that it was really humid? Hot and moist like a good cake (but bad weather). My curly hair was getting really curly from the humidity, which I don't like. I have what Jerri calls a "Jew-fro." This, like my Schwinn Varsity and love for the Beatles, is a gift from my father (one Jerri obviously couldn't burn in the fire).

Upstairs, the kids were laughing.

So I did it. I called Peter Yang. Peter doesn't have a cell phone, and he has like a hundred brothers and sisters, all of whom are as boring or more boring than Peter, and I don't like talking to any of them, so I was very pleased that Peter was the one who picked up. He sounded happy when he answered "Hello!"

"Wassup, Peter?"

He sounded less happy when he said, "Oh. Um. Hey, Felton. What's happening?"

"Not much, my man. Summertime, right? You must really be missing Gus, huh? I'm surprised you haven't called me! Ha ha. You want to go hang or something?"

"Um, I'm kind of busy."

"With what?"

"Debate club."

"Aw, Jesus, Peter. It's summer. There is no debate club."

"Well, we're going to go to the pool together—me and the debaters—to build team cohesion."

"Okay. Sounds great. Can I come with?"

"Well, I guess."

"Great, Peter. Fantastic. Can you pick me up?"

"Uh, I have a full car."

"Fine. See you there, okay? I'll ride my bike."

"Yeah, we'll be there, Felton. See ya."

I went to sleep.

At around noon, I got up, changed into my swimsuit, which was *way* too small for me, grabbed a towel from the closet, and then went upstairs to grab lunch before riding my bike to the pool. Instead of finding a crew of quiet super-geek orchestra freaks eating sandwiches, which is what I assumed I'd find, I only found Andrew sitting at the dining room table, picking at a piece of wheat bread, looking totally mopey. "Where's your band of brothers, bro?" I asked.

"Jerri told them they couldn't stay for lunch."

"Really?" I was sort of dumfounded because Jerri loved it when Andrew's dipshit pals were over.

"She claims to have a migraine."

"That's weird."

He pulled off his plastic nerd glasses.

"I think it's because you're making her crazy, Felton."

I paused and squinted at him. Andrew looked sincerely sad.

"Me? I don't think so."

"Yes. You. You're rude to her, and you're lazy, and I think she's had it."

"Shut up, Andrew," I said.

"She never tells my friends to go home. Why today?"

"Maybe Jerri doesn't have enough money to be feeding every last geek at Bluffton Middle School. That's a lot to bear on a part-time crossing guard's salary."

"We have plenty of money, and you know it. You...you..." Andrew's face got really red, and he worked hard to say something.

"What Andrew?" I asked. "What do you want to say?"

"...you ass brain."

"What did you say?" I asked.

"You heard me," he said.

"Uh, I don't know, Mr. Dickweed. You think we have money? Why do you think Jerri is making me do this paper route? We're probably broke. We're probably going on welfare. I'm likely the main breadwinner here. You see what I'm saying? Paper route money is floating the boat. I'm like your dad now. You should call me Dad."

Andrew's cheeks flushed even hotter. His eyes went watery. He stood, looking like he wanted to punch me. Then he bit his cheek and said, "Why are you such a retard, Felton?"

I paused for a moment and thought about killing Andrew. Then I thought about what he'd just asked me, why I am such a retard. It was a good question.

"I don't know," I said. Then I left the house.

Jerri was lying on a lawn chair out in the middle of the yard, her whole head covered up by a towel.

"I'm going to the pool with Peter Yang," I called.

Jerri sat up, pulling the towel off her face, and said, "Oh, good. Good, Felton." She didn't actually sound good though. Crazy town.

I got on my bike and rode toward the pool.

• • •

What kicked off the big change that day? First, the voice in my head, which said this as I biked: You are causing everybody pain and suffering, you jerk. *You cause Andrew to mope and to say ass brain and to stop playing music with his friends. You cause Jerri to call you names and stare at walls and cover her face up with towels and kick out Andrew's friends because she has a migraine (which you caused).*

Shut up, brain! Shut up, voice! Jesus!

What exactly did I do to make everybody suffer? What? I didn't know.

But I did. Gus was the only one who didn't suffer around me. My family, what's left of it, suffered. Why?

I wasn't a criminal. I'd only been in trouble once (bathroom stall breakdown, which was really Gus's idea, although I heartily agreed with it and also did the deed). I didn't fight or drink or do drugs or have sex of any kind or stay out too late or do anything even remotely approaching deviant. I just watched a lot of cable alone, and I slept a lot, but that hardly seemed a reason for my family to suffer.

As I biked, I wondered if Jerri would feel better if I did get in trouble staying out late and having sex. *Hey, look who's a normal Suckville teen! Felton!!!* I also wondered when it was I began to hate my teeny weenie brother Andrew. I felt sincere hate for him. Why? *Sure, he's a jerk, and he's arrogant, and he's a pain in my ass. But that's no different than how it's always been. I've never hated him.* A few minutes earlier, back when he was mad at me about his friends, I had to escape him or I might have punched out his light bulb, which is definitely not the kind of trouble Jerri would want me to get in.

Then I thought: *I've always made her suffer, all the way back when I had heart attacks. Maybe I'm just old enough to see how much she hates me?*

At that moment, I got such a big gust of energy from my insides that I just absolutely let loose on my Schwinn Varsity. I tore down the road a million miles per hour, which is an exaggeration because nothing goes a million miles per hour. But what isn't an exaggeration is this: I biked so damn fast I actually passed a car on the main road. The old man driving the car rolled down his window and cheered as I passed him. That was pretty damn cool.

• • •

The second thing that kicked off the change was Peter Yang's treachery.

Let's get this straight. I don't love Peter Yang. I'm still not good with him. In fact, maybe he isn't my friend at all anymore. Maybe he hasn't been for a while.

Last winter, I hung out with him a lot because we could all go out driving together. I think I enjoyed Peter's company only because he had the car to drive Gus and me around in. Gus had a lot of funny stuff to say when driving around. Lots of observations. Gus was pure comedy gold in the car. Peter was not so interesting. He had nothing to say except "Come on, guys" when he thought Gus and me took things too far with our wry observations or whatever. Maybe I've never been that interested in him. I guess he's been at every birthday party I've ever had in my entire life up until this year, and his dad and my dad were friends, etc. Maybe I'm just really mad. And maybe it was good to be mad because it helped kick off my change.

I got to the pool, put my T-shirt and flip-flops in a basket, walked out to the deck in my much-too-small swimsuit, and saw that it was packed out there because of the high humidity and climbing temperature. I couldn't see Peter Yang anywhere.

Jess Withrow was there, though, in plain view, and so was Abby Sauter. They were all half-naked in their little bikinis, showing off on their towels. I almost lost my nerve but didn't want to go home, so I kept moving. They whistled at me when I walked past. Abby said, "Looking hot, Felton Reinstein. Super hot."

Jess said, "Nice short shorts, fur ball."

God, they were unbelievably mean!

I didn't say a word back or even look at them. I was socially smart enough to know when no response was necessary. But for some stupid reason, I did look down to see if my privates were showing, which elicited a big howl from the two of them. How did they know where I was looking?

I got a little dazed, a little unsteady in that heat. I had to calm down. I breathed deep and exhaled and, crap, accidentally said "Om shanti shanti shanti." Abby and Jess rolled around their towels, laughing. I walked a little quicker.

Some of Jerri's life lessons (*om shanti*, for example) have been extremely detrimental to me socially.

Okay. Steady. I was at the swimming pool for a reason. To hang with my old pal, my second best friend Peter Yang. And together we'd hang, apparently, with his new friends, the entire debate team, who I didn't know or like. I walked and looked and walked. But Peter Yang and the debaters were nowhere to be found. All there was at the pool, it appeared, was a wall-to-wall carpet of honkies.

Still, I lingered, walked, and looked, hopeful of finding Peter Yang.

I walked completely around the main pool. The water reflected cool blue and refreshing, and the deck was really hot on my feet. Little kids jumped, splashed, shouted. They were having an excellent time. The lifeguards, who were all just chuckleheaded kids from the high school but liked to act like gods, stared down at me from behind their mirrored honky shades. I did not see Peter. I walked over to the slides and the little pool where moms park it with their toddlers. Still no Peter.

I was getting pretty annoyed with the whole situation. Have I mentioned that I am not a big fan of Peter Yang?

As I was taking a last turn around the pool, someone called "Hey, Reinstein. What's up?"

Okay, here's the third thing that brought on my change.

I looked toward the pool house and saw Cody Frederick, jock-o, jogging toward me. He was with Jason Reese, a large fellow, who I believed to be a bona fide chuckleheaded dumbass. My chest got tight.

"Oh. Hey. What's going on, Cody?" I said.

Reese stared at me like a mountain gorilla.

"I was going to call you," Cody pulled off his sunglasses. He was sweaty. "You missed the first summer weights."

"Yeah?" I asked, even though I knew that. I didn't want to lift weights.

Reese nodded.

"Yeah. I'm organizing passing drills too, after baseball practice on Wednesdays. Maybe add a day or two as the summer goes on. Think you could hit that?"

"Why didn't you invite me to passing drills?" Reese glared at Cody.

"Because you're a lineman, idiot. Jesus. You gonna be running pass routes?" Cody looked back at me. I could smell that smell of his. Vague pee. "What do you think, Reinstein? It would be cool to be in sync when the season starts, man."

"I see your point. Uh huh. Can you text me or something?"

"What's your digits?"

As I was nervously giving Cody my cell number and he was plugging it into his phone, who should walk out of the pool house but that jerk Ken Johnson, fastest man in the state (midsized schools division) two years running. This year, he won in both the 100 meters and 200. (I should have been there to beat him.) His 100 meter time was faster than even all the big-school Milwaukee kids. (So? I could've taken him…maybe.) I was not happy to see Ken, as you can imagine. He'd just graduated and was on his way to Iowa on a football scholarship, and I, being a great optimist, of course, figured I'd never have to look at his stupid white-blond head again.

"Uh, I gotta roll, man," I said to Cody.

Then Ken shouted, "Hey Rein Stone Squirrel Nut. Dad said you missed weights already. You gonna flake?"

"Uhhhh," I responded.

Ken walked up and put his arm around Cody but kept looking at me.

"Bullshit, dude. I keep telling everybody not to count on you. Why are you bothering with Rein Stone?" he asked Cody. "Rein Stone is no football player, for Christ's sake. He's a jumpy little squirrel nut, that's all."

"I don't know," Cody looked down.

"Yeah, Squirrel Nut," that idiot Reese said.

Right then and there I thought I would barf. I felt my insides twist and upheave into upchuck position, and my eyes bulged out of my head and I got instantly sweaty, and I opened my mouth and almost said "Om shanti" but actually said "Gotta go." I took off jogging, with jerky Ken Johnson and chuckleheaded Jason Reese, horrible honkies both, laughing behind me.

Okay. Here's the change.

Laughing at me? I mean, what the hell? Why? What did I do?

Man. Piss me off. Seriously.

What the hell are they laughing about?

Piss. Me. Off.

I was so mad, I almost barfed. This was new. Generally, I barfed (or almost barfed) from being scared, not mad.

As I ran back to the pool house, I felt it. As I entered the building, I seriously felt it. I had to stop running. Once inside, I took two big steps and stopped cold right in the middle of the changing room, right in front of the little naked boys and their dads. No. Didn't want to do it. Didn't want to barf. Didn't want to bahhh like a sheep in front of these people. Not for any reason, mad or scared.

I was so freaking mad!

Piss. Me. Off.

What in the hell are you laughing at?

And I did not barf. Why? Because the voice in my head got huge. Instead of calling me an idiot, it called the honkies names. *"You gonna let these weak-ass dipshits control your biology? You gonna let the pig pricks make you barf? You should make them barf. They should see you and barf and barf because they're so scared. Don't take this crap from honkies."*

Yeah, voice! Yeah! That's a good voice!

I breathed deep and then walked the hell out of the pool house, slow and controlled, my head held high. I went right over to my bike to ride it home. Then I turned, just as slow and controlled, and walked back into the pool house almost hoping I'd see that jerk Ken Johnson again. Then I picked up my T-shirt and flip-flops from the basket, which I'd forgotten to do the first time I left the pool house. Then I left for real, got my Varsity, and rode it home, slow and angry, shaking my head slow, repeating this fine little mantra: "I'm gonna make you barf. I'm gonna make you barf. I'm gonna make you barf." That's a little different than *om shanti shanti shanti*, which is about peace, not terror. Oh hell no. "I'm gonna make you barf." That's not Jerri's mantra.

No peace, no justice. I'm gonna make you barf.

Hey! Ho! I'm gonna make you barf!

I, Felton Reinstein, was hot. Seriously hot. Boiling angry. Me, a good, very fast, potentially funny young man, with no naturally occurring ill intent toward anyone, had been completely mistreated forever. I'd had enough.

Hell no! We won't go! I'm gonna make you barf!

I rode slow past dumb little houses and the ugly little golf course, simmering and steaming. I got to our drive and pedaled slow up the hill. When I made it to the garage, I stepped off my bike and let it drop right there.

"Goddamn chuckleheaded honkies," I said, pausing for effect, folding my arms across my chest.

Jerri shouted from the garden, "Felton, Coach Johnson just called."

But then the voice in my head said something extremely important: *"Wait. Wait. It's not just the honkies. It's not just fat ass Reese or that jerk Ken Johnson. What about Peter Yang?"*

What? Peter Yang? Peter *freaking* Yang.

"Honkies are not the only problem," I shouted.

"What?" Jerri called from the garden.

I walked up and into the front door of the house, past Andrew plunking the piano like a robot, then down into the basement, where I called Peter's house. Mrs. Yang answered with her Chinese accent.

"Is Peter there?"

"No. He went with Mindy to play the game."

"The game, huh? You tell him Felton called."

"Okay."

"You tell him he's a damn jerk, okay?"

"Okay."

And then Mrs. Yang hung up.

That's right, Mrs. Yang. The truth hurts.

Then I didn't really know what to do with myself, with all my anger.

I turned on the TV, but nothing interesting was on. Then I got on my computer and emailed Gus:

> i got no use for peter yangs of world. no more peter yang.
> done. over. called his mom and canceled subscription.

• • •

It took Gus about two hours to respond:

> way to go. we two pees in potty. zero friends between us.

I don't need bad friends, Gus. You got that?

But by night, I felt really lonely, and the anger made me crazy.

CHAPTER 10:
I'D NEVER SEEN ANYONE
DO ANYTHING THAT WELL,
NOT EVEN ANDREW

In some ways, the night that followed the pool day was kind of like tonight. I am listening to music like I did then. I can't sleep (it is 2:13 a.m.!) like I couldn't that night. But I'm not thrashing around. I broke a bunch of shit in my room that night.

Yeah.

The morning after I told off Peter Yang's mom, I had a really hard time getting up for the paper route. Yeah, I'd spent the entire evening barricaded in my room, all emotional and homicidal, pacing, breaking old toys (poor *Star Wars* action figures), considering the things I had to do to feel good about the world or to destroy the world: get a driver's license, drive to Mexico, etc. (or fire bottle rockets and Roman candles at Ken Johnson in his stupid car).

I listened to my dad's old CDs. (Andrew found them in a box in a closet a couple years ago—this was several years post-bonfire, and Jerri barely reacted to them.) Lots of Beatles but also some other stuff, like the Pixies and Nirvana and the Smiths and Sonic Youth and punk music like Minor Threat that nobody else even knows about really (except Jerri, of course, who said she never liked any of it). Andrew took all Dad's classical CDs. I got all the rock ones. And a lot of it is angry-sounding, and I was angry, a Gus-less wonder adrift and abused. I liked Sonic Youth. It's what Dad listened to in the Volvo after he ran up the Mound that time.

Jerri came to my closed door at some point in the night, knocked loud, asked me to turn down the music, then shouted "You all right in there?"

"Yes. Leave me alone."

"What's that music? You having bad thoughts?"

"No. Just need to be alone."

"I didn't mean…You know…I thought you'd want to know that Coach Johnson called."

"Who?"

"Coach Johnson called for you today, Felton."

"I don't care about any Johnson. I don't care about Coach. And I don't give a shit about his stupid son, okay?"

Jerri paused outside the door. I imagined her staring blankly at the wood.

"Umm, do you want to talk about it?"

"I'm listening to music here!" I shouted, then cranked up the tunes. I guess she went away.

Yes, the head football coach is Ken Johnson's dad.

Too much Johnson, man. Too much Johnson. "I'll pound all you Johnsons!" I shouted. Then I pounded on my chest. *Why the hell do they think you want to play football?* the voice in my head said. *What a bunch of idiots!* Sonic Youth exploded from my little computer speakers. I glared and clenched my fists and looked in the mirror.

It was truly exhausting to be so mad. Plus, I was awake until like 5 a.m. And, thus, I was really completely exhausted for the paper route the next morning. (I got up to go at 6:45—not enough sleep!) I was very late delivering. I didn't get to Gus's house until almost 7:30.

The people who were living in there had the door open and the curtains were pulled. The living room had every light on, even though it was plenty light outside by that time, and the wood masks were staring out the window. I sort of zombie-walked up the stoop to drop the paper off. I heard a noise when I pulled the screen door open. And I couldn't help it, my exhaustion left me without my natural fleeing defenses, so I sort of popped my head in to see what the noise was.

The black girl in her white nightie was pulling herself up to Gus's piano.

Gus is a terrible piano player. Awful. He has no natural rhythm, and he is tone-deaf, and he can't see the keys very well because his hair wad is in his face. He bangs and shouts and makes me laugh until I have a headache and want him to stop.

This girl, who I now know so well, is not even slightly terrible. She's got great rhythm and knows how melodies should sound. In fact, she is completely amazing.

Stop. Listen to me. Completely utterly amazing.

I watched. She paused, drew in a deep breath, then just exploded onto the keys, exploded into this classical music thing, which I would not normally like, but oh my holy shit.

I stood there sort of tingling, I'm sure with my mouth hanging open, just staring at her like a total dork while she played. I recognized something in her. Maybe genius? The music was like a wave that hit me in Florida when we were visiting Dad's parents right before he died. The music made me kind of cry. I'm sort of crying now. Seriously. What a dork I am. This girl, who I love, used every bit of the length of both her arms going up and down the keys. Then I heard this deep voice say "Can I help you?"

I looked up, and there was this huge dad staring at me (Ronald).

"Um, yes. Paperboy," I mumbled.

"Aleah plays well, doesn't she?"

"Holy crap," I replied.

"Well put," he said.

And then I nodded, handed him the paper, turned, and took off like a stupid-ass jackrabbit.

She's so good. She's so good. She's so good.

I couldn't stop thinking about the girl in her nightie and her dad and being caught staring at her and how I was alone and how I can't play piano or anything.

You're just jumpy. That's all you are. Jumpy, jumpy, jumpy.

I tore through the rest of the route, hurtling off my bike, dropping papers off at houses, then to the nursing home. Inside, old ladies were out of their rooms, heading to breakfast because I was late, and they called to me: "Help!"

"Shut up, old ladies," I told them. "I've got nothing. You're just old."

CHAPTER 11:
I FELT BETTER UNTIL JERRI DROPPED THE F-BOMB

When I got home, Jerri was drinking coffee and reading an old magazine on the front stoop. It was already too hot out there, and she was sweating. It was obvious she was waiting for me. I tried to walk right past her, but she grabbed my arm and looked up into my eyes.

"You're getting home late," she said.

"Why did you make me take this stupid job?" I asked.

"Did it feel good to listen to your dad's music yesterday, Felton?"

I didn't answer immediately. I looked at her face, which was pale.

"Yes, it did."

"Sure brought back some memories for me," she said. "Not good memories."

"Oh, yeah?"

"You were listening to some pretty angry music."

"Yes."

"Do you ever wish you were with him, Felton?"

"With him? What are you talking about?"

"Somewhere not here?"

"Jesus, Jerri."

I didn't know what she meant at all, of course. So I tried to tell her what was up.

"Listen. Jerri. I feel like a…Sometimes, I feel like a trapped squirrel, okay? I'm a damn friendless squirrel nut that doesn't know how to do anything."

"Squirrel nut?" Jerri raised her eyebrows for a moment. Stared at me. "What do you mean?"

"I don't know."

"Do you want to talk about it?"

"There's nothing to say really," I told her.

"Can I help you, Felton?"

"I'm hungry."

"You wouldn't eat dinner."

"I know that."

Jerri stared at me, squinted, then let go of my arm.

"Go inside. I'll make you a big omelet, okay?"

"Okay." I opened the door to go in.

"You know I'm really trying," she said.

"Why?" I asked, stopping. "Why are you trying?" *Why do honkies laugh? Why does Jerri need to try? Why can't I do anything well?*

"You know I'm going to a therapist, Felton?" Jerri said.

"No."

"That's where I went on Friday. She's worried about you too."

Oh. Oh. "Who? Who's worried, Jerri?"

"My therapist."

"Your therapist?" My stomach dropped.

"Yes."

"Good. You need a therapist, Jerri." I didn't want a therapist. I've had a therapist. My therapist caused me to whisper Gus's name

58

like he was my girlfriend when I was in fourth grade. My therapist made my heart attacks worse. I went inside and tried to slam the door, but it didn't really slam.

Andrew was already up doing what he does, singing off-key while playing one part of a song over and over on the piano. He calls the parts he plays over and over "phrases," but I don't hear anything like meaning in them or even a complete thought, which I know, from seventh grade English class, a phrase should have. Hearing him and seeing him and not feeling so good about myself anyway, I was mean, which I completely regret. I regret a lot, which maybe is unhealthy. At least he didn't get I was being mean at that point.

"Hey, Andrew," I said. "You're not that great at piano."

He stopped playing and sat up straight.

"Why?"

"I saw a girl play a hell of a lot better than you just this morning."

"How did you see her? She practices in the morning? Did she ask you inside?"

I was confused.

"Um, sort of."

Andrew swiveled around on the bench, eyes wide open.

"Aleah Jennings," he nodded.

"Oh. Aleah Jennings. She's black?"

"Uh huh. She lives in Gus's house. Aleah Jennings, Felton!"

"Yeah."

"She's probably the best sixteen-year-old piano player in the universe. I read her blog."

"Aleah Jennings?"

"She won the Chicago Competition last spring. I watched it on YouTube."

"I heard her."

"She makes me…She makes me want to be a zookeeper."

"What?"

"She's too good, Felton."

"What?"

"I should be that good."

"You're thirteen. She's older."

"Or an astronaut or a veterinarian. I like animals. I'd be a good veterinarian. I don't like how they smell."

"You're a great piano player, Andrew. You're probably the best thirteen-year-old piano player in the universe."

"Not even close." A look of pure ice fell on Andrew's little kid face, a look of pure unadulterated ambition. "But I'm going to be. I mean…I mean…I can't believe she lives here. I made Jerri call over there yesterday. I made Jerri…I invited Aleah Jennings to come over for tea tomorrow. I had to invite…Jerri was mad because she's not feeling herself lately but…"

"Really?" I blushed at the thought. "She's coming here?"

"I hate Aleah Jennings!" Andrew cried. Then his face turned red and his lips trembled. Andrew's whole body trembled. "I hate her! I hate her!" he cried.

Wow. Freak. Out.

I watched him for a moment, observed him. This went through my head:

Who carries around a leather pouch full of shiny rocks and crystals?

Me.

Why do I carry around a leather pouch full of shiny rocks and crystals?

Jerri.

Who is crying like an insane baby because there's a good piano player in town?

Andrew.

Whose mother makes him call her Jerri? Whose mother stares at him while he sleeps? Who found his dad hanging like a suit coat in the garage?

Who wouldn't be jumpy in these circumstances?

Maybe no one?

Why do the honkies laugh?

Because you grew up thinking crazy was normal?

• • •

Weird, huh? I'd never thought of it before. It never occurred to me that I am not the source of the problem, but maybe I'm, you know, just a branch of a big ugly tree. I mean, Andrew was sincerely flipping out. This is also weird. Watching Andrew freak, I kind of felt better.

"I hate her!" Andrew screamed. He was pounding his fists on the piano bench. I stood back and stared at him, feeling my muscles relax.

Jerri ran in the house.

"What did you do to Andrew? You leave him alone, Felton! Just because you're depressed doesn't give you the right to hurt other…"

"I hate her!" Andrew shouted.

"You hate me?" Jerri cried.

"No! Her!"

"He hates her," I nodded, earnestly.

"Who is her?" Jerri cried.

Just then my cell went off. It chimed and buzzed, and I flinched (because it was the first time it had gone off since Gus left town). I pulled it out of my pocket and looked at the number. It wasn't one I recognized. Because any conversation had to be better than the freak show happening in front of me, I said "Gotta take this one" and then jogged to the bathroom and shut the door. Jerri and Andrew shouted about "her" outside. I answered my phone. It was Cody Frederick.

"Sorry Ken Johnson is such a jerk, Felton," he said.

Let me pause here and state the obvious: At that moment, life was quite confusing. The only person who had been nice to me in several weeks was Cody Frederick. Let me also say this: I am stupid fast. That is a fact. Is there another single positive thing that could've been said about me? I don't really know. Although I wanted to be a comic, no one found me funny, which is a hindrance and thus not positive. Perhaps this: If you like hair, I have a lot of hair, and I was in the process of growing it very fast. So that could've been seen as positive on a very limited basis. Of course, the day before, two very beautiful (and, sorry, very mean) honky girls at the swimming pool had called me fur ball. No. Superior hair growth was not positive. Anything else? Not really. Suddenly, only two things made complete sense: Cody Frederick and my speed.

I took a breath and said easily, "Ken Johnson has always been a jerk, man."

"He used to beat me up at little league practice," Cody said.

"Ass effing hole," I said.

Cody agreed.

While Andrew and Jerri carried on outside the bathroom, Cody and I talked, and he asked me to go to weights with him the next day. I told him I would. We made a plan. And I didn't even feel nervous about it. What did I have to lose? My friends? The stability of my family? I left the bathroom in time to see Jerri and Andrew hugging and sobbing and apologizing to each other.

Then Jerri made breakfast. During breakfast, she stared at me without blinking. Her face was all pale, her eyes watery.

"Can I help you?" I asked.

"You remind me of…You need to ask for help if you need it, Felton."

"I don't need help, Jerri."

"Your dad committed suicide. I'm sorry," she whispered.

"That was over ten years ago. What's wrong with you?"

"Leave Jerri alone," Andrew said.

"I don't know," Jerri said. "You're right. It's my problem."

"You know, Jerri," I said, "I'm just a small part of a much larger problem." I really had no idea what I was talking about, but right then, something jarred loose.

Jerri stared at me, clenched her jaw a couple of times, and then nodded slowly.

"Right. You're right, Felton."

"I am?" I asked.

"Help me with dishes, Andrew," she said really coldly, standing up.

"Why do I have to? Why doesn't Felton have to?"

"He's going through a time—a time of growth," Jerri said, weirdly calm.

"Please stop the freak show," I whispered.

"You watch your mouth," Jerri snarled. She glared. She curled her lip. Then she said "Fucker" under her breath.

I think that was the most scared I'd been in my life. At least until a couple of mornings later (and then until the end of July). Well, probably not if I think about it because I've seen some terrible stuff and also the heart attacks, but it was scary.

Andrew stared at me with his mouth open. Jerri stood with her back to the table. I stood up and went downstairs.

CHAPTER 12:
MAKING A LIST, CHECKING
IT TWICE

Downstairs in my room, I pulled the leather pouch out of my sock drawer and almost pulled out shiny rocks (semiprecious stones from Brazil) and crystals to try to relax but then caught myself. *Don't do that.* I jammed the pouch back in with the socks.

Then I found my notebook where I always meant to take notes about life and whatnot, which I'd never done. I wanted to write something about how I wasn't the problem. I wanted to write about Jerri, but I couldn't. The notebook was completely empty. What are you supposed to write in these things? I emailed Gus:

> there is strong possibility that i'm nuts primarily because my
> mother and brother have made me nuts, not to speak of my dad,
> who was also likely nuts (or maybe had been driven nuts by my
> mom). it's not my fault. do you keep a journal of your thoughts?

Gus responded an hour or so later. Extremely out of character, he wrote like a million words, way too much to read. Clearly, he was bored out of his cabbage. Here is some of what he wrote:

> i own nothing but my thoughts (and also my pants)…you
> ever hear of hugo chavez? he's el presidente and he hates
> america because we love money and mcdonalds (i want a

quarter pounder) and he took away american tv so i cant watch
anything i understand…i'm writing a book about spies who eat
tacos and hide in large house plants…grandma moans and farts
and swears at dad in spaniard HILARIOUS…use notebook to
write to-do lists. dad does that…

None of what Gus said made any sense. Not even my oldest
friend made sense? I remember being at his house for dinner with
my parents when we were toddlers. (Yeah, his dad and my dad were
friends—at least colleagues; there were always colleagues around
and parties and picnics—that's something I remember from
when Dad was alive.) I remember Gus had white baby booties
with bells on them, and I chased him around because he made a
jingle noise, which I liked, and both our dads were totally dying
laughing because Gus didn't want to be chased, but I wouldn't stop.
Gus's dad said "Chasing booty. Chip off the old block" to my dad.
I remember that perfectly. That might be my first memory actually.
But even Gus had become incomprehensible.

Well, at least he mentioned I could use my notebook to make a
to-do list of my goals and plans, etc. So I did. This is all I wrote. I'm
reading the original right now (it seriously took me about three hours):

1. Lift weights with Cody.
2. Get driver's license.
3. Consider giving up comedy, as comedy isn't even funny
   anymore.
4. Stop talking to Jerri and Andrew.

Then because I was so exhausted from not sleeping the night
before and from what Jerri called my "time of growth," I went

out and flopped onto the couch, flipped on the TV (truTV, not Comedy Central), and went to sleep. I had no dreams. I slept like a rock all afternoon (while the sound of *COPS* reruns played in the background), only waking a couple of times before morning— once to sneak upstairs and jam about a loaf of bread, a pound of cheese, and a banana in my mouth and once when Andrew poked me so he could show me a YouTube video of Aleah bashing a piano keyboard like a goddess. Even from Andrew's laptop, the sound was like that Florida wave crashing on me.

"She's too good," he said. "She's really, really good."

"Uh huh," I agreed, getting goose bumps. (I said uh huh— grunts, not words—so as not to break my plan to not speak to him or Jerri.)

"Yes," Andrew whispered.

Before I fell back asleep, I replied to Gus's mammoth email. I wrote: *beautiful girl in nightie lives in your house and plays your piano.*

I'm very certain that Jerri didn't check on me or watch me sleep.

CHAPTER 13:
IT IS 2:35 A.M.

I'm the opposite of how I was that day. I am the opposite of tired. No sleep. No sleep.

Jerri couldn't check on me if I did sleep. Jerri isn't in the house.

Maybe I will be able to sleep soon. The air in the basement is getting cooler or maybe I'm finally cooling down. I was so freaking hot. I was a pee pan full of sweat. It's possible I sweat more than most people because of my high metabolism (eat and eat and eat). Holy crap, I would kill for food. I'm going to get some food. Going to the kitchen.

• • •

Eating now. Ham and cheese in a sundried tomato wrap.

Painful trip to the kitchen though. I've got cuts and bruises on my shins. My foot hurts (stomped on). My left hand is throbbing. It's swollen. I've got a big bruise and bump on my hip.

I've never been this beaten up, not even when I crashed my Schwinn Varsity and slid on the gravel. Beat to hell!

2:38 a.m.

Story. Story. Story.

CHAPTER 14:
THE HILLS ARE ALIVE WITH
THE SOUND OF MUSIC

The morning after I wrote my to-do list, I seriously got up at the butt crack of dawn. It wasn't really intentional—I'd just slept so much of the day before that I couldn't sleep any longer. *Why not hit the road, get it over with?* It, of course, being the paper route. So I rolled out of bed, checked to see if Gus emailed me back (he hadn't), and picked up the papers super early and then went silent through the neighborhoods.

The route skirts the edge of town where there's a mixture of new and sort of old ranch-style houses. Jerri hates ranch-style houses. I don't know why. On the route, when it was later and people were awake, I really liked those houses because they have really big front windows, and I could look in and see what the people were up to. All these houses have lots of very dark, prickly evergreen bushes in front of them, which sort of scared me the first few days I did the route because they seemed like good places to hide if you wanted to surprise and kill the paperboy. But I'd begun to like these bushes because they smell really good. They smell like the holidays, I guess. Really piney. That morning, most of my route smelled like Christmas in the summer (not the farm poop smell that Bluffton usually has). And I couldn't see in houses because nobody was awake yet, but I could imagine all those normal people cuddled up in their beds, sleeping, which was kind of comforting too. And there wasn't much noise, no radios or TVs or lawn mowers or anything, but I could hear farmers in their tractors, probably miles away, and the occasional semi driving down State Highway 81. I liked how dark it was. I was unseen in the dark, sliding from house to house like a ghost.

It was still pitch-black dark when I got to Gus's house. Aleah wasn't asleep though. She practiced. I could hear her for a couple of blocks before I arrived. The sound wasn't loud, but it carried. Piano floating on dawn air. Sort of spooky, and classical music sounds really old, like something ghosts would listen to, and so I might have been scared if I didn't know it was her.

Like the day before, the front door was open, and Aleah Jennings—because it was definitely, no doubt, the same girl Andrew showed me on YouTube winning the Chicago Competition—was at the piano playing in her white nightie. And once again, I couldn't help it: I set down my bike, walked to the door, pulled open the screen, and leaned my head in so I could watch her hit those keys. There was something sort of angry and ferocious in the way she pounded that piano. There was like this "Don't eff with me, mother effer" feel to it. Amazing. More than that. I guess hypnotizing is a better word. My mouth was open, and I was probably drooling. I was halfway breaking and entering to hear her, and I couldn't help it because I was glued in that spot and then she promptly stopped and spun around on the piano seat. She looked directly at me.

"Daddy said you stopped to listen to me yesterday too."

"Uh!" I felt my muscles coil. I could feel the animal spring about to happen, that damn squirrel nut donkey leap. But instead, I breathed out slow and said "No."

"You didn't watch me yesterday?" she asked.

"No. I did. Uh. This is my best friend's house."

Then, Aleah jumped. She leapt from the piano bench, a shocked look on her face.

"And I think I'm a little freaked by you guys being here in Gus's house."

"I thought…Daddy and I thought that you were slow."

"Slow?"

"Retarded."

"No. I mean, maybe a little."

"Because you ran away like that and can't talk."

"I can talk."

"Well, that's obvious."

"Actually, I'm trying very hard not to be retarded."

"Oh. That's admirable." Aleah stared at me hard.

"Yeah. It's hard work."

"Yes. I know." Aleah stared at me harder.

"I have to deliver more papers, okay?"

"Okay." Aleah stared at me so hard I thought my head might catch fire.

"You play piano really, really, really well," I said, saying the final "really" really slow so she could tell I meant it.

"Thank you."

"I know too because my little brother is the best piano player of his age group in…in the world, I'd guess, and he isn't even close to as good as you."

She walked a few steps closer, across the living room. She spoke slowly. "Is his name Andrew?"

"Yes." I backed up a step, out the door.

"Do you know your mom called here?" Aleah got to the door and put her hand on the screen to hold it open.

I backed to the edge of the stoop.

"Yes."

"Then maybe you know that me and my daddy are coming over to your house this afternoon."

"I do. I'm going to deliver my newspapers, Aleah."

"And you know my name," she said.

"I do. I'll see you later."

I turned, jogged to my bike, got on, and pedaled away.

"Wait," she called. "I don't know your name."

"Felton," I called back.

"What?"

But that was enough. Man. Then I delivered all the rest of the papers in mere minutes because I was on beautiful fire.

When I got home, the sun was exploding orange in all its glory over the bluffs east of town, and Jerri was out on the stoop drinking coffee.

I forgot my pledge to not talk to her.

"Good morning, Jerri," I said.

Jerri squinted at me. Maybe she made a similar pledge she hadn't forgotten.

"Umm," she said.

Okay.

I went in and ate two enormous herb bagels I found in the fridge. I ate them with mounds of cream cheese. The bagels were great. Super fresh. And the sun was bright and the sky clear, and I actually talked to a girl, a pretty and talented girl, without running away immediately, which I hadn't done since fifth grade when Abby Sauter was actually my friend for a few weeks. I mean, what a great morning!

Then I remembered Cody Frederick and breathed deep and fought the response to be worried.

Weights. Coach Johnson. Maybe Ken Johnson? That chuckleheaded fat fart Jason Reese for sure. Fine. Fine. No problem. You can do it.

Then Jerri walked in and looked in the fridge. "Did you eat both bagels, Felton?"

"Yes."

"One of those was for Andrew. You're selfish."

Then Andrew walked in and shouted, "You ate my bagel? You ass brain jerk!"

I continued to chew and look out the window. Aleah Jennings playing piano in a white nightie—that's what I thought about. And also this: My family is nuts. I'd better not be here when Aleah comes for her visit. It will likely be a complete disaster.

After my breakfast, I checked email again. Gus had not returned my message. I wrote: *listen up…a beautiful girl our age plays piano in your house and sleeps in your bedroom.*

I didn't really know where she slept but hoped that bit of info would at least pique his interest.

It didn't seem to.

CHAPTER 15:
SO BIG!

I say this respectfully because Cody Frederick is probably the best person I know, seriously, but Cody's truck smells vaguely like pee in the same way he smells vaguely pee-like. Sorry. Maybe my nose is just super-smelling, which is bad?

At 9 a.m., the vaguely pee-smelling Cody Frederick came by the house and picked me up in his vaguely pee-smelling pickup truck, which was sort of cool. I'd never ridden in a pickup truck, pee-smelling or otherwise. You get to ride really high in the air compared to the low Hyundai Sonata that Jerri drives. You get to see stuff. I considered the possibility that I should buy a pickup truck after figuring out how to get my permit and then getting my driver's license (and saving money from the paper route so I have money for a truck). I wouldn't run over honkies in this truck, I decided, because honkies can be okay. We drove toward the school to lift weights.

"You ready for this, Reinstein?" he asked.

"I guess," I said, although I had no idea what we were going to do at weights except for lift weights, which seemed painful and ridiculous.

"I remember that you're a pretty good catch," he said as we made it off our gravel drive and onto the pavement of the main road. "At least, back when we were little. Can you catch a football, you think?"

"I can catch pretty well," I said. Then I said something dumb. It just popped out. "Are we big now?" I immediately wanted to take it back, but Cody didn't respond like a jerk.

"You are," he said. "You seem big. Bigger than me, I think. We'll find out because Coach is going to measure you and take your weight this morning."

"It's possible I'm big," I said, nodding, thinking. Even with all the growing and eating and hair growing I'd done over the months, it hadn't exactly dawned on me that I might be "big." I mean, I knew I was bigger because my clothes didn't cover my body. But actually big? I'd always been small or at best average, and I'd always felt tiny.

We drove through town high off the road, and I felt big.

At school, we walked along the west side on a sidewalk I've never been on before to a side entrance I didn't know existed. From there, we climbed up a back stairs to a loft overlooking the gym. (I'd noticed this place before from the gym floor but had never been in it.) This was the weight room.

I almost folded right then and there.

I can't even begin to say how bad it smelled. Oh, to smell that terrible smell. I've never in my life smelled anything so terrible, not even when we visited the Milwaukee Zoo and all the monkeys in the monkey house took dumps within like thirty seconds and then started flinging it around on each other, which got the poop smell thick in the air, which means we were getting monkey poop particles in our mouths and noses. I mean, that was totally gross, but this jock-o weight smell was even smellier. (I couldn't even tell what kind of particles I was getting in my nose and mouth, like nut sack particles? Yeeeeeek.) The smell burned my eyes. But I knew I would have to power through it. No folding. I couldn't gag, although I wanted to. I couldn't turn around and run back down the steps. Where would I go? Over to Peter Yang's fish-smelling house to hang out with his sisters and his mom?

Everywhere I looked, pee-smelling honky jocks and poopstinking farmer boys, who are football players, sweated like crazy and screamed and pushed all kinds of weight up on bars.

"Gaaaaahhhh!"

"Push it! Push it!"

I've known every one of these people for as long as I can remember but haven't talked to any directly in several years and had no idea that they spent any of their time doing this weird thing, pushing weight up on bars, while sweating animal smells and screaming "Gaaaaaahhhhh!" I stood there blinking. Cody said, "Smells terrible up here, doesn't it?"

"Uh, yeah," I said.

"Let's find Coach."

Coach Johnson wasn't in the weight room. We ended up downstairs in the coaches' office in the locker room. And, oh, shit, his son, that jerk Ken Johnson, was in the office with him. Ken crossed his arms and curled his lip when Cody and I walked in. I thought about Aleah Jennings pounding on piano keys. I smiled at him big and fake, which made my heart pump. *Take that, honky!*

His dad, the large-assed Coach Johnson, was happy to see me though. He said as much.

"Reinstein, I'm sure happy to see you."

"Thanks."

"You're the missing link, we believe."

"What?"

"You're a weapon. Potentially. A big gun."

"Big gun," I said.

"Frederick, you're showing great leadership for this team. Thanks for bringing Reinstein in."

"Yes, sir," Cody said.

"Reinstein. First things first. Pull off your shoes and socks. Let's get your measurements."

I did what he said and then stood against a wall with a bunch of numbers on it.

"Yes, sir, just about what I figured," Coach Johnson said. "Six feet, one and one-quarter inches."

"What?" I shook my head. "Say that again?"

"Six feet, one and one-quarter inches," Coach Johnson repeated.

"I'm six-one?" I said. I couldn't believe it. "Are you kidding me?"

"That's right," Coach Johnson said. "You're an inch taller than Kennedy right now."

"Who?"

"Ken Johnson? My son? You ever hear of him? Ha ha ha."

"Yeah. Hah," I said. Ken glared at me. I smiled back, heart pounding. This time, my heart wasn't pounding because of conflict with Ken Johnson though. This time, it was pounding from non-squirrel-nut adrenaline. I had no idea I'd gotten so tall.

"Get on the scale, son."

I walked over and got on the scale. Coach Johnson kept moving things around, weight things, to put the scale in balance. He kept saying "Yup." Finally, the scale balanced. "Felton Reinstein," Coach Johnson said. "You weigh a hundred and sixty-eight pounds."

"Whoa," I said, startled. "Am I fat?"

"You're a beanpole, Reinstein," Ken Johnson said.

"I've gained like forty pounds," I said.

"Seems to me your puberty went steroidal, kid," Coach Johnson said. Both Ken and Cody giggled when Coach said puberty. "You've got no fat on you. None."

"No muscle either," said Ken.

"Well, some muscle," Coach Johnson said, "He's about as fast as you, Kennedy. But we can do better."

"Beanpole," Ken whispered.

"Jerk," Cody whispered, looking at Ken.

"We can do a lot better," Coach Johnson nodded.

"I grew seven inches and gained forty-three pounds since the beginning of gym last year," I said, thinking back to Coach Knautz measuring us right before our Ping-Pong unit started last fall.

"Reinstein, you've got a frame. You hit the weights, keep eating and growing, and you could be carrying two hundred easily by your senior season."

"Is it good to be so fat?" I asked.

"That's D-I sized," said Cody.

"Pfff. Yeah," said Ken Johnson.

"And with that speed?" said Coach Johnson. "You're telling me. D-IA."

"D-I?" I asked.

"Division I college athletics, my boy. You could get much bigger too. Two-hundred and twenty isn't out of the question. You might get taller, of course. When do you turn sixteen?"

"End of July," I said.

"My goodness, you're big," said Coach Johnson.

Ken Johnson, who was shorter than me but probably weighed over two hundred, just glowered. I didn't smile at him. I was lost in swirling thought, guilty, crazy thought:

How did I grow so much? Am I driving Jerri crazy by eating every-thing? Maybe Jerri really needs my paper route money? I probably ate ten thousand pounds of food in the last year. Oh my God. We're running out of money, and that's why Jerri is so stressed out and has to go to a therapist and is crazy and calls me the f-bomber. I am eating Jerri and Andrew out of house and home! I ate that bagel! I ate an extra bagel! Oh, Jesus, I'm eating my family! Oh my God!

Coach Johnson talked, and Cody talked, and I spun out in my brain, and Ken Johnson shook his head, and then Cody motioned for me to follow him, which, thankfully, I did.

As we climbed the stairs to the weights, Cody said, "See, I thought you were big, Reinstein."

"I don't feel big, man."

"You gotta start carrying yourself like you're that big. Really, Reinstein. Nobody will ever mess with you again."

"Nobody messes with me now."

"Are you kidding me? Everybody does. I used to, and I don't mess with anybody because I think messing with people is dumb."

"Really? You messed with me?" Duh. I knew that. People messed with me all the time, and I hated them for it. That's why I spent an hour drawing a picture of Ken Johnson getting shot with bottle rockets two nights before.

"Carry yourself the way you really are, though, and it won't happen."

"How am I really?" God, I said stupid stuff. Pee-smelling Cody could've made shit of me, but he didn't.

"Here's the truth, Reinstein. Without ever setting foot on a football field, you're a Division I prospect. You've got unbelievable speed and a big frame. I'll never have any of what you've got."

"No. I'm a beanpole. You heard Ken."

"You're maybe a beanpole for an eighteen-year-old but not for a fifteen-year-old. You're just plain big for a fifteen-year-old."

"That makes sense."

"So carry yourself like a real athlete, and everyone will treat you that way. Okay? I'll let everybody know that you are a serious D-I prospect and then you just act that way."

"Uh huh," I said.

The voice in my head was still barking at me a little. It was going on about how I was eating Jerri and Andrew.

Then Cody stopped climbing and grabbed my arm, which shocked me out of my head completely.

"But you have to do something for me. You have to lift weights and practice all summer. You have to learn the playbook. If you do, we're going to be unstoppable come fall. That's what I want. I want to be unstoppable. We've got a huge line. Karpinski's sort of an ass, but he's an awesome receiver. I'll get him the ball. And you? With you, Reinstein? Nobody's gonna know what hit 'em. Jamie is going to be pissed to lose his spot, but you're our tailback, Reinstein. No doubt. Will you work hard?"

"Yeah," I nodded. I meant it.

"Thanks, man."

Cody looked deep into my eyes. It was sort of weird. I got a surge of adrenaline.

"I really appreciate it," he said.

I swallowed hard. I seriously meant it. I'd work my ass off.

We started climbing again toward the weight room, and I thought.

Who is Jamie? Oh, Jamie...Jamie...Jamie Dern...honky...grade older than me...dentist's son. Have I ever said a word to him? Is he in the weight room now? What the hell would Gus think about this? He'd hate it. He'd make mean jokes. Should I tell him? He might not even respond to my email. I don't have to tell him anything. Why don't I hate it? Why do I want to do what Cody says? How did I get so damn big? When will I stop growing hair? What if I keep growing and growing and growing? What if I turn into King Kong? (Accidentally smash Ken Johnson?) What if I have to move to an island away from people because I crush them if I live among them?

We popped into the putrid-smelling weight room.

"When's your birthday, Reinstein? It's coming up, right?"

"July 31st."

"I'm going to throw you a party."

"Oh, thanks." I wasn't sure I liked the idea.

And then we lifted weights. Jamie Dern was up there, pumping it like the rest of the yahoos. At one point, after a couple poop-stinkers prodded him, he came over to where me and Cody were. He said he wouldn't give up his spot without a fight, but he didn't look mad or anything. Maybe he looked relieved? He actually shook my hand. And even though I could keep up, pumping weight and shouting gah and sweating and stinking and lifting because I'm apparently naturally strong, at the end, I was so exhausted that I could barely walk.

"That's what I'm talking about! That's what I'm talking about!" Cody shouted.

Sort of couldn't walk. Before we left, Cody made me go down to the gym. He handed me a basketball. He said, "Dunk it, Reinstein."

"I can't. I can barely touch the net."

"No. Dunk it."

I looked up. Half the honkies of the world were hanging over the weight room railing, staring down at me. I got a burst of adrenaline. I bounced the ball once, looked up at the rim, took about five steps, sprung up, and stuffed the ball through hard with my right hand.

"Holy effing crap!" I shouted.

"Woooo!" Cody shouted.

"Jesus, Rein Stone," someone shouted from above.

"You're big," Cody smiled.

Then my legs turned to rubber, and I almost fell over. Cody and I shuffled to his truck, and he drove me home. When he stopped in front of my house, he said, "This is going to be a great summer."

"Yeah," I smiled and then climbed down from the cab. "Thanks, man."

I went in through the garage door and avoided Andrew and Jerri, who were upstairs talking. I showered but couldn't get the smell out of my nose. Pee smell. I wondered if I would smell vaguely of pee for the rest of my life? A brawny pee-smeller with fur and muscles. I wondered if it was worth it. I figured it was. I already knew it was. Definitely. *"Did you notice your brain didn't talk to itself the entire time you were lifting?"* the voice in my head asked. That's great. Maybe I'll learn to enjoy the pee smell. I thought of my dad and the smell in the Volvo. I sniffed and crinkled my nose. Weird smell. Then I coated myself in deodorant. I literally put deodorant on my whole body. Slip slop. Smelled like flowers soaked in pee. Gross.

The doorbell rang.

Oh, no.

Aleah.

Andrew.

Jerri.

Me.

CHAPTER 16:
WE COULD ONLY SEE EACH
OTHER, SERIOUSLY

Yeah, what a huge day.

From the bathroom where I'd just applied deodorant to my entire body, I heard Aleah and her father enter my house. I'd had no intention of "visiting" with them. Before. But wasn't I large? Wasn't I a Division I football prospect? I dunked a basketball. Holy Christ, I dunked a freaking basketball! I liked what Cody said too. I had to carry myself like an athlete. Jesus.

Before doing anything, I went into my bedroom to check email. Surely Gus would have written something hilarious by now. I opened it up. Nothing. Where the hell was Gus?

I wrote: *beautiful piano girl from your bedroom is upstairs in my house.*

From downstairs in my bedroom, I could hear Jerri play cheery, although I knew she was not.

"Oh, wonderful! Oh, lovely! What a beautiful dress!" She actually sounded kind of psycho (not surprising). I couldn't hear Andrew at all, which made me think he was acting strange, probably just staring unblinkingly at Aleah from behind his plastic nerd frames and thinking about how jealous he was of her.

If I let Andrew and Jerri represent the family, there was no way

I could face Aleah Jennings, super genius, at her house for the rest of the summer.

Om shanti shanti shanti, I mumbled. Then I slapped myself in the face. *No, no, no! Not freaky om shanti! I am big. I am huge. I am an athlete.*

I stood straight. I broadened my shoulders. I looked at myself in the full-length mirror that hung on my bedroom door. I said, "I am really big." What was weird was this: I looked really big. For real. I looked like a young man you might believe is fast. I clenched my jaw and glared and looked sort of mean and ugly and, potentially, sort of smelly, which was accurate.

• • •

You know, I've never had any particular dislike for people who play sports. When I was little, I even watched football on TV. Green Bay Packers. I asked for a Brett Favre jersey once for my birthday (a request Jerri totally ignored—I believe she got me a Shel Silverstein poetry book that year). I've watched basketball too. I like big dunks. Sure, jocks smell funny. But animals don't smell good, and I never blamed them for that fact. It's nature. I never would've even cared that Ken Johnson played sports if he didn't knock me off my damn bike when he was the one who parked half sideways in the swimming pool parking lot. Yes, it pissed me off that jocks called Gus names and me names and that Karpinski broke Sam Peterson's finger in seventh grade (I'm sure on purpose, but he never got in trouble for it). None of that has to do with sports. I don't mind sports. I like sports. I can be good at sports.

In the mirror, I expanded my chest, stood straight, and said, "I am huge."

• • •

Two minutes later, I'd thrown on sweats (not to look like a jock but because all my pants were too short and they made me feel dumb) and I was upstairs, ready to face Aleah and her dad, to show that Reinsteins aren't just a bunch of freaks.

I walked into the living room. Jerri and Aleah's dad were sitting in the leather chairs talking about the college or something. Not a terrible scene. Aleah, who was wearing an orange sort of airy kind of sundress and looked completely, utterly awesome, sat across the coffee table from Andrew. They weren't saying anything.

"Hello," I said and smiled while I walked in.

"It's the paperboy," Aleah's dad said. "You look bigger in the daytime."

"I'm growing," I told him.

"You do look tall," Jerri said, then stared at me and cocked her head a little. She breathed out really hard. "Umm, I guess you've met Aleah?"

"Yeah," I smiled.

Aleah's mouth was open. Her eyes were watery. She looked sort of stunned.

"Uh, hi…you…"

"Hi. It's Felton," I said.

"Hi, Felton," she said.

And then I blushed. I couldn't take my eyes off her eyes. We were in this tractor beam of eyeball heat.

"I could be a zookeeper," Andrew blurted. "That wouldn't bother me in the slightest. I could pick up animal poop all day. I'd be happy working at the zoo."

"Oh," Aleah sort of whispered, still looking at me.

"I could be a veterinarian or an astronaut or a..." Andrew nodded.

"Andrew. Have you played anything for Aleah?" I asked without looking at him.

"That'd be great, Andrew. Play something for me," Aleah said without taking her eyes off mine.

"I wouldn't want to be a medical doctor. I don't like people," Andrew said. Then, he got up and played piano.

Andrew is really good. People hear him and they can't believe he's thirteen. He's small, like I'd always been before the fur growth, but with big hands (I also have really big hands), and he puts his face close to the keys and looks up at the music and then back at the keys, which is sort of intriguing because it is so odd, and it seems impossible a tiny guy, so frail, can get so much sound out of a giant piano.

Neither Aleah nor I heard a single note he played. He must've played for ten minutes while Aleah and I stared at each other.

Then Jerri applauded and Aleah's dad said, "Boy's got chops." Then there were crackers and cheese, which I didn't eat. Andrew talked and Aleah nodded. I made a joke and Aleah laughed. Her dad laughed. Jerri laughed, not in a psycho way but in the sort of sweet, singy way she used to laugh. Aleah and I looked at each other.

"I don't miss Chicago so much today," she said.

"I don't miss my old friend Gus that much," I told her.

Aleah and I looked at each other. Andrew talked. Jerri and Aleah's dad laughed. Jerri smiled huge. Andrew stopped talking. Andrew left the room. Jerri talked. Andrew came back dressed in his white orchestra jacket, wearing a bow tie. I laughed. Andrew played piano some more. Andrew bowed. Aleah and I looked at each other. Aleah's dad said it was about that time. Aleah gave me her cell number and told me she'd be playing piano for me in the morning. I walked her to the door, and I guess her dad was with her, and I guess Jerri and Andrew were probably at the door too. But I honestly don't remember. All I remember is Aleah walking to the car, backward walking so she could look at me and smile at me, and then she was gone. And I stared up the road, where dust from the Jenningses' car hung in the summer air.

"Felton?" Jerri asked.

"Ass brain," Andrew said.

"Hello," I nodded at them both.

CHAPTER 17:
IT'S 3 A.M.

I just turned my light off.

I'm achy and would like to fall asleep thinking about Aleah at my house that first day because that was good. But I can't sleep. I can't. I can't!

In the past, after Andrew had a piano recital, which I would go to very grudgingly because I can be a jerk, he'd stay up until all hours of the night replaying the songs to try to burn it all into his memory or something. Jerri used to stay up with him, and she'd applaud after every replay and shout "Bravo!" They'd talk, and he'd play, and she'd clap and shout. I'd lie in the basement buried in pillows, going crazy, trying to get some sleep (even with my door shut, I'd very easily hear the piano vibrating through the floor like it was right next to my ear). He'd play and play and play. Crazy.

I understand.

I turned my light back on.

3 a. freaking m.!

Go. Go. Go.

CHAPTER 18:
I LIKE ME SOME FRIENDS

After the Jenningses left that day, I sat stunned in my room for a while. I wanted to tell someone about Aleah. Gus was the obvious choice, but I didn't want to send him email after email without him ever replying because I'd feel like a dork. I checked email again, hoping for Gus. No Gus.

I did have email though.

Cody sent me a link to a YouTube video of a dude named Jay Landry who is on St. Mary's Springs, the team Bluffton was to play in its first game of the season. Cody wrote: *check it. he's a safety. big time. going to notre dame after next year. we'll beat him.*

The video was set to some kind of screamy speed metal and was just a bunch of clips of this Jay Landry hitting people on the football field, totally killing them, knocking the ball out of their hands, hitting receivers trying to make catches, standing over kids he's knocked totally stupid, shouting, and flexing.

Oh my Jesus God, I thought. Is this really what's going to happen to me? Does Cody think I'm going to like football after watching this? I do not want to have my whole curly Jew-fro head knocked off my shoulders by Jay Landry. Jesus.

I closed the YouTube window and looked back at email.

No, no, no. Nothing from Gus. Man!

So I decided to be a dork. I wrote: *what if i said i love beautiful piano girl who lives in your bedroom and also that i am on football team and i am d-i football prospect and i jammed a basketball and i am smelly and in love?*

His response came back in two minutes: *what in hell you talking about? mom annoying as crap and i cant be on computer and grandmas apartment smells like poop and everybody hates me. i hate…*

Before I finished reading Gus's message, I received another email and went back to my inbox. Three messages in one day that weren't all from Gus (only one was from Gus)? I was on record pace!

It was from Cody again: *me and karpinski going to grill and watch longest yard (bad football movie) sometime next week. you wanna hit that?*

I responded right away: *sounds good, man. thanks for video. jay landry is an animal. scary!!!*

Cody messaged back right away: *landry is good, but you'll be better.*

I jumped out of my chair and then sat back down. I shook my head. I'm going to be better than that animal? Then this occurred to me: I might suddenly have friends and a girlfriend. *Are you kidding?* That sounded really good, even if I'd have to grill out with Karpinski, one of the worst honkies on record (sorry).

What a day!

• • •

I mean, this is really the thing: I'd never had a girlfriend. The closest I ever came was in fifth grade when Abby Sauter lived in a house on the golf course, and we walked home from school together every day for about six weeks. One day, she said, "You're my boyfriend. I wrote it in my diary." After that, I almost passed out every time she was within twenty feet of me. I stopped walking home with her, running out the door after school to avoid her but tried to smile when I saw her in the hall.

By the next year, she was sticking pencils down the back of my pants and calling me Rein Stone in Mr. Ross's independent study hour, which I totally didn't get. Why is Rein Stone funny? It's just my name with a vowel changed. When I cried, Jerri told me that kids have funny ways of showing they like each other. Oh, right, Jerri. She liked me *because* she stuck pencils in my pants. Great! I harbored the totally ridiculous notion that Abby was my girlfriend for another year.

Then in seventh grade, Abby, who had just gotten really tall and gotten boobs, shoved me against a locker so hard my head bounced off the metal. She pinned me there and breathed on my face because she'd just eaten a bag of Doritos. Jess Withrow shouted "Gross!" I figured at that point, Abby had broken up with me. My stomach hurt for a month.

But not long after, me, Gus, and Peter realized that honkies were honkies and were different than us and that we hated them.

In eighth grade, I got called Gay Boy Rein Stone so much that I began to figure I was gay, even though I was attracted to girls, especially Abby Sauter, who I believed to be a terrible person, but I couldn't help it. I thought about how I'd like to smell her Doritos breath again.

Then, in high school, the upper classes changed my name to

Squirrel Nuts or Squirrel Nut and didn't invoke Rein Stone as much, and I felt like Squirrel Nuts—jumpy and flinching, staring out across the lunch room, nibbling my food fast. My shiny, secret rocks and crystals were squirreled away in my leather pouch in my pocket, and I was so wary of the dangers present—ready to hop and hightail it.

Romance, gay or otherwise, didn't occur to me, not even when I searched for Ladies in Swimsuits on the Internet (which I did a lot all sophomore year).

Then I grew tall and strong and hairy and fast and a famous African American pianist, the most beautiful person I've ever seen in my entire life, told me she'd be playing music for me when I showed up at her house in the morning to drop off the paper.

As I lay in bed that night, I thought, "Aleah Jennings, you are my girlfriend." Yes, that was a little…What's that word? Presumative? Presumptive? Let me look it up.

Presumptuous!

Then, because I'd lifted weights and changed into another human being completely in one day (evolved from squirrel nut donkey boy to big) and was thus completely exhausted, I slept like a freaking rock.

CHAPTER 19:
JERRI DRINKS SOME WINE

I can't say that any real alarm bells had gone off before then. Yes, Jerri had called me an f-bomber, and yes, I'd made a pledge not to speak to her or Andrew ever again. But as I've said, Jerri had always been a little strange, and I'd just figured out that normal for me was not normal at all, not remotely, and I suppose I figured we'd just keep rolling along and we'd all figure it out or whatever, and I didn't follow through on not speaking to my family, and Jerri had seemed warm and happy while the Jenningses were over.

But the next morning was the first morning of the rest of my life.

My alarm went off, and I turned to stop its music but could almost not turn at all. "Whoa. Ouch." I struggled and had to basically fling my hand at the alarm clock because I could not control my shoulder muscles. "Owwww." I moved to leave bed, but everything burned. All my muscles were on fire. "Ahhhh!" I cried out. Had I caught polio or multiple sclerosis or cystic fibrosis or cirrhosis of the liver? Every little piece of me just totally killed. "Ahhhhh!" I had to lift my legs with my aching arms to get them out of bed. "What the hell is going on?"

I lumbered into shorts and a shirt and a windbreaker. I stumbled up the stairs, using my aching arms to steady me so I wouldn't fall over. I stumbled down the hall into Jerri's room, convinced she'd have to drive me on the route or I wouldn't make it because I'd caught multiple sclerosis.

But Jerri's room was empty.

The light was off. I pressed on the bed, but she wasn't in there. I moved to the door and leaned out into the hall. "Jerri?" I whispered, trying not to wake Andrew.

No one answered.

I lumbered back down the hall, holding myself against the wall. "Jerri?" I said louder.

No one answered.

The light was out in Andrew's room, but the door was open a crack. I pressed my lips into the crack and whispered, "Andrew?"

No one answered. No one made a noise.

Andrew didn't seem to be breathing in there. I reached through the door and turned on the light in his bedroom. I poked my head in. His bed was made. He was gone.

"What the hell is going on?" I shouted. No one responded.

As fast as I could on my broken limbs, I rumbled through the house shouting, begging for a response. The house was totally empty. I began to panic. Had aliens attacked us overnight? Had they taken Jerri and Andrew and poisoned me so my body would not work, so I could not pursue them (I pictured poor Andrew and Jerri undergoing total butt probes and screaming in pain)? Had kidnappers released gas into the house, knocked us all out, robbed us blind, taken my little brother and mother? I flipped on light switch after light switch, shedding light in every room.

Nothing was out of place. If robbers had robbed us, I couldn't see what they'd taken.

I tripped back downstairs calling for my family, nearly in tears from the pain and the loss of my potentially butt-probed family.

I do have experience with the world turning inside out. This was all so weird, like the day when I was five when my dad died. I was five. Five. But everything felt out of whack, was out of whack. Bizarro world.

While I stumbled around the house, everything felt out of whack.

Should I call the police, I wondered? I couldn't do it. Not yet. Maybe Jerri was outside. Maybe she was gardening at dawn. Maybe Andrew was helping her. Andrew never helped her, but maybe, because he knew he wasn't the best piano player in town, he was looking for a new career. As a gardener. Or a butt-probe victim.

"Oh my God. Oh my God," I mumbled, stumbling down the hall to the garage door.

I kicked open the garage door, terrified of what I might see on the other side (as I saw something terrible in the garage once before). This is what I saw: The light was on. Jerri's Hyundai was gone. Andrew was standing in there next to his bike, looking out the open garage. He turned to me and said, "Good morning, Felton. Ready to deliver some papers?"

"Where's Jerri?" I shouted.

"What's wrong with your head?" he asked. "It looks crooked."

"Where the hell is Jerri?"

"You look like Quasimodo. He's the hunchback of Notre Dame."

"Andrew. Where. Is. Jerri?"

"I heard her leave around midnight."

"Where'd she go?"

"I don't know. It's really none of my business. She's an adult, you know."

"God dang it!" I shouted. I didn't know what to think. I had no idea what was going on. I stumbled over to my Schwinn Varsity. I had to do my paper route.

"Why are you dragging your leg like that?" Andrew asked.

"It's really none of your business!" I shouted. I grabbed my paper bag, hunched my head, and let the bag drop painfully over my shoulder. Then I grabbed my bike and leaned it way down, using my left arm to pull my left leg over the seat.

"Okay," Andrew said. "Let's deliver some papers!"

Before I pedaled away, I turned to Andrew and said, "You wait right here. You wait for Jerri. If she shows up, call my cell."

"Can't do that," Andrew told me. "I'm going for a bike ride."

"Stay here!" I shouted. I biked away down the driveway, my aching legs straining against the pedals. At the main road, I stiffly looked back over my shoulder. Andrew was pedaling down the hill, about a football field behind me.

"Oh my God," I whispered, shaking my painful Quasimodo head.

• • •

At each stop on the paper route, I'd look up the street and find Andrew ghost-like about a block away, riding his bike in circles, waiting for me to move on. He never got any closer because he knew I'd go off on him. I sort of knew what he was up to. He either:

A) wanted to see Aleah play the piano, or B) wanted to make sure I didn't spend time with her alone. I believed the correct answer was "B" because he could've ridden directly to her house, skipping all the Felton tailing, if he just wanted to see her in action. In either case, I was terribly irritated and freaked (Jerri).

If my muscles weren't killing me, I'd charge you like a drunk elephant. I'd go gorilla all over your little monkey ass.

Fortunately for Andrew, I didn't have the strength to charge, and I was preoccupied with Jerri's absence, which I found really scary.

Jerri had never been gone when I woke up in the morning. Up until that moment, she'd been there every single morning of my life. Before she turned weirder recently, she wouldn't let me start a day without hugging me. After she turned weirder but before I got the paper route, she'd have breakfast for me in the morning, and she'd stare at me and try to say something nice, even if incomprehensible. Since the paper route, at least I knew where she was because her car was in the garage when I'd go out there, and it didn't seem remotely possible that she'd ever leave me. But now gone? Left at midnight? Jesus Christ! Where the hell did she go?

Her absence didn't faze Andrew one bit.

After hitting the first half of the route, I noticed that my muscles were loosening. By the time we got to Aleah's block (or the block next to Aleah's block, in Andrew's case), the kinks in my neck and shoulders were pretty much gone. My chest and biceps and thighs still hurt, but I felt looser. It occurred to me, coming around the corner, that my muscle disease could have something to do with the weight lifting the day before. The looseness might have meant two things: 1) That I could make my gorilla charge on Andrew, and 2) I could enjoy Aleah's playing, etc., in relative comfort—if my brain wasn't torturing me about Jerri's absence, of course.

But speaking of Jerri, as I rounded the corner, something stunned me so hard I stopped thinking at all and nearly crashed. Jerri's Hyundai was parked on the street in front of Gus's house. That is, Jerri's car was parked in front of the Jenningses'.

I squeezed the front brake on the Varsity so hard that the back wheel came off the ground, threatening to flip me completely over. I jumped off the pedals and steadied myself, staring at this most horrifying sight. Behind me, Andrew had come to a halt. I waved him toward me, my breathing getting thinner and thinner. Andrew kept riding in circles until I hissed, "Get over here, Andrew!" Then he slowly, nervously biked toward me.

When Andrew got to me, he whispered, "I don't know why Aleah would even like you, you athlete."

I pointed down the street at Jerri's car. "Look."

"Jerri? What the ass?" Andrew's mouth hung open.

"Come on," I said.

There was no piano sound floating as we biked slowly forward. The whole neighborhood was still, totally silent. I actually feared noise. I imagined Jerri sitting in that living room, babbling on to Aleah or Mr. Jennings, showing off what a freak show she actually is, talking about *Tayraysa* and turnips and "engagement" and Tito.

But it was worse than that.

As I approached the car, I saw Jerri's body folded over the steering wheel. "Oh, no. Oh, no. Andrew." As Andrew pulled up next to me, he began to scream.

Immediately, Mr. Jennings came bounding out of the screen door.

"Quiet," he shouted, trying to whisper at the same time. "Steady kids. Steady," he said. "Your mother's okay."

"Jerri's dead!" Andrew shouted, both of us staring at Aleah's dad.

Out of the corner of my eye, I saw movement in the car. Jerri looked up at us and rolled down the window. "I'm not dead," she said so quiet. "I'm stupid."

"Um, Felton. You have a paper for us?" Mr. Jennings asked.

I was so confused, but I reached in my bag and handed Mr. Jennings a paper.

"Andrew," Jerri said, popping open the trunk from inside, "put your bike in the car. Let's go."

"Are you sure you're okay to drive, Ms. Reinstein?" Mr. Jennings asked.

"I'm Mrs. Berba," Jerri said.

"I'm sorry?"

"I'm sorry, Mr. Jennings. I'm so sorry," Jerri said. "I'll take Andrew home now. Finish your route, Felton."

"Okay," I said. But I didn't move. Mr. Jennings stared at me holding his newspaper in both hands in front of him. Andrew stared at me. Jerri slumped in the front seat. I thought of her hugging me back when I was little. I thought of her singing John Denver songs by the campfire at Wyalusing.

"Jerri," I said. "Are you okay?"

"Andrew," she said, "get in the dang car."

Andrew's eyes were huge. He looked at me and shook his head. I looked over at Mr. Jennings, who was stuck in place.

"Go, Andrew," I said. "It's okay."

"Okay," he said, then put his bike in the back of Jerri's Hyundai.

"Have a good morning, Mr. Jennings," I said to Mr. Jennings. And then I biked off, totally shaking.

When the mail comes to our house, it's addressed to Jerri Berba because my mother never took my dad's last name. They were married though. Andrew established that fact later in the summer.

At the nursing home, that sort of young lady inmate screamed when I walked through the door. I didn't even pay attention to her.

I rode my bike home slowly because I wasn't exactly looking forward to getting home. My stomach hurt more than my achy muscles. I'd already thought Aleah and I were together, which was, yes, *presumptuous* because she didn't know me. I was sick over our breakup, even though we'd never been together for real. I was also sincerely, completely, totally terrified of what I'd find at home. What Jerri would tell me about what she did. What the consequences would be if she was even at home—*she might be gone. What if she left?*

As I got to the top of the hill on the main road heading down to our place, there was a buzz in my pocket. I stopped my bike.

I was wrong about Aleah. It was a text from Aleah. We'd exchanged cell numbers the day before. I couldn't believe it.

We sent several texts as the sun came up, me standing over my Schwinn Varsity, facing the east bluffs.

It went like this:

> That was weird.
> Sorry. Don't know what happened. What happened?
> LONG STORY. Stop by tonight. 8pm?
> What about your dad? Sure OK?
> Understands domestic drama. Too much. Worried about you.
> Andrew too.
> OK. Definitely. 8pm.
> See you then...

The voice in my head simply said *I'll be damned*. Yes, *unbelievable*, I responded to my own voice. Aleah Jennings, Aleah Jennings, Aleah Jennings. My heart swelled!

Dang, yeah, how freaking selfish. My own mother was suffering some unknown breakdown, and I was up on the hill by our house all swollen in love. I don't know what to say about that, so I'll just move right along.

If I hadn't been facing a serious domestic drama back home, I might have exploded all squirrel nut crazy and biked a million miles an hour down the hill. But the terror...the terror...Home was at the bottom of that hill. So after my swelling, I stared down at the house, swallowed, and then rolled down the hill slowly.

I was totally right to be terrified.

• • •

I rolled my bike up into the garage and found Andrew sitting on a lawn chair in there, his face totally red and his eyeballs red from crying. I know this because he was still sort of crying. Andrew cried out as I flipped down the kickstand on the Varsity.

"Jerri's an abusive alcoholic!"

I stopped in my tracks. Paused. I couldn't believe that.

"Did she hit you?"

"No."

"What do you mean alcoholic?"

"We drove home, then she barfed, then she drank wine."

Jerri was no drinker. Not at all.

"Where'd she get wine?"

"She bought like ten bottles for Aleah's dad for their visit yesterday."

Jerri hadn't served wine when the Jenningses were over the day before. This was completely out of character. Jerri could barely stand the smell of alcohol. Her own dad was an alcoholic, and she hated it. We could never go out for pizza because she thinks Steve's Pizza smells like beer.

"Okay. Okay. How is she abusive, Andrew?"

"I went to...I began to..." Andrew could barely get this out. "I played piano because I thought it would make her happy because it always makes her happy, and she told me to go make my crappy noise someplace else."

"That's bad," I nodded at Andrew. It really was about the worst thing you could say to the poor kid.

I went inside, even though I didn't want to. I found Jerri upstairs sitting on the couch with a wine bottle in front of her. She was staring out the picture window across the room.

"Um, hey, Jerri. Having some wine?"

She turned and looked at me.

"Felton, you look just like your father."

"I'm six-one," I said.

"Yeah, you are."

"He was short. Remember?"

"Right."

"Uh, you okay?"

"What do you think?"

"No."

"Right again."

"You really want that wine?" I asked.

"I do, but it makes me throw up, which isn't really that great, Felton."

"Did you drink wine before you went over to the Jenningses' last night?"

Jerri looked out the window again. Then her cheeks began to tremble. She spoke out the window too, like she wasn't talking to me at all.

"I haven't had a decent conversation with a man in years," she said.

"No. You have…Tito…"

"Don't you bring up that ass."

"Okay. You talk at the grocery store."

"That's not what I'm talking about!" she shouted. Then she started sobbing really hard, which was terrible.

"I don't know what to do, Jerri."

"You don't have to *do* anything, Felton. You're a damn kid."

"I want to help."

"It's not your problem! It's not your problem! You got that, kid?"

I stared at her.

"Please go away, Felton," she said, sobbing.

So I did. I went downstairs. What was I supposed to do?

I could've called Grandma, but that didn't occur to me.

CHAPTER 20:
I REALLY DIDN'T KNOW
WHAT TO DO

Jerri was an only child. There were no aunts or uncles or cousins to call, which I only thought about recently because Cody Frederick seems to be related to about ten percent of everyone in Bluffton, so this kind of thing couldn't have happened to him.

My dad, of course, was not around. His parents and sister didn't call us or write us or probably even think about us.

Gus and his parents, who were the closest thing me and Jerri had to people who cared about us, were in Venezuela.

Jerri's dad was dead.

Grandma Berba, Jerri's mom, lived in Arizona, and she seemed to hate Jerri. She really did. Jerri had always pretty much said Grandma Berba hated her (and I took that to mean she hated me and Andrew too—why wouldn't she hate us? Who wouldn't hate us?).

I should have called her right away. I didn't know.

Andrew is the one who suffered.

I'm sorry. I went about my business then. I mean, I tried.

3:21 a.m.

CHAPTER 21:
I CAN CATCH A DAMN FOOTBALL

Andrew was still out in the garage. Jerri sat silent in the living room. I stretched in my bedroom.

My body still hurt, but it was time to get going. I had to meet Cody Frederick and the other backs and receivers for pass routes after baseball. It was 8 a.m. Baseball practice finished at 10 a.m. Even though I could get to the field in ten minutes, I knew it was time to get going.

"What are you doing?" Andrew asked when I entered the garage.

"I have passing drills," I told him, getting on my bike.

"You're leaving?" he asked. "What am I supposed to do?"

"I don't know. Whatever you want, I guess."

He stared at me.

I left and biked up to Legion Field, where the baseball team was practicing, and Cody immediately shouted, "Yo, Reinstein! You're a little early."

Then all the honkies who had caused me pain and suffering for all those years started shouting, "Hey, Rein Stone! What's up, Rein Stone? How's it going, Rein Stone? Heard you dunked, Rein Stone."

They used that "funny" name Rein Stone in a brand new way. It was like I heard it wrong all those years. They weren't making fun of me. It was a good name. Rein Stone was like another word for pal or dude.

During practice, when somebody picked up a hard grounder or hit the ball hard, they looked up at me to see if I noticed, and I'd clap.

At one point, while the team was doing base-running drills, Coach Jones—a big fat ass gut buster with a country singer goatee who had once apparently pitched for the Chicago Cubs (not in the major leagues)—came over and said, "Can't take you this year, Felton. Roster's set. You practice a bit, and we'd sure be happy to see you out here next year."

I said, "Okay, Coach." Because I'd heard jocks do it all the time, I figured that it's cool to coaches if you call them Coach, even if they're not your coach, instead of calling them Mr. Jones or whatever. It must make them stand out from what they are at school otherwise, like driver's ed instructors, lunch room monitors, keyboard teachers, etc. Coach.

Coach Jones wasn't a regular teacher. He was the driver's ed person at the county tech school.

"Hey Coach," I asked, "How do I get my driver's permit?"

"Stop by practice tomorrow, and I'll bring you the paperwork," he said. "Think about baseball next year?"

"Definitely, Coach," I told him.

• • •

At one point, I believed nobody had noticed that I'm stupid fast. This was not the case at all.

Between baseball practice and pass routes, honkies galore came up to me and said stuff about my D-I prospects. "Wisconsin contact you yet? You on Rivals.com? Have you got your 40 time yet?" I answered no, not yet, to every question but only really understood the first one. The idea that the University of Wisconsin football team might contact me made me sweat a little, made my heart beat funny.

Uh, I didn't know how to play football. Didn't anyone realize that?

As far as Rivals.com and 40 times, I had no clue what the honkies were talking about.

• • •

I didn't disappoint the honky class during routes though.

At first, I was a little unsteady and totally uncomfortable, and I could feel my face getting hot because it was embarrassing in a squirrel nut way. Cody would show me a route in the playbook and would tell me where to run, and I'd run it as fast as I could, and the pass would end up ten feet behind me and I'd try to twist around and get it, which would almost knock me down. "Slow down," Cody said. "You can go all jackrabbit after you catch it. The only time you should take off like that from the line is if we're going downfield."

"Okay," I nodded, but I wasn't sure what he meant. (Face was frying hot from feeling stupid—honkies were whispering.)

So I breathed and slowed down. And that was it. It was there.

I sort of jogged the routes. And then somehow, it felt like there was nothing more natural in the world than running and receiving a football. Right away, when I moved more slowly, Cody threw it right to me, and I found out I can catch really well. I have really huge gorilla hands. (In the past, when I was shorter, I actually walked with my hands all balled up so nobody would think to call me gorilla.) Andrew has huge hands too, which is one of the reasons he's so good at piano. Gorilla hands are perfect for catching a football, by the way. Catching a football felt like falling asleep when you're super tired or taking a pee after you've just put down like ten gallons of water. So easy and so good. Catching a football felt like a huge relief.

Even though I was jogging, nobody could even come close to keeping up with me. Toward the end, Karpinski tried to cover me. I'd always hated Karpinski but had plans to grill with him and watch a football movie, remember, so I didn't want to embarrass him. I didn't really think I'd embarrass him. He's a jock. And he's a really good catch. But, it would seem, he isn't very fast. I jogged around, and he stumbled all over himself. Cody threw the ball, and I caught it.

"Jesus Christ," Karpinski shouted. Then he walked up to me and smacked the ball out of my hands, which I wasn't ready for. I sort of tensed because it was an asshole thing to do, something Karpinski would do to Squirrel Nuts. But then he said, "Nobody can cover you, Rein Stone." He was totally breathing hard like he was going to barf. "We're gonna kick everybody's ass." That put me back at ease.

At the end, Cody said, "Coach doesn't want me to do this, but just for fun, let's do a fly." Everyone else was drinking water out of bottles, lying around on the ground, sweating.

"Okay," I said.

"Line up about in the slot."

"Where?"

"Thirty feet that way," Cody pointed, "When I say go, just goddamn gun it. I'll try to hit you."

"Downfield?" I asked.

"Yup."

Everyone watched. I stood like I'd seen receivers stand on TV. When Cody said go, I let loose. I hadn't run like that since track, and it felt unbelievably great. When I was about twenty yards down the field, Cody threw the ball. I tried to keep one eye on it and one on the ground, which didn't work, and I stumbled a little. I balanced myself and kept running. Looking up, it seemed like the ball was a thousand feet in the air, and it seemed like it was going to pass me by and land way in front of me, so I just strode out as hard as I could, kept my eye in the sky, the little brown blob against the clear blue—and then it got bigger and bigger, and it was falling in front of me, so I stretched my arms way out and watched the ball drop into my hands. The honkies all cried "Woo!" Somebody shouted "Holy shit!" I turned around and jogged back toward the group like that catch was something I've done my whole squirrel nut life. Inside my chest, though, my heart exploded, not with heart attacks but with everything.

Catching a ball is the best. "That was the damn bomb right there," Karpinski said, high-fiving me as I got to them.

Honkies smiling everywhere.

I smiled so hard I thought my face would break.

• • •

After pass routes, Cody put my bike in the back of his truck.

"That's a hell of an old bike," he said.

"It's from when my dad was a kid," I told him.

"It's from when you were a kid. You've been riding that bike for like three years. You used to look hilarious on it."

"Um." Why did Cody remember my bike? Did I look that dumb? "Yeah. I could barely reach the pedals a couple years ago. Now it fits perfectly."

"It was your dad's?"

"Yeah."

"He must have been tall too."

"I don't think so," I said.

Me, Cody, and Karpinski then drove over to Main Street to grab a sub. We listened to rap music. I'd never listened to rap music. I felt like I was in some kind of bad ass rap-jock movie. Thump. Thump. Thump. Rap sort of makes things in slow motion. Heat came off the streets, which were reflecting the sun. The speakers boomed kind of lazy and scary.

Along the way, Karpinski—who was seriously sitting on my lap ("You pop wood, Rein Stone, and I'm going to have to punch you."), which was gross, he was completely sweaty—said, "Erin Bellmeyer on the right." Erin, a honky girl, walked down the street. Karpinski slid over me to get to the open window and then shouted, "Hey, Erin! Hey, Erin! You're my Balls' Mayor!" She laughed and flipped him off.

I don't completely understand honky humor, which is maybe why I've not been funny.

At Subway, Karpinski was totally loud, swearing constantly, jamming a sandwich in his face, spitting food out, firing wet pieces of bread out of his straw at younger kids, who looked at him and smiled like they enjoyed it. I could see the fear in their frightened eyeballs though. I've been one of those kids. Me and Andrew got hit by spit wads by jocks way older than us when we were at Subway two years ago. I smiled like the poor dumb kids here when Karpinski did it. Even though he was only eleven, Andrew actually said, "You are so immature." Andrew's pretty fearless. I was mortified and told Andrew to shut up. I was still kind of mortified when Karpinski did it, even though I was no longer the target.

"You're such a pig, Karpinski," Cody laughed.

Karpinski snorted and jammed food in his mouth.

And I fake-laughed my entire ass off. Ha ha ha ha ha. Ho ho ho ho! My ass is falling off! Ha ha ha! *Thank God Gus is out of the country. He would skewer you for laughing.* Ha ha ha ha!

I'm an asshole.

When we got up from the table, my muscles were in walnut balls again.

"Ahh. Jeez, I'm sore!"

"Good. You worked hard enough. More weights tomorrow," Cody smiled.

Cody and Karpinski drove me back to my house. (*Thump. Thump. We are Honky Gangstas. Thump.*) As we drove up the driveway, Karpinski, who had, of course, been a mammoth asshole to me as long as I can remember, said, "You're not as big a dickweed as I thought, Rein Stone." We did some kind of weird handshake.

I decided he wasn't that big a jerk really (seriously, he isn't). Then we got to the top of the driveway.

Andrew was still outside the house. He was sitting upside down in a lawn chair, with his back arched so his straight hair touched the gravel. He had his arms crossed over his chest. He stared at the truck.

"That kid is a dickweed," Karpinski said.

"He's my brother. He's a little pissed off today."

"That's why he's upside down?" Karpinski asked.

"Probably."

Cody jumped out and helped me get my Schwinn Varsity out of the back of the truck. Upside down, Andrew stared the whole time.

After Cody and Karpinski left, I wheeled my bike passed upside down Andrew. I said, "Jerri still drinking wine?"

"I wouldn't know. I'm an animal. I live outside, pee in the yard, and steal cucumbers from gardens."

"Jesus, Andrew. You're acting like a freak."

"Oh, am I?"

"Yes."

"Then I'm a freak."

I parked my bike in the garage, entered the house, and found it dark and quiet.

CHAPTER 22:
I CAN BE A NORMAL DAMN TEENAGER, SORT OF

Jerri was out cold the whole rest of the afternoon. I checked on her a couple of times. She was breathing. It actually occurred to me that I was acting like Jerri when she'd stand there watching me while I watched TV (pretending to be asleep so I wouldn't have to talk to her). *Is she really sleeping?* One time, I got real close to her and put my hand in front of her face to see if she'd flinch because maybe she was pretending to be asleep so she wouldn't have to talk, but she didn't move. Plus, there was no TV in Jerri's room at that time, so there wasn't anything she could be squinting at.

I spent most of the afternoon watching TV myself, a Big Ten Network replay of the 1994 Rose Bowl game, where Wisconsin beat UCLA. Wisconsin had this little bowling ball running back who ran over people and stomped on their heads. *He's tougher than you, but you're faster.* As I watched, I stretched my legs because they seriously hurt. Andrew never came inside.

Around seven, I took him out a goat cheese sandwich. He still sat in that stupid lawn chair out on the driveway.

"Why don't you come inside?" I asked.

"I'm not welcome in my own home," he said.

"Yes, you are, Andrew. Just come in and watch TV, okay?"

"I don't think so," he said.

About ten minutes later, he did come in though.

"Can I watch cartoons?" he asked.

I got off the couch, motioned for him to sit down, then went into my bedroom to email Gus from my laptop. I wasn't sure where to start. So I just said: *jerri lost her marbles today. might be in trouble.* I hit send and went into the bathroom to shower. While I scrubbed my fur-bursting, pee-smelling jock body, I figured Andrew had stayed out of the house for over twelve hours. He's no dickweed. He's tough as hell. I also thought, Gus will reply with something good. He'll help me figure out what to do about this crazy shit.

Gus is only sixteen too, of course. What was I expecting?

I dressed in the biggest jeans I could find, not that they were big. They were far too small for my body. Jerri bought them for me in late May, just a month before. I was still growing like a weed (not a dickweed). All this growth and too small pants, etc., made me wonder if I could seriously take that jerk Ken Johnson in the 100 meters. My guess was yes. If only I had the chance. I pulled on the longest T-shirt I had, so as not to show off my furry belly button, and headed out past Andrew watching *SpongeBob*.

"Where are you going?" Andrew asked.

"Bike ride. Call if you experience any trouble."

Andrew pulled the phone off the side table and sat it in his lap but didn't say anything else; just kept watching the sponge.

Of course, I couldn't tell him I was going to see Aleah.

• • •

Why couldn't I tell him? Because he'd probably have wanted to come with me, okay? Or he might have tailed me and gone all peeping tom in the windows. He had my cell number if something went wrong, and Jerri had it on speed dial on the phone, so he could just press a button, and I'm very fast. I could get back to the house in mere minutes if need be. There was clearly no reason to bring up the sore subject of Aleah. What if he woke Jerri? What if Zombie Jerri was in a Frankenstein mood and got the word from loose lips Andrew and decided to lumber over to the Jenningses' again? ("Give me some wine!") I sincerely doubted my relationship with Jennings, both father and daughter, could withstand another dose of drunken Franken-Jerri. It was good judgment, sound judgment on my part not to tell Andrew anything, okay?

Crap.

So I biked toward my ridiculous paper route, not to deliver papers but to see a girl who plays piano and who lives in my best friend's house. The sun was still pretty high because it was summer. I sweated in my tight jeans because it was summer. I smelled the pee-smell of my own athlete's body. I biked to see a girl, it occurred to me, who may well not want to see me at all, who may well be under instructions from her father to bring me to her house for purposes not even remotely regarding the love I had in mind.

I haven't yet reported on the sound of my anxiety fantasies. Sounds like this:

What if this is some kind of intervention? What if Mr. Jennings called a social worker, some harsh-looking old lady who tells me that I'm going to be pulled from my home and stuck in foster care or the care of the state because Jerri is obviously an unfit mother because we call

*her Jerri and she doesn't really work ("What kind of work is being a
crossing guard, Felton? That's not real work."), and she has hair under
her arms, and she sleeps in her car when she's drunk ("Jerri Berba
is entirely unfit."). This could be it, Felton. This could be the beginning of a nightmare without end. Andrew and I will send letters back
and forth from shag-carpet country homes, rundown, stinky, dirty
homes owned by dirty people who make money taking in defenseless
foster kids. They'll use the money to buy beer and cigarettes, and they'll
blow cigarette smoke in my face and burn Andrew's forearms with
their butts, and they'll force him to drink beer too. I'm sorry! I'm sorry!
The letters between me and Andrew will be filled with our love for
each other and be filled with the severe abuse we're enduring. But it
won't matter because the abuse will eventually break us down, kill our
brotherly love, because we're not strong enough, and we'll grow apart
and get hardened and do crimes and get no cards or calls from Jerri.
Poor Jerri—screaming for wine, crying, stuck in a straitjacket in some
rat-sack dirtbag asylum in some dirty city. This is crazy. Come on.
Snap out of it, Felton. Come on. No! No! You're not being crazy at all!
This is not implausible and stupid at all! You found your dad hanging
from a beam in your garage! Five years old! You know the whole wide
world of horror isn't something from a stupid movie. It's reality. It's true!
The whole wide world of horror will open up. It's ready to swallow
you whole at any given moment, particularly this particular moment
because this moment with Andrew saying he's an animal that pees in
the yard and Jerri buying ten bottles of wine is just the kind of moment
when...*

"Are you planning to park your bike?" Aleah was standing at the end of her driveway, her arms hanging at her sides, her mouth open, her eyes blinking. I realized I'd been circling her block for like ten minutes.

I can be a serious head case. Truly.

I stopped my bike and breathed (*om shanti shanti shanti—dang it*).

"Sorry. I was just thinking."

"What about?"

"Bad stuff."

"I figured that. Would you like some iced tea?"

"Yes. Thank you."

"Come inside then."

"Okay. Thanks."

• • •

Aleah is an odd person. I found that out right away. She's extremely intense all the time. This is not reserved for piano playing. Her piano playing is just a normal part of how she is second to second, minute to minute, day to day. On fire.

"I love human drama," she told me.

"Oh." I wasn't sure I agreed.

"Your family's weird."

"Yes. That's true." She was certainly right.

"I'm weird. It's okay to be weird."

"I don't know."

"I embrace being weird."

"Oh." Huh?

We sat on opposite ends of Gus's couch in the living room. She'd poured me some really sweet iced tea that tasted almost like blueberry juice. She sat cross-legged, facing me. She was wearing a white V-neck T-shirt and jeans and a red bandanna tied over her hair. I couldn't exactly turn toward her because my legs are long. They felt twenty feet long. *I'm spaghetti man.* So I had to keep them on the floor in front of me because if I tried to sit cross-legged, I'd fall off the couch. I didn't tell Aleah, but just three years before, Gus and I had made a fort out of this couch's pillows. We'd written out a list of people who weren't allowed in the fort, which included our mothers. We then played with super balls inside the fort. We named the balls after honkies (a couple of whom I'd eaten lunch with that day), and we threw them hard against the wood floor, saying crap like "Take that Karpinski!" Several times, the balls bounced off our faces, which hurt and which made us even madder at the honkies. *You want to hear about weird, Aleah?*

"I've always been weird," Aleah said. "But I'm weirder now than ever."

"Where's your dad?" I asked.

"He's teaching. Then he goes for a glass of wine with another English prof."

"Wine?"

"Yes."

This was not to be an intervention.

"Does your dad know I'm here?" I asked.

"Of course. Daddy suggested I invite you over. I would've anyway. He's worried about you, you know?"

Okay. "Tell me what happened last night, okay?"

It wasn't as bad as I thought. There was no screaming or breaking and entering or talk of turnips or engagement or Tito. Jerri didn't mention me or Andrew at all either. She'd just knocked on the door sometime after midnight. She said she only knocked because the light was on. She looked like she'd been crying. She told Aleah's dad, who's named Ronald, that she had a lovely time talking to him. He agreed it was nice to talk. Then she left. "Daddy said she smelled like alcohol, but she wasn't acting drunk," Aleah said. "We both thought it was odd, of course, but not that odd. My mom acted much crazier than your mom."

"Oh. Okay. That's not so bad. I figured Jerri kicked in your door and killed your cat or something," I said.

"We don't have a cat."

"I mean, not literally."

"Yes, well, there's a little more." Aleah nodded.

Aleah was playing piano around 3 a.m. when the doorbell rang again. Ronald came bounding out of his bedroom in his pajamas, looked at Aleah, and said, "This is a little much," assuming Jerri was at the door. But it wasn't Jerri. It was a police officer.

"Sorry to bother you. Saw the light on. Just wondering if you know Jerri out there?" The police officer turned and pointed to Jerri's car, parked out front.

"Oh, shit," I said.

Ronald told the officer that he did know her. The officer asked Ronald to dump out the bottle of wine he'd found on the front seat.

"She's asleep," the officer said.

"That's the bottle of wine she brought over when she came for dinner," Ronald told the officer, which was a lie, of course. "She didn't drink much of it."

The officer paused for a moment, stared at Ronald, looked over at Aleah, then told them to be nice to Jerri. He said that he'd known her all his life and that she's a good girl. He said she's had a rough life.

"Oh my God. That cop was Cody Frederick's dad."

"The policeman said he'd call your mom in the morning to check up on her."

"I don't know. I don't know if he did."

"Why has your mom had a rough life, Felton?" Aleah asked.

"Ummm, suicide?"

"Suicide. Your dad?"

"Ummm, yes. But Jerri's never been…She's never been bad off. She's always been okay until this year. I think."

"It's getting dark! Let's go for a walk!" Aleah said, jumping off the couch.

• • •

There is one social class in Bluffton I've failed to mention. It's the class, I guess, that Jerri probably belonged to, at least when she was a really young girl. You've got your honkies. You've got your poop-stinkers. You've got your college kids. Then you've got this big group of sort of hidden kids whose parents work at Kwik Trip or Subway or in bars or not at all. It's a pretty fine line between honkies and these people sometimes, and the big difference is parents that drink a lot of beer and are noisy when they do, which is maybe why Jerri was sort of one of these people. (My grandpa, who died of lung cancer when I was a baby, owned a bar, made a lot of noise, drank a lot of beer.) The reason she wasn't exactly one of these people is that her mom, Grandma Berba, who now lives in a condo in Arizona, sold insurance, divorced my grandpa, and didn't drink a lot of beer. Plus, Jerri is really smart and was really good at school, which means she turned honky, or almost college kid, from how she described it. This class in Bluffton tends to ride in the back of ugly cars, live in ugly houses close to Main Street or in trailer parks on the outskirts of town, wear clothes from garage sales, swear a lot, get into fights when they're in middle school (or pregnant in eighth grade), then sort of disappear when they're in high school. If they don't disappear, it's either because they're serious criminals, or loud, raspy girl-drunks, or because they've migrated into honkiness, which means they're probably okay at school or sports. You might call them townies or burners or druggies. Gus calls them dirt balls, but it didn't catch on with me because the name made me feel bad for my grandpa and for Jerri. It's the serious criminals you have to watch out for.

Herein lies the story of how Aleah was made aware of townies (or dirt balls) because of an interaction with a couple of serious criminals, Rick and Rob Randle.

Aleah and I left her house and walked out onto Hickory Street. The sun was setting, and the sky was all orange and purple. It was really pretty.

"I really love how the air smells here," she said.

"Like poop?" I asked.

"Is that poop?" she asked.

"I've always thought of it as poop," I said.

"It smells like the country," she said.

"Like poop," I said.

"Chicago smells worse in the summer," she said.

"Chicago smells worse than poop?"

Aleah laughed.

"Uh huh," she smiled and nodded.

"Do you miss Chicago?" I asked.

"No. Not really. I've had a bad year."

"Why?"

"My mom."

"Suicide?"

"No. Not even close! Too much life in her. That's what Daddy says."

"Oh."

We turned right on Davis Street and walked along the curb. There aren't many sidewalks in this newer part of town.

"So," I said, "how does it feel to be the best piano player of your age group in the universe?"

"I don't know," she said, and she tilted her head and squinted like she was thinking.

"Do you think there might be really good piano players in China or Russia or something, so you can't be sure you're the best?"

"I sometimes wonder, I guess, about other pianists. Not very much though."

"I guess you won't know for sure until you're older and can fight it out with them in competitions for adults."

"No," she said. "I don't think about that."

"No?"

"No. I practice at night."

"That's pretty dedicated. That probably tells you you're the best, huh?"

"No, no, no."

"No?"

"Stop saying no!"

"No."

"Stop!" She grabbed my arm and squeezed. She laughed. Then she slid her hand down and grabbed my hand. We walked holding hands, which made me totally dizzy and sort of sweaty.

Om shanti shanti shanti.

"Go on please," I exhaled.

"While I'm playing, I sometimes wonder if there's a girl like me in London—that's where my mom lives."

"Wow. That's cool."

"Yes. Not really. I mean London is cool, but my mom isn't."

"Oh. Because she's got too much life in her?"

"I guess. And she's crazy and mean."

"I hear that," I laughed. Aleah laughed too. I'm not sure what we were laughing at.

"So I wonder about a girl playing in London or in Germany or Japan or something, who's playing during the daytime because it would be daytime there while I'm at the piano, and maybe she's practicing the same piece as me, a girl who loves it as much as I do."

"I bet you beat them with a stick," I said.

"That's not what I mean," Aleah laughed.

Just then there was a loud booming sound behind us. Loud guitar and drums, heavy metal music. We both spun around, dropping our hands. The sound came from an old car that was driving really slow. The car stopped and then its engine revved.

"Who's that?" Aleah asked.

"Townies," I said.

Then whoever was driving jammed on the gas and accelerated like crazy, heading right toward us. Aleah and I jumped up on the curb. As the car passed, someone within shouted "Squirrel Nuts!" An egg crashed at my feet.

"The Randles," I said.

"What?"

The car squealed around the corner. We heard it accelerate down the block and then squeal around another corner.

"Hmm," I said. "They're probably coming back around."

"What are they going to do?" Aleah asked.

"Just be jerks," I said. "Let's cut through yards back to your place."

We walked quickly behind the nearest house, tripping in the dark. The car came squealing around the corner onto Davis Street. As it passed, someone yelled, "You doin' Aunt Jemima back there, Squirrel Nuts?"

"Oh my God. I'm so sorry. I…I can't believe they said that," I said. We cut through several backyards, heading in the direction of her house. I was a little worried that we'd trip motion sensors and get caught in spotlights.

"Said what?" Aleah asked.

"That Aunt Jemima thing. This town sucks."

"I hear worse than that at my private high school in the city, Felton."

"You do?"

"I'm more concerned that you're part of a gang fight."

"What are you talking about?"

"Why did they come after you?"

"They didn't."

"They threw an egg at you."

"That's Rick and Rob Randle. They throw eggs at everyone. They're criminals."

"Are they your friends?"

"No. Of course not."

"How do you know their names?"

"This is Bluffton. I know everybody's name."

"Weird."

We crossed another couple of yards and then were back on Hickory Street, Aleah's street. As we got to her house, another car squealed around the corner and skidded to a halt under the street-light at her corner. It was a new Honda. There were three smashed eggs on the hood. Jamie Dern leaned out the window. "Yo, Rein Stone. Have you seen the Randles? They egged Reese's car." Jason Reese was driving. A couple of other honky football players sat in the backseat. They leaned over to look at us.

"Yeah. They were just over on Davis."

"Who's that?" Jamie nodded at Aleah.

"This is Aleah."

"Okay. Nice to meet you," Jamie said to her. Then he shouted "Let's go." They were obviously pretty mad.

"He's very polite for a gangbanger," Aleah said as we stood in her driveway.

"Jamie? His dad's a dentist."

"Do you think he'll shoot the Randles when he finds them?"

"No," I laughed. "Plus, he won't find them. There's like a million miles of streets and highways and county roads, not to mention all the gravel roads. Jesus, the Randles could drive all the way to the Mississippi on gravel roads. Reese will just drive around and around and around until they get tired and stop for a Quarter Pounder. Then they'll probably go to Kwik Trip for a slushy or maybe to Walmart to walk around.

"What if they do find the Randles?"

"Probably cut them."

"Really?"

"With their knives."

"Shut up."

"Okay."

"Seriously, Felton. What will they do if they find the Randles?"

"There could be a fight but probably not. The Randles don't want to fight football players because they'd get smeared. Football players don't want to fight the Randles because they'd get in trouble. There could be some shouting, I guess. Probably somebody will flick the bird, shout some names, you know, "You jerks, clean up this egg from my mom's car or I'll punch your nuts off!" But it won't be a big deal. Tomorrow night, the same thing will happen all over again. Eggs. Chasing. Quarter Pounders. Crap goes on and on. Ten years from now, Jamie Dern will probably be a dentist."

"Weird. What about the Randles? What will happen to them?"

"They'll go to jail for stealing cigarettes. Their stinky kids will eventually be on Main Street playing video games."

"Really?"

"That'd be my guess."

"Weird."

"It's the circle of life."

"I like this town."

"Are you crazy?"

"The stakes are low."

"That's true. Low stakes. Yup."

I followed Aleah back up toward her house. I wanted to go inside with her. She stopped me on the stoop.

"It's time for me to practice," she said.

"Piano?"

"Yes."

"Okay." *Oh, man! No!*

"I'll be playing for you when you drop off the paper."

"Don't you ever sleep, Aleah?"

"All day long, all summer long." Then she leaned over and kissed me on the cheek. "See you in the morning, Felton." She opened the door and went in.

I stood there for a second, stunned. Then I called after her, "I'll tell Jerri not to come over tonight with her wine," but the door had already shut behind her.

Then my cell started buzzing in my pocket.

• • •

"Where the hell are you? You left two hours ago. Aren't you tired of riding your bike?"

I'd just answered my cell and was in Aleah's driveway climbing on my bike one-handed so I could speak. "Why are you awake, Andrew? Are you okay? What's wrong?" I was sincerely scared.

"I'm hungry."

That's not so bad. I exhaled. "Is Jerri awake?"

"No. She hasn't been up at all."

"Get yourself something out of the fridge."

"I don't want to go upstairs. Can you come home please?"

"I'll be there in a couple of minutes."

Andrew hung up. I rode home slowly, sort of split between the monkey elation of Aleah's lips touching my cheek and wariness over the Randles making a return and a mess of me with their eggs and also wariness over the Reinstein-Berbas making a mess of me with their true-life drama. The stakes weren't really so low either. There aren't low stakes. Jerri grew up in this town and married a professor that killed himself. The Randles probably wouldn't die in gang violence, but they could easily get drunk and explode their Chevy against some tree out in the country. That definitely happened from time to time. Are the stakes low for the poop-stinker kids who get their arms ripped off by farm machinery? "Oh, no problem. I've got a whole other arm, Pa. Let's bale that hay!" Easy come, easy go. Just another day in rural Wisconsin. I told Aleah a whole bunch of crap about driving around and being a honky or a criminal, and the fact is, I don't know anything about it. Me, Peter, and Gus used to drive around sometimes, and I witnessed honkies shouting at the Randles and the like, but I have no idea what they do afterward. Would I find out, now that I'd been adopted into Honk Honk Honky culture?

Her lips touched my face. The stakes aren't low.

I entered the house from the garage. Andrew was lying on the couch watching a horror movie. He didn't even look at me. I pushed up his legs, sat down on the couch, grabbed the remote control out of his hand, and flipped the channel.

"Don't watch that crap," I said.

"Why not?"

"You're afraid to go upstairs as it is."

"Just don't want to see our mother," Andrew said.

"Yeah, she's a horror movie," I said.

"She certainly is."

I pushed myself up and climbed the stairs to the living room. No lights were on. With a twinge of fear, I moved to the hall light switch. The last thing I wanted to see was some grizzly death scene involving Jerri. But when I turned on the light, she was nowhere to be found. I moved down the hall and could hear Jerri breathing in her room.

A voice came from her bed.

"Felton, is that you?"

"Yeah. You okay, Jerri?"

"I feel like shit. Probably shouldn't drink wine."

"I guess not."

"Is Andrew okay?"

"Yeah. He's watching TV in the basement."

"Good. I'm going to get some sleep."

"Sounds like a plan."

I turned and walked back into the kitchen. Jerri sounded a little better. I felt better. In the kitchen, I gathered a bunch of chips and salsa and junk and some sparkling waters out of the fridge and took it downstairs to Andrew.

"Jerri isn't dead," I told him, putting the food on the side table.

"We're truly blessed," Andrew said.

Man, he looked beat up. There were dark circles under his eyes, and there was some dry grass in his hair. He had smudges of dirt on his cheeks. The light from the TV made him look pale and fragile. Man, he just looked bad! I honestly felt a little guilty for being so happy. I almost couldn't keep it inside. I almost said, straight up jackass style, "Aleah Jennings kissed my cheek. This cheek! This one on my face!"

I didn't tell Andrew anything. We watched *George Lopez*, a show we both hate, in silence, except for the crunching of our chips.

CHAPTER 23:
MAYBE I DON'T NEED GUS?

Andrew fell asleep immediately after he ate the chips. Poor little dipshit. He snored sort of soft, and I stood up to go to bed. I couldn't sleep though, so I checked email, hoping to find something from Gus. He hadn't responded. There was another message from Cody: *dad told me about your mom. you ok, man? check this out.* He sent a link to a website with a bunch of videos of asswipe Ken Johnson playing football. More crushing tackles and fumbles and touchdowns and crap that made me nervous. It had all kinds of recruiting information, height and weight and track times and other physical tests and an interview with Ken where he acted all cool and serious and good about helping his college team be great. Bullshit. Cody wrote that I'd get a page on this site too. *I've never played football!* I closed Cody's email.

Andrew snored outside my room. Jerri slept upstairs. Tough day.

But really, Jerri actually seemed okay. I figured she'd had her little blowup and things would go back to normal, which was not normal but was normal for me. I couldn't wait to get up and see Aleah playing piano. I couldn't believe that at *that* moment, a few miles away, she was awake too, practicing. Even though Gus hadn't responded to my earlier email, I wrote to him: *I am a very lucky young man with a girlfriend.*

Gus immediately responded by email: *what girl wants you? must be cow.*

Was that supposed to be funny? Why didn't Gus respond to my serious email about Jerri being crazy? What a jerk! Cody asked how I was doing. Gus said only a cow would like me.

Then I started wondering why Aleah would like me. She didn't know anything about me, except I have a weird family. Then I tried to go to sleep, but I couldn't sleep because anger boiled in my gut about what Gus said, and I wanted to yell at him for being a jerk, but I couldn't because he was on another continent. I worried that Aleah wouldn't like me once she figured me out because there wasn't much to like. What if I do date cows? Real cows? What if they moo and chew grass and smell terrible?

I suppose I drifted off to sleep but not for a long, long time. Gus had gotten all my emails and responded to just that one *and* he responded like a total jerk.

• • •

Because I had such a hard time falling asleep, I got up very late. Most of the night, I hallucinated about Aleah's piano and feeding Andrew chips and getting crushed on recruiting websites and dating cows. Awake, sort of, but having nightmares! Finally, when I had to get out of bed, I couldn't get out of bed. Jesus! I was so late for the paper route!

No problem. Going to her house. She'll be playing piano for me.

But Aleah wasn't playing piano for me when I arrived.

I was dizzy with sleepiness, even though I'd been gunning it, running up to doors, handing the paper to angry dudes dressed for business. *"Just want to check the Brewers score before work. That too much to ask?" "No way, Mr. Dickweed! Sorry I'm not here earlier! Much prefer to hand you the paper when you're in your boxer shorts so I can see Wee Willy Wanky poking out."* Like they couldn't just check the Internet anyway.

By the time I got to Aleah's, the sun was completely up, and although it looked like morning, it was definitely the day part of morning, not dawn anymore.

The garage door at Gus's place was open, and Aleah was resting against the back end of her dad's Volvo. She was wearing purple bike shorts and a tiger-striped bike helmet. "Holy cow. There you are! I've been waiting for an hour!"

"Holy cow?"

"Oh, does that sound dumb, farm boy?"

"Um, no. I don't like cows."

"Why not? They're cute."

"Yeah. What are you doing?" I sort of laughed because of her crazy bike attire.

"I want to go on the rest of the paper route with you."

"Where's your bike?"

"I don't have a bike. We were going to buy a bike for me when we got here, but haven't yet. I do have my bike helmet though!"

"I can definitely see that. And bike shorts."

"They have a butt pad, so I'll be comfortable on your seat."

"Am I supposed to run along beside you?"

"No."

"I mean, I will."

"No, you're going to chauffeur me."

I got off the bike and ran a paper up to the stoop. Ronald Jennings opened the screen door before I could. "Yo, Felton!"

"Hi, Mr. Jennings."

"Aleah's hell bent on going with you. Make sure she drives some. I'd like her to get a little exercise too."

"Okay," I said.

Aleah was holding my Schwinn Varsity steady when I got back. We had to try like five different ways, but we finally figured out how to get both of us on it. Mr. Jennings laughed his ass off at us.

"Hold it steady, Felton. Get Aleah perched on that seat first." He was right. That worked.

I had to press on the pedals like a dang elephant to get us moving. Aleah held on to my hips to stay balanced. We were totally unsteady and were laughing and laughing.

As we biked down the block toward the next house, it occurred to me that Ronald was being pretty nice.

"Why's your dad so nice to me?" I asked.

"He knows about your dad from the college," Aleah said. "He told me all about it this morning. He knows you're a good kid too."

"Oh." All about it? What all about it? *You're a good kid?*

"And, of course, he's dying for me to be a happy girl."

"Why?"

"Duh! My mom moved to England last winter!"

"Oh. Yeah. Was she living with you before she moved?"

"Yes. She left right out of me and Daddy's apartment after she spent about five years yelling at us."

"Nice."

"Uh huh. Daddy said she was too young when they got married and she didn't know who she was, and when she figured it out, she had an apartment and a husband and a little girl, and it drove her crazy."

"That's a lot of information."

"Too much?"

"No. No. I mean, I'm surprised you know all that stuff. That your dad told you."

Just then we rolled up to the next stop on the route, and I leaned the bike, which completely toppled us. Thankfully, we fell on grass next to the curb, not on a sidewalk.

"Oh my God!" Aleah laughed. We lay there on our backs laughing, spread-eagled on the yard. Then I did it. Just a burst. I rolled over and gave her a kiss on the lips.

"I didn't mean at all that you were telling me too much."

We stared at each other, my face like two inches above hers. Heart pounding. She's so beautiful. We were probably lying there staring at each other for two weeks when somebody spoke above us.

"Excuse me. Could I get the paper?" It was the lady who lived there. She was none too pleased.

I jumped up and pulled a rumpled paper out of my bag. The woman grabbed it out of my hand, turned, and walked back to the house, mumbling, "Kid thinks he's on a date. He's got a job. This isn't a date."

Aleah and I quietly mounted the Schwinn, repeating our successful procedure from her driveway. About twenty feet down the road, Aleah whispered in this nasal tone that mimicked the woman, "This is a job, kid. You want a date, go to the roller rink. A paper route isn't a date."

"You're funny," I turned back to look at her, smiling my ass off.

"Oh, yes, I am," Aleah whispered dramatically.

Then we hit a parked car (we were going really slow, of course).

It seriously was pretty smart of Aleah to wear her helmet. We could've sustained major head injuries no fewer than fifteen times as we teeter-tottered, occasionally crashing, through the rest of the stops.

Finally, we arrived at the crown jewel of the route: the nursing home.

"Do they really read?" Aleah asked.

"I don't think so, but they get the paper."

We both limped toward the front door. I actually had a welt on my thigh from the car collision. Because it was late, the old ladies were milling about in the common area at the front of the home.

"Let's move fast. I don't like the smell in here."

"I don't like it in here period," Aleah said.

We rounded a corner, dropped off a paper in one room, then hit another spot down the hall where one of the only old men in the place lay sleeping on his back, the TV on in front of him, his mouth wide open. We dropped another off in an empty room (the one where I almost always find a half-naked lady who wants me to help her escape) and then high-tailed it toward the front to drop two off at the nurses' desk. We flew around a corner and were instantly face-to-face with the younger woman who freaks when she sees me. On cue, she screamed bloody murder, turned, and ran down the hall, spitting and mumbling.

"What was that about?" Aleah asked.

"She's a total nut bag," I said. "She screams like that every time."

"She's like my mom's age. They take just flat-out crazy people here, not just old ones?"

"I guess they do."

We dropped the papers off with the nurses, hit the security code on the front door (1, 2, 3—*Genius! No one will ever figure it out!*), and then left the building. We were finished with the route.

As I held the bike to let Aleah get on, she paused.

"You mind if I do an experiment?"

"Uh, I don't know."

"Wait here a second please."

Aleah went back into the nursing home. She was gone for about five minutes. I had no idea what she was up to.

When she returned, she was nodding.

"That lady in there is terrified of you."

"Well, yeah. That's apparent."

"I mean, just you. She didn't look at me at all when she screamed. She was staring only at you."

"So?"

"So I found her sitting at a table tearing a picture of George Clooney out of a *People* magazine, and I asked her how she was, and she smiled at me and said her breakfast was mushy, and she hoped they had something better for lunch."

"Maybe she's scared of men?"

"Hello? Tearing out a picture of George Clooney?"

"Maybe she was tearing it up."

"Don't think so. She gave George a kiss while I was standing there."

"Maybe she's scared of real-life men. Flesh and blood men. Real big hairy and muscley men." The conversation was actually making me nervous.

"You're not that hairy."

"I'm pretty hairy. You should see my belly button." Okay, I was sounding stupid. *Shut up, Felton.*

"I don't know. I saw two male orderlies in that place, and they were both plenty big and hairy, I'm sure."

"Do you think I did something to her?"

"I'm just saying she specifically doesn't like you."

"Can't win 'em all, I guess." I felt sort of pissed. I looked down.

"It's very important to me to figure out the mysteries of life," Aleah said.

"Sometimes, it's better not to know." I continued to look down.

Aleah reached up and put her hand under my chin, raising my face so we made eye contact.

"I specifically do like you," she said. "Specifically a lot." She smiled.

"Why?" I could feel intense heat in my face and ears. I must've been blushing like a Christmas bulb.

"I don't know yet. But it's a mystery I'm interested in figuring out."

"Me too," I smiled. *Then I'll write Gus to tell him why, the jerk.*

140

"But that lady sure doesn't like you."

"Shut up!" I laughed.

We teeter-tottered home, nearly hitting the curb and nearly straying out into traffic. But we didn't crash again, which sort of sucked because I wanted another excuse to roll over to her. I did consider intentionally crashing, but I didn't want it to be forced and for me to seem like too much of a dork (after all, I'd already told her I have a hairy belly button).

When we got back to her house, we expertly slid off the bike.

"We're good," I said. Aleah and I fist-bumped. "And that was so dang fun."

"Yes. It was great," she said.

"Maybe I can stop by tonight?"

"Oh, well, actually, I wanted to say that I can't really do anything at night except for Fridays and Saturdays because that's my weekend."

"Why?"

"If I want to be a professional pianist, I have to act like one. I couldn't focus very well after last night. I kept thinking about you. I need to focus."

"No, okay. That makes sense." I felt a little sad. I don't know what I was expecting. That we'd spend every last minute with each other for the rest of our whole long lives, I guess.

"You can come in for breakfast if you want though. Daddy's probably left for school."

"Oh, crap. What time is it? Oh, shit," I said.

"What?"

"I've got weights. It's late, right? Cody's coming to pick me up."

"What's weights?"

"Weight lifting. Weights."

"You lift weights?"

"Football."

"You play football?"

"Uh, yeah. I'm a D-I prospect. That's the only reason I can even talk to you."

"What?"

I stopped my scrambling, looked Aleah straight in the eye, and said, "I like you specifically. A lot. I can't say any more without making a total dipshit out of myself, okay?"

"Very mysterious," Aleah smiled. "See you soon, my football player."

That's right! That's it! I'm not a football player. I'm her football player. I'm Aleah Jennings's football player! I'm very close to acting like a complete retard! Go! Felton! Now!

I totally bolted.

"Well, maybe you can watch me practice sometime," Aleah shouted after me.

This is turning into a great summer, I thought. I biked home bursting, without any consideration of what I might find there.

CHAPTER 24:
THE DAY BEFORE WAS NO DREAM—THE HOUSE WAS UNWINDING

It's 4:02 a.m., but we're into this thing.

Okay.

Really, I should have been prepared for it, but I wasn't. Jerri's quietness the night before and Andrew's little boy snores made me think everything was going back to normal.

But Andrew sat in a lawn chair in the driveway as I biked up to the house. Oh, no. I rode my bike up to the garage and got off. Andrew stood and spun the chair around and then sat back down so he was facing me.

"What's happening now?" I asked.

"Good news, Felton."

"Really?"

"Jerri won't let me play piano in the house."

"That's not good news."

"Yes—and more good news. Jerri has also informed me that she's given away her entire life to us boys and she has nothing left to give."

"What?"

"She doesn't want the responsibility anymore."

I was stunned. Then I was pissed off. Not at Jerri exactly but because I had stuff to do and was tired of the drama.

"Unfortunately, Andrew, I have no time for this crap."

"It's crap, huh?"

"Yes."

"That our mother has decided that she's got nothing left to give to us?"

"Right."

"Do you know I'm thirteen, and legally and emotionally and morally, I need a parent?"

"Why don't you call your friends? Take a bike ride. Take a shower. You need to re-engage, Andrew."

"Shut up."

"That sounds like Jerri, right? I'll be your mother. Go do something with your summer, kid!"

"I need *my* mom, not yours."

"And I need to get my sweats on."

"I won't take this sitting down, Felton."

"You *are* sitting down, Andrew."

"Only so I can figure out what to do when I stand up."

"Fair enough! Great! Get busy! Go get 'em, son!"

"You're an assface."

I ran inside and changed clothes as fast as possible. I honestly didn't have time for the crap, which is harsh, I know, but I wasn't sure anything really bad was going on—Jerri might snap out of it at any moment—and my paper route had taken tons longer with Aleah in tow. Not that I minded. Plus, I started seriously late. Cody would be at the house any second. It did worry me that Andrew might do something stupid like overreact and call the police on

Jerri, tell them she'd decided not to be a parent anymore and then we'd get carted off to some home just when things were getting good for me. I did feel bad for Andrew too. No piano? What the hell?

I figured we'd better have a family meeting or something. I decided to tell Andrew we'd talk sincerely and seriously later in the day.

As I was about to leave, Jerri yelled, "Felton?" She was obviously in the living room upstairs.

I paused for a moment and thought…*Should I answer?* I did.

"Yeah, Jerri?"

"Tell your brother to take a chill pill."

"Okay. You bet, Jerri." *Chill pill? What's a chill pill?*

I ran out the door into the garage. Just in time. Cody was pulling up the driveway in his truck. Andrew's chair sat empty. He was nowhere to be seen. This made me feel bad. Andrew was just a little kid after all. I wanted to tell him we'd have that family meeting, and I wouldn't have told him to take a chill pill. I opened the truck door and jumped in.

"Everything okay?" Cody asked.

"Other than my family going totally ape shit loony tune, it's great," I said.

"Yeah, Dad told me during supper that he found your mom sleeping in her car. Did you get my email?"

"Yeah. Thanks."

"Did you see the Rivals.com stuff about Ken Johnson?"

"Yeah. Pretty cool." *Not that cool.*

"Coach Johnson will get that set up for you too."

"Okay." Then I thought, *Why?* I had to ask.

"Hey, why would colleges be interested in me before I've even played football? There's no video of me of breaking people's necks or running or stomping heads or doing anything."

"Pretty obvious."

"No."

"Yeah. Would you rather have a raw talent with huge speed and size that might totally make a difference on the next level or someone experienced like me who's short and slow and, no matter how much I know, won't be able to compete with big, fast dudes? You're a wet dream to a recruiter. Someone huge and fast who nobody's talked to yet. Plus, your track times are already out there, so people know who you are."

"Oh, shit."

"You okay?"

"Yeah."

At the corner of the main road, Cody stopped. He looked at me.

"Really, man. You okay?"

"I think."

"Your mom okay?"

"She's fine."

"You know Dad talked to her yesterday?"

"I heard something about it."

"She seemed okay to him."

"Okay," I nodded. I seriously hoped Officer Frederick wouldn't tell anyone else about what happened. I changed the subject.

"Hey, what's a chill pill?"

"I don't know. Is it some kind of drug?"

"Maybe. Jesus Christ."

"Seriously, Reinstein. Let me know if you need anything, man," Cody said.

Then we drove to weights, stopping briefly at the junior varsity baseball practice so I could pick up pamphlets and paperwork from Coach Jones that might earn me my driver's permit.

At weights, that jerk Ken Johnson said some snide stuff to me, but I can't even remember what it was. *He's like dandelion fluff. He's nothing.* I pumped iron like an angry gorilla. They had to throw thirty pounds extra on the bar every time it was my turn. The weight room didn't smell to me. The weights' heaviness just made me want to fight harder, so I lifted more. I shouted, pressing up the final lifts. Between lifts, I thought: *Check this out, Jerri. Eat my crap, Ken Johnson. Don't worry about chill pills, Andrew. Nobody better mess with me.*

• • •

You know what? I'd been a D-I prospect for only forty-eight hours. In that time, my life had turned completely upside down. Seriously, I was nothing more than a friendless squirrel nut like three days before that.

• • •

Back home, I looked up chill pill online. According to urbandictionary.com, it's something someone says to another person to tell them to relax *or* it's something someone says to another person to tell them they're an asshole *or* it's LSD, which I also had to look up. According to drugzczar.com, LSD is a psychedelic drug that makes you hallucinate, dance really well, and sometimes fall off of buildings to your death.

I was pretty sure Jerri wasn't suggesting little Andrew take LSD, so she probably meant the first definition or maybe the second. Neither of them was that big a deal.

Hmm.

At that point, I did have a very bad feeling about the situation. I wasn't blind.

CHAPTER 25:
WHAT SEEMS TO BE THE
PROBLEM, OFFICER?

The last like week and a half of June slid by without terrible incident. Jerri wasn't even remotely normal, but she wasn't exactly hostile either. She just didn't do mother stuff or Jerri stuff.

Mostly, she stayed in her room in bed or out in the living room on the couch. She read what appeared to be romance novels or sort of sex novels, judging from the covers (lots of bare-breasted muscle men with long hair carrying half-naked ladies). They were library books, so I know she must have left the house at some point, but I didn't see her leave.

Reading these books was definitely, totally out of character for her. But so? She'd spent years reading philosophy books and spirituality books and poetry books. *Look where it got her,* I thought. She didn't have any friends. Her not talking to Andrew and me was weird. But okay. Talking to us clearly got her nowhere too. Her not mowing the lawn was really weird. But not that big a deal. I sort of thought she was doing what I was doing—trying on a whole new lifestyle. *Good for her!*

Yeah.

Andrew thought it was a huge deal.

"She's completely lost her mind," he told me.

You've lost your mind, Andrew. I didn't say that out loud.

He sort of had lost his mind. Jerri wouldn't let his friends come over, and she wouldn't let him play piano because it apparently rattled her nerves, and he didn't go anyplace, although I'm sure he was free to go, and he started winding up really hard. Every time I saw him, he called me a name or slung some kind of serious insult at me. I considered telling him to take a chill pill because he was such a jerk.

I don't know.

Jerri stopped cooking and stopped grocery shopping, which was a problem. Andrew and I ate bread and cheese for the most part. Then cans of kidney beans, then green beans, then peas. Then cans of corn, which we don't like. Then there wasn't a single can of anything in the cupboard except sauerkraut, which I eyeballed but didn't open.

"You going to get groceries anytime soon?" I asked Jerri one afternoon when she was lying in bed reading.

She looked up from her book. Looked at me all confused. Shook her head like she was trying to shake out the cobwebs and then looked back down and started reading without saying a word.

"Jesus Christ," I hissed.

Okay, I was worried.

Huge thistles grew. They grew up like three feet high in one week and were here and there all over the yard and a lot in the garden. They were taller than any of the plants Jerri put in during spring (yes, she'd stopped gardening).

"Those thistles remind me of you," Andrew said one morning late in June when I rolled up on my bike after the paper route.

He was digging around in boxes Jerri had piled in the corner of the garage years ago. "You grew really fast, and you're ugly."

"Andrew, come on. That's not very nice."

"So sorry. Really I am."

"What are you looking for?"

"The key to life as we know it."

"What? You're weird as hell."

"So?" he shouted, standing straight and turning toward me. He breathed hard and glared over his plastic nerd glasses. His cheeks were red. I didn't say anything, but I stared hard back at him. He turned and went back to work sifting through junk, his little skinny body bent in an awkward looking way, his legs spread wide. "Are you going to football practice again?" he asked.

"Weights. Weight lifting. I have to change."

"Can I come?" he asked without looking up.

"You want to come with me to weights?"

"I really should leave the property at some point."

"Why don't you visit your friends?"

"What friends?"

"Music friends."

"Janie left with her parents for the summer. She's the only one with a serviceable piano."

"You've got other friends."

"I don't," Andrew spat, turning his head, glaring. "I don't have friends, okay?"

"Okay. Whatever. You can't come to weights with me. You're too young. You'd hate it up there anyway. It smells bad."

"You smell bad."

I felt heat rise in my face, but I really didn't want to fight poor Andrew.

"I know. I'm a jock. Jocks smell, right?"

"Very bad," he nodded.

"Fine," I said. I went inside, slamming the door, and changed into lifting clothes. When I got back out to the garage, Cody was pulling up the driveway. Andrew was still digging through junk.

"Your smelly friend is here," Andrew said without looking up.

"I know. I'll see you later, okay?"

"Yes, you will, Felton. I'll be here with Jerri sex book, digging through dirt piles, trying to find the key."

"What are you talking about?"

"Let's roll," Cody shouted.

"Never mind, Felton."

Andrew was very irritating, okay?

Ken Johnson wasn't at weights that morning, and that meant I could be totally free to concentrate and pump iron because I loved pumping iron and that second week of lifting, I could already feel this big difference—like my arms were muscley jungle snakes that could crush stuff. *Yo, check out my pythons!* And I just wanted to lift more and more weight.

After weights, Cody threw passes to just me and Karpinski. We went up on the field furthest from the school, where we could see the big M, the big Mound, the big bluff east of town where Dad jogged all those years ago (and I ate a rock), and me, Karpinski, and Cody just did pattern after pattern. Because Cody didn't have a baseball game until Monday of the next week, he threw and threw and threw, and we ran and ran and then Karpinski fell over because he was going to barf if he ran anymore, and I just kept running and catching and running and catching, never dropping the ball, never stopping, not thinking at all. It was seriously like breathing to me, like taking a big breath and letting it slide out. *Run, catch, run, catch, breathe, breathe, run, catch,* and nothing else existed except the ground, my legs, my hands, the ball. I could've gone on forever. Cody could've too. We wouldn't have stopped except Karpinski shouted, "Goddamn it, I'm hungry! Aren't you done yet? Let's get the hell out of here!"

He sort of woke me up. I sort of felt like I was in a trance.

"That was awesome," Cody said.

"Yeah," I nodded.

"Recruiters' wet dream," he said.

Then we went to Walmart to get a sandwich and water.

Karpinski shouted out the window the whole way, at everyone, everything, people, cars, trucks, dogs.

"Hey, dawg," he shouted at a barking dog, which was jumping behind a chain-link fence on Mineral Street. "You want a piece of me, dawg?"

The owner was on the front stoop of the house.

"You leave my dog alone!" he shouted as we rolled past

"Stick it in your ass!" Karpinski shouted, hanging out the window, flipping the bird back at the man.

"Jesus Christ, stop," Cody said. "My dad's a damn cop."

At Walmart, I got an extra couple of sandwiches for Andrew.

Thank God for my stupid, ridiculous paper route so I had money. I left them on Andrew's bed. I saw him sitting at the dirty kitchen table eating them late in the afternoon, but he didn't say thanks or anything. I walked down the hall and listened to Jerri breathing in her bedroom.

That night, I drove over to Karpinski's with Cody to grill and watch an old football movie. Karpinski wouldn't shut up. While we ate burgers that Karpinski's mom (big hair lady, wears short shorts) grilled for us, Karpinski talked and talked and talked and talked, and everything that came out of his mouth was so stupid that I sort of felt like choking him to put him out of his misery.

"Shelby Adams is pretty hot, don't you think? She's got a big ass, but I like a big ass because what's the point of a small ass. You might as well be dating your little skinny ass brother, and the last thing I'm going to think about when I'm all over Shelby Adams is your little brother, Rein Stone, so stop talking about him when I'm trying to talk about a chick's ass. Just kidding, man. You know I'm kidding. You know who else is hot is that Katie Koehler. She's going to be a freshman. You know her? Her ass is small, but I'm okay with that if…" and on and on and on and on. I chewed and nodded. Cody just chewed and looked across the yard.

And the freaking football movie? Even though I couldn't really hear it because Karpinski was talking ("That's a helluva hit—remember when I hit Bennett in the Dodgeville game? That was that kind of hit), I could see it fine. Pretty much horrible. There was some running and catching, which I like—high-arching passes in slow motion across the big blue sky—but it was mostly close-ups of total brutality times like five hundred, and there was a lot of blood and broken legs and noses and snot and stuff. Even though the movie was supposed to show how cool football is, I think, it more showed how terrible it is and how mean and mad everybody who plays football is. I totally loved running and catching a football but actually playing football? I didn't like the idea of broken noses and snot and blood pouring out everywhere.

Thankfully, on the way home, while he drove, Cody shouted over the sound of night air blowing in through the windows, "Football's not really like that at all, Reinstein."

"What?" I shouted.

"Football isn't that crazy. Your legs aren't going to get broken," he called.

"Yeah, but, isn't that Jay Landry dude from St. Mary's Springs going to try to break my legs?"

"Sort of, but legs just don't break that easy, man. I've been playing tackle since Pee Wee, since I was seven, and I've never gotten hurt even a little other than getting the wind knocked out of me."

"Oh. That's good to hear, man." The hot wind blew in. What did he mean wind knocked out?

Then Cody smiled big and looked at me.

"Karpinski never shuts up, does he?"

"No."

"Did you notice?" Cody asked.

"What?"

He started laughing.

"My experiment?"

"What?" I started laughing too, even though I didn't know why.

"I wondered if I could go to Karpinski's house, have supper, watch a movie, and leave without saying a single word."

"Did you?"

"Not one word in like four hours!"

"I didn't notice!"

"Not even hi or bye!"

"I didn't notice!"

"How could you? Karpinski never shuts up." Cody smiled huge.

And he completely cracked me up. Totally hilarious. I really liked Cody. Seriously. He sort of made me like Karpinski too.

When he dropped me off, he said, "See you tomorrow, brother."

Speaking of brothers: Andrew was digging in the storage area under the stairs when I got home. That wasn't a surprise. But something did catch me off guard: my TV wasn't on the stand in the basement.

"What did you do to the TV, Andrew?" I hissed.

"Jerri took it," Andrew responded, still digging through crap.

"She took my TV?"

"I'm working here, assface," Andrew said, continuing to dig.

I went to bed and looked at the football team's playbook Coach Johnson gave me a couple of days earlier. I tried to figure out all these crazy arrows and Xs and Os that were supposed to show where me and the other players were supposed to run. It looked like algebra and geometry combined, and it made me tired, which was good because I was so mad about the TV that I didn't think I could sleep. *What gives you the right to just take my TV? It's always been mine. It's mine, Jerri. Mine!* Cody told me I wouldn't really figure it all out until we were on the field in pads and helmets when there'd be a defense there trying to break my legs, like Jay Landry is going to break my legs, except legs don't break that easy. But he might knock my wind out, which doesn't sound very pleasant at all because I need my wind—*wind is breath, wind is air, wind in the clouds.* I fell asleep.

• • •

Outside of spending a ton of time with Cody and Karpinski doing football stuff (and listening to Karpinski rant and rant), I spent a lot of time with Aleah the last week of June. Both weekends at the end of June, because she didn't practice on weekends, we hung out a lot, taking walks all over town (yes, townies shouted at us, which Aleah loved), eating stuff she made, watching movies (all of it at her house because I didn't want her to see what was going on at mine).

She still didn't get out of bed until about dinnertime on weekends, so we did everything at night.

In a way, the fact that Jerri was sort of out of it was really good because she didn't know or care where I was. If I was out until 2 a.m. before, she would've totally freaked. She had no idea where I was. She probably didn't even notice I was gone. Jerri took my TV and then it was on in her bedroom twenty-four hours a day, and there was no way she could hear me come and go.

I spent most of the weekday mornings with Aleah too. (Probably like two out of every three days, she'd stop practicing by the time I got to her house.) She rode on the back of my bike when she went, and we got good at it. I'd accelerate really hard, and she'd hold on and scream and laugh. One time, she even said, "My football player is so strong," which totally made me happy because I liked being somebody I'd never been before; someone not connected to what was happening at home; somebody who is obviously not a Reinstein because, I thought, Reinsteins aren't football-playing powerhouses who make their girlfriends squeal with the massive power of their god-like thighs!

We never smashed up after the first day, though, which was kind of sad because I never had a chance to roll over and kiss her, which I really, really wanted to do. I spent almost all my non-football time when I wasn't actually with her thinking about kissing her: when I biked, when I tried to sleep, when I watched Andrew digging through boxes. I began to worry that I'd never ever get another chance to kiss her. I mean, Jesus, how are you supposed to kiss somebody if you haven't fallen over on the ground? Tickle fight? *Tickle her. Tickle her.* I didn't tickle her because it didn't seem respectful.

Hi, I'm Felton Reinstein, football player on the outside; Squirrel Nut Donkey Ass on the inside.

Of course, I didn't come up with the solution. Aleah did.

The last Saturday of June, we watched *Casablanca* in her/Gus's basement. We watched that particular movie because her dad was writing a paper about it and had the DVD. When Rick, the old dude in the movie, kissed the young beautiful one, Aleah totally grabbed me and kissed me. Then we kissed for a while until we heard Ronald get up and walk across the living room.

Then Aleah stared at me and said, "Haven't you wanted to kiss me?"

"Yeah, I think about it all the time."

"Why haven't you kissed me?"

"Uhh, I didn't want to seem like a dork?" Of course, I totally seemed like a dork by saying that.

"Don't worry about being a dork with me," Aleah said. "I'm a dork."

"Okay."

Then she got really serious. "When you ask me questions, do I hold anything back?"

"I don't think so." She clearly didn't. She talked about everything.

"You hold back though. Is that because you're worried about being a dork?"

"I don't hold back. I talk! When don't I talk?"

"When I ask how your mom is, you just say fine."

"Because."

"Because?"

"Because she's fine."

"And when I ask how exercise went…"

"Weight lifting."

"Whatever! When I ask how that was, you say pretty good."

"It's just lifting crap. It isn't very interesting."

"I'm interested."

"Why?"

"Because I like you."

"Why?" *Here we go, Gus. I'll give it to you.*

Aleah paused. She looked at me and didn't say anything.

"Because I'm mysterious and you like mystery?"

"No. Because you come from a musical family and…"

"I'm not musical, Aleah." *This isn't good. If she knew about my family.*

"That's not what I'm saying. I like you because you're really gentle and…"

Blood rushed to my face. My eyes watered. I was so embarrassed. What kind of kid am I that a girl would call me gentle?

"You're blushing."

"Well, yeah."

"Don't be embarrassed, Felton. After the year I just had with my mom, I really love gentle."

I looked down.

"I don't mean you're weak because you're not. I know you're not."

I looked back up.

"How do you know?"

"Because what you went through with your dad and how you just seem like a normal kid who likes football, and you're not all messed up. That's strong."

Then Aleah touched my face. Then she kissed me again. I was really aware of her face being so close to mine. Her face was right up against mine. She smelled like lilac bushes. We kissed for a while longer until Ronald, her dad, called down the stairs, "Getting real late, kids."

I biked home through cool 2 a.m. air thinking about being gentle and about how I'm strong.

• • •

When I got home, I found Andrew awake with junk spread out all over the basement room where the TV used to be.

He looked up at me. His face was pale. He had dark circles under his eyes.

"I don't think there's a single picture of our father in the whole house, Felton," he said. "Jerri got rid of him."

This wasn't news to me. I knew that. I remembered the bonfire.

"So?" I said.

"So?" Andrew snarled. "You don't care what happened to our dad? That's repulsive. I'm going to ask her. I'm going to ask."

"Ask what? I found him hanging. I know what happened."

"I'm going to ask her the hard questions!" Andrew shouted.

"Do whatever you want, Andrew." I slammed the door to my room and put on music.

I didn't feel very gentle.

CHAPTER 26:
THINKING ABOUT COMEDY
AGAIN

People who don't like you don't find you funny. (For example, when nobody liked me in seventh grade, they booed when I did Jerry Seinfeld.) People who like you find you funny, sometimes even when you're not trying to be funny.

How do I know? Suddenly, lots of people laughed whenever I made a joke (and sometimes when I didn't make a joke). Aleah laughed. The honkies? I seriously made them cry. Even a poop-stinker lineman or two would crack a smile when I joked in the weight room.

If Ken Johnson didn't show up at weights, which was about half the time, I'd joke along with Karpinski (bad jokes). *So a bare-boobed blond with a parrot on her shoulder walks into a bar…*I'd spend most of my evenings driving around with Cody and Karpinski, letting whatever ridiculous stupid dumb thing that popped in my head slide right out. I called Karpinski FishButtBoy because his name sounds like Polish for fish butt. He didn't think it was funny, but Cody did, so I called Karpinski FishButtBoy all the time, repeatedly, over and over, even whispering it under my breath when no one else was talking. Like when all the honky backs and receivers were at Steve's Pizza or at Subway or out at Walmart and were eating, not talking, me chewing and whispering at the same time—FishButtBoy—until Karpinski freaked and grabbed my head and told me he was going to punch me in the nuts if I didn't shut up (everyone just dying).

Repetition, I realized, is the key to honky humor (if the honkies like you—Gus probably wouldn't have success with this technique). Be annoying! Don't stop at any cost! FishButtBoy FishButtBoy *Fish Butt Boy.* The honkies would die laughing.

I'd become a honky, so it was funny.

With Aleah, I had to use a subtler, smarter humor—well, maybe not that subtle.

"I used to think pianists had something to do with penises, like the fact Andrew wanted to be a pianist meant that he'd be touching himself all the time. I pictured him on stage playing piano with no pants on, and when he'd stand to take a bow, he'd throw back his head and hands, revealing his privates, and the crowd would ooh and ahh because he's such a great pianist."

"Shut up!" Aleah shouted, laughing.

Aleah constantly laughed and told me to shut up. She'd cry from laughing.

"You should be a standup comic," Aleah said one night while we sat on her couch, while I made jokes, while tears of 100% pure blueberry joy rolled down her pretty face.

"I used to think that," I said.

"No, you really should!"

• • •

People who don't like you don't find you funny, and chances are you don't find them funny either. Like Gus, for example (not that

I don't like him, but I was mad—and he was mad). After two weeks of not hearing from him at all, he wrote: *why you never say a word? you just replace me?*

I responded: *you only say stuff like girl who would like me must be cow! i have serious problems in my house! i have fire pirate brother and psycho jerri! and you tell me only a cow would like me???*

what you talking about? are you trying to be funny? i don't get joke. Is all he wrote back.

I didn't even respond to that. I wasn't joking. I was telling the truth, but Gus wouldn't listen. Maybe that's what I mean—people who like you listen to you?

• • •

I was serious about Fire Pirate and Psycho.

One night in early July, I came home from watching Aleah practice piano, which she let me do on occasion (I'd sit next to Ronald while he graded papers, she'd play, I'd get hit by giant waves of music, which blasted my Jew-fro down to my head). As I biked over the hill on the main road above our house, I could see a glowing orange. I stopped and focused. It was a fire. A very large fire raging in the distance. It was obviously on our property. *Oh, shit. Oh, no.*

It had to be Jerri. Jerri burning. That's all I could think. I pictured Jerri in her yoga clothes, soaking herself with gas like I'd seen an Indian monk do on TV. (*Om shanti shanti shanti*, she says.) I pictured her lighting herself up. (Good-bye, boys.) *Oh, God.*

I took off on my Schwinn, jackrabbit, toward the house. By the time I got to the end of our drive, I could see the huge fire was at least contained in our fire pit, which meant the house itself wasn't burning, which was a relief. Still, the fire was too big, roaring and lighting the side of the house and the yard around it. It actually made a roaring sound like a windstorm.

Also lit by the fire was Andrew. He stood there in his glasses and his tighty-whitey underpants, reflecting orange in the flame. He had no clothes on otherwise. He looked so skinny and bony. He poked a long stick, more like a tree branch, into the flames. I dropped my Schwinn and ran up to him.

"What the hell are you doing?"

"Getting rid of my baby clothes and other artifacts of my past."

In the fire, I could see the collars of the dorky polo shirts Andrew always wore. I could see pairs of his little jeans burning. I could see all his striped socks and his Mozart sweater and also a picture he'd drawn in art class last year that Jerri really liked. There were other papers burning too.

"Jesus Christ, Andrew. You're crazy! Is that all your clothes?"

"Definitely," he said, stirring the fire from ten feet away.

"I'm telling Jerri."

"Mother knows."

"Jesus!"

I ran into the garage and into our dark house, not a light on, up the stairs into the hall and to Jerri's room. She half-reclined, covered up in the bed, no light except from the TV (my TV) in front of her. She was half asleep.

"Jerri! Andrew has gone crazy."

"No," she mumbled. Then she tried to look around me to the TV, which was playing some kind of crime drama.

"Uh, yes. He's out there naked burning his clothes, Jerri."

"I know."

"You going to let him be naked? Is he going to school naked in the fall?"

"He bought new clothes today. Could you move a little to your right, Felton?"

"He's not wearing them!"

"I'm trying to watch TV," Jerri yawned.

"You're crazy!"

"Get out of here, Felton," she said, not mean, not angry. She was totally mumbling.

I turned and stomped out of the room and back down to the basement. Andrew was coming in from the garage. He had no hair on his head (to match his clothes-less body). Of course, I already knew about his hair. A couple of days earlier, he'd shaved it all off.

"I'm getting a hot dog to cook," Andrew said, which would've been a funny thing to say if I thought he was funny. "Do you want one?" he asked without laughing.

"Where'd you get hot dogs?" That's all I could come up with.

"I bought them."

"When?"

"After I stole Jerri's wallet and walked to the thrift store to buy some pants and a shirt, I went grocery shopping at Kwik Trip. The hot dogs will be quite good cooked on the fire," Andrew said, again without laughing.

"They'll taste like the bugs in your clothes."

"Duh, Felton. Fire burns all the germs away."

166

"I was making a joke."

"Yes. I know," Andrew stared at me.

I stared back and then said, "I'm going to bed."

I heard Andrew banging around for another couple of hours before I actually fell asleep. To relax, I tried to imagine Aleah still playing the piano, with her dad still on the couch reading poetry essays. But I didn't sleep until the house was silent.

• • •

I was a little late on the paper route the next morning. Aleah waited for me in her yard, with her little Walmart mountain bike lying on the grass next to her. (She determined it would be good for her to get her own bike so she got some exercise instead of having me do all the work; because he's an attentive dad, Ronald bought it for her immediately.) She sat up, wearing her dorky tiger-striped bike helmet. She said, "Good morning. I was just thinking that we should watch a movie at your house this weekend. It's kind of rude to make you come to me all the time."

"I prefer to come to you," I said.

"But I want to!"

"No, you really don't. Andrew has gone utterly psycho, and he might kill us both if you come over," I laughed.

"Really?" Aleah said, eyes wide. "But he's so cute!"

"No! He's a pyromaniac, and I don't even know what horror he's capable of!"

"You're funny," Aleah giggled.

Hilarious.

• • •

When I got home, Jerri was out of the house for maybe the second time in a week. She was covered head to toe (hat, sunglasses, long-sleeved T-shirt, jeans, socks) lying on a lawn chair in the yard, about ten feet away from the scorched fire pit. Next to her was the giant weed-infested jungle garden. The thistles were five feet tall. Other weeds climbed the thistles, flowering, shading all the vegetables below. But really, at least she was out of the house. I stood looking at her for like a minute but didn't speak to her. She was so still.

In the house, I found Andrew rifling through the rock CDs in my room. He was wearing a pair of black trousers (I can only describe them as trousers) and a black T-shirt with a skull and crossbones on it. I grabbed his arm and squeezed, "What do you think you're doing, you jerk?"

He pulled his arm away and glared at me.

"Taking Dad's CDs," he said.

"You midget pirate," I shouted. "Drop 'em!"

"Eat crap," he shouted, then pushed past me carrying my CDs.

"Goddamn it! Bring those back," I shouted.

Andrew didn't respond.

I could've stopped Andrew. Easily. But I didn't.

The voice in my head said: *Be careful. Be careful. You could kill him.*

I wanted to wrap my hands around his throat and squeeze and squeeze and squeeze.

I changed clothes, left the house, and walked to the road, where Cody picked me up.

Even though Andrew dressed like a pirate and cooked hot dogs on a fire fueled by his own socks, I didn't find Andrew funny.

• • •

When I came home from lifting weights two hours later, Jerri was still in the yard in the same place as she was when Cody picked me up.

"Your mom still resting?" Cody asked, dropping me off.

"She probably did a lot of work while we were gone," I said.

"Didn't mow the lawn, did she?"

"Ha ha ha. No."

While I lifted, Andrew's piracy had sapped all my energy. What was happening to him? He scared me. I couldn't concentrate.

As Cody pulled away, I decided to seriously address the Andrew situation with Jerri. She's his mother after all. I walked up to her.

Jerri stirred as I approached.

"What now?" she said.

"What now?" I asked.

"What. Now," Jerri spat.

"Andrew stole Dad's CDs out of my room," I told her.

"He took my wallet yesterday," Jerri mumbled.

"We've got problems."

"Yes."

"What are we going to do?" I asked.

"Me? Nothing," Jerri said.

"You have to," I said.

"No," she said.

"Yes," I replied.

"I'm just a small part of a much larger problem. Remember when you said that, Felton?"

Yes, I remembered saying that. It was part of the conversation a few weeks earlier that ended with her calling me an f-bomber. That wasn't what I was talking about.

"Jerri, you're his mom. You have to do something."

"You're his son. What are you going to do?" she hissed.

"Andrew's son?"

"Shut up, Felton."

"What do you mean?"

"Shut up."

"Your stupid kid is turning into a disaster and a pirate, and you have to do something, Jerri," I shouted.

"Maybe I'd rather my kid turn into a pirate than a damn tennis player."

"What the hell are you talking about?"

"Shut up, Felton."

"Mom."

"Go away. I have to weed the garden," she trailed off.

I started shaking.

"You can't do that on your fat ass, Jerri," I shouted.

"Shut up, asshole. Shut up!" Jerri screamed, struggling to sit up.

I turned and ran to the garage. I grabbed my bike and biked so fast. I tore up the hill.

Comedy, it seems, is a lot about situation and who you like and don't like. Sometimes, midget pirates who cook hot dogs on their burning socks aren't funny.

CHAPTER 27:
4:38 A.M.

Why in the hell am I doing this tonight?

I can't help it.

But I should be happy and asleep, letting my beat-up body heal.

I don't like dark tales. I like funny stuff. Gus says funny stuff is always dark.

Is this funny?

Here's that to-do list again:

1. Lift weights with Cody.
2. Get driver's license.
3. Consider giving up comedy, as comedy isn't even funny anymore.
4. Stop talking to Jerri and Andrew.

I definitely did number one. I considered number three a lot (I still am, except I *do* think comedy is funny). Coach Jones gave me the form to get started on two, but I needed to get Jerri's signature to get the permit, which she wouldn't give me, and then she'd have to have teach me to drive—which also wasn't going to happen. It was at this point in July that I tried to implement number four.

CHAPTER 28:
THE ROAD RUNNER RUNS
UP CLIFFS

That day Jerri called me asshole out in the yard was the first day I ran up the Mound (the same one Dad ran up).

Let me describe it a little.

This Mound is a seriously huge-ass hill on the east side of town. It's a county park, so anyone can go there. A really long time ago, college kids whacked down a huge tract of trees on it and made this huge M on its side out of big rocks. Then they painted the rocks bright white so the M can be seen from like a thousand miles away, if you've got the right view. Every few years, the engineering department from the college goes up there and paints it white again so it's always really white.

I have no idea why they put an M on it. M obviously doesn't stand for Bluffton. Maybe it just stands for Mound? I don't know.

There's a steep path that runs next to the big M so lovers of the letter M can climb up the hill. The path has got to be like a football field and a half long, maybe longer. It's a hell of a place to run. I'm sure my dad would tell you the same thing if he could.

After Jerri called me asshole, I didn't really know where I was going. All I knew was that I couldn't stay in the house with her and Andrew around. I biked past the baseball fields and saw some honkies playing, but I couldn't stop there because I was bawling and would look stupid. I biked past the schools, the track, the practice football field, and the tennis courts. *Tennis player?* Then I got on County Road D, saw the big M in front of me, and gunned it out into the countryside. I biked the several miles out there in no time flat. One pickup truck filled with poop-stinkers shouted "Rein Stone" as they passed. I didn't wave or anything. Just kept pumping.

When I got to the Mound and the big M, I was completely out of breath. I lay down on a picnic table and sweated in the sun.

I thought about Jerri and Dad, and I got sick but couldn't stop. Then I thought about Aleah.

Why is she so lucky? Yeah, her mom is gone, but Ronald takes care of everything. He's great and she's always happy—almost always happy. At least she knows why her mom left—too young when she got married and had to leave because she was so unhappy—and at least her mom didn't totally abandon Aleah because she didn't kill herself and she actually calls Aleah sometimes and sends her postcards. Ronald and Aleah talk about Aleah's mom every day. Aleah told me. They talk and talk and talk. We never talked about Dad. Jerri never said anything except leave the past behind and re-engage. Aleah is so lucky to know why her mom left.

And why is Cody so lucky? His dad makes sure everybody's safe. His mom works at the bank and probably buys groceries.

Even Gus is lucky. Sure, he has to do a paper route. Sure, he gets shipped to South America. But his mom would never call him an asshole.

She called me an asshole. She called me an asshole.

My legs started feeling twitchy.

Why are you so damn crap out of luck all the time? Jerri hates you. Your mom hates you. Your mom totally hates you.

I jumped off the table and ran toward the path next to the M. Within seconds, I exploded up it, running the rail stairs, accelerating up rocks and dirt. This is going to sound really dorky, but I felt like a mountain lion, and I was balanced like that. Trucks could've rolled at me and I would've dodged them, punched them on their sides and sent them tumbling away down the hill. I accelerated like crazy, even though I was going straight up. Up up up up! I probably looked like that Road Runner in that old cartoon. Up! Up!

At the top, I bent over to catch my breath. Sweat poured off my face and stung my eyes. My muscles shook. Ants scrambled on the ground below me. How easily I could've killed them all, all those ants. I stood straight, put my hands on my hips, and breathed, and looked out over a thousand miles of Wisconsin and Iowa and Illinois. Then I jogged back down so I could run up that Mound again.

I ran until I was dry-heaving, spitting, breathing so hard, groaning, cramping up in my guts. At the top, I collapsed onto the ground, face down, sucking air. And then I rolled over and stared at the sky. Deep breath. Deep breath. Breathing is good. Lying in the dirt is good.

Believe it or not, the sky was blue. The few clouds up there were white, as you might guess. It was exactly what I expected to see. Jerri felt far away. Just a ghost of somebody I didn't know. Andrew could take what he wanted from my room. It didn't matter.

Everything was a thousand miles away. I relaxed on the ground on top of the big M. The sky was blue, as it should be. The clouds were white.

Then my phone buzzed in the pocket of my shorts. It was a text from Cody. Apparently, he'd sent it to all his honky friends:

> party my place july 31 celebrate rein stones 16 bday. 7 oclock.
> no alchies!!!

I know he sent it to a bunch of honky friends because Karpinski, Jason Reese, and a number I didn't recognize all texted me immediately:

> legal to drive get some hookers
> gonna be fun rein stone
> reinstein is big boy now!!! :0

The first message was from Karpinski. I texted back and asked him to pay. I said "will be fun" to Reese. "who this?" I asked the other.

Abby was the response.

Abby Sauter sent me a text. My friend planned me a birthday party. I could run up a cliff like the Road Runner.

This is my life, Jerri. That's what I thought.

CHAPTER 29:
ALEAH

On the following Friday night, after managing to spend three solid days without saying a word to either Andrew or Jerri (actually, barely seeing them at all—this was the same strategy I used with classmates through just about all of eighth grade and freshman year—don't look, talk, appear in front of them), Aleah and I watched this adventure movie with Nicholas Cage where he's trying to figure out some mystery. I have no idea what else happened because Aleah invited me over not to watch a movie in the basement but to pretend to watch a movie. What she really wanted to do was lie on Gus's giant beanbag chair and make out.

As we were kissing, she reached under my shirt and ran her hands over my skin, which raised all kinds of bumps, and I also put my hands under her shirt and touched her skin. I pulled her onto me, and we kissed until my mouth hurt and my lips were chapped, and I couldn't see straight, and my legs hurt and my hips hurt and other stuff hurt, and I almost felt sick to my stomach because it was so great.

At around one, Ronald shouted down the stairs, "It's about time for Felton to go home. There's a paper route to be done in the morning."

Aleah rolled off of me, and I stood fast because Ronald's voice scared me and then I almost fell down because I was dizzy. Aleah almost couldn't stand up because she was so twisted up. But we smiled at each other and didn't say a word, and I ached and then climbed the stairs with Aleah right behind me.

Ronald squinted at my face as I walked out the door and said good night.

I biked home through the cool air, with blood running the right way through my body again.

It never occurred to me that I might ever actually have sex. The proposition had always seemed so totally remote and completely unreasonable. *How would that ever happen?* Suddenly, in one night, I knew how that would happen. Not that I thought Aleah and I were about to have sex or anything because I didn't really want to. I was sure Ronald would walk down the stairs and see us and then I felt really terrified and explosive and crazy. *Oh, man, Aleah.*

At home, I could hear the TV on in Jerri's room, and I went right to bed. But I didn't go to sleep, not at all. But I guess I was asleep when the alarm went off.

• • •

On the paper route the next morning, right after I'd handed Ronald the newspaper and he'd stared at me and squinted again, as we biked down the street together, Aleah said, "Daddy gave me the third degree. Hoo, boy!"

"What's that mean?" I asked.

"He wanted to know exactly what we were doing down there."

My stomach dropped.

"Oh, man. Jeez. How'd you get out of that?" I could feel myself blushing, and my mouth got dry.

"I didn't. I told him what we did."

I stopped my bike, leaned and stared at her.

"What? You realize I can never look at your dad again."

She stopped right next to me.

"Why? He didn't mind. He said it's normal."

"He wasn't mad?"

"Maybe a little uncomfortable?"

"Oh my God. Oh my God."

"He did say that if we went any further, he'd lock me up until I graduate high school."

"Well, we're not going to. I won't touch you again. Seriously. He doesn't have to…Tell him not to worry about…He won't be seeing…"

"He said not to go any further. But you are going to kiss me again, Felton. You got that?" She grabbed my forearm and squeezed.

I tried not to smile because I was seriously concerned, but I did smile because I couldn't help it. Then I said, "Okay. Yes. I'll kiss you."

Aleah smiled.

"You're sexy."

"Uhh, yeah."

"Aren't you going to talk to Jerri about it?"

"No," I said.

"Why not?"

"Because."

"You should talk to Jerri. It's important to get an adult's perspective."

"I don't know any adults," I said.

"You know my dad. He's an adult."

"You want I should talk to your dad?" I asked, putting on a TV gangster accent, which made Aleah laugh and forget about poking at me.

CHAPTER 30:
THE MOUND

I started going every day for hours, no matter what. I ran up while lightning shot across the sky and thunder rumbled down, the rocks, dirt, and rail ties slick with huge rain. I ran up it when the sun was burning hot, burning a hole in the back of my head, blinding me (even though I'd purchased some mirrored honky lifeguard shades). I ran up when the clouds were so low I was in fog at the top, sweating in the stillness and stinky humidity. It didn't matter what was going on with the weather. Nothing else mattered. I ran and ran and ran.

Once, I ran up with that leather pouch of hippy rocks and crystals that dumbass drummer Tito had given me to help me relax (which made me a freak in the eyes of my classmates), and I dumped them in my right hand and whipped the whole handful down the M so they disappeared. (I threw the pouch in the weeds.)

Because I didn't want to be at home (Andrew had, in fact, started asking Jerri "hard" questions. Jerri had, in fact, begun to scream like hell at Andrew), I'd stay out there for hours every day.

Every now and then an old couple or some family with kids or some tourist from another part of the state would show up and climb while I ran. Always, always, always, whoever was there would say, breathing hard, "I can't believe you can run up and down this hill. It's amazing."

I'd nod, smile, keep running. Meep meep.

Mostly, though, I was alone out there. And that was good. No ghosts to freak me out with their pirate/zombie wailing about the past. Nothing to do but what I loved doing. I felt like an adult. It felt perfect to be out there. So much so, I began protecting the whole afternoon.

CHAPTER 31:
ALEAH AGAIN

One early morning in the middle of July, at the end of the paper route while we were slowly rolling home, sort of zigzagging our bikes and crossing real close, Aleah said, "I'm considering changing my schedule, Felton."

"Why's that?" I asked, pedaling past her.

"You know, summer isn't that long."

"Already seems like forever," I said.

"Well, summer term at the college ends at the end of the month. Daddy is aching to get back to Chicago."

I hit the brakes and skidded to a stop. Then Aleah stopped a few feet ahead of me. She turned back and stared.

"You're leaving at the end of July?" I asked, my stomach sinking.

"Maybe not exactly at the end. But pretty soon. Daddy's got article deadlines in August, so he wants to get back to work with his co-author. You knew we were leaving."

"Yeah, but I just figured it'd be later…Like the day before Gus comes back, right before school starts."

"No," Aleah shook her head.

"Oh, no."

"That's what I'm saying, Felton. I want to change my schedule so I'm awake during the afternoon so I can see you more."

"But I'm not around in the afternoon," I said, feeling dizzy.

"Where are you?" she asked.

I got off my bike, and rolled it up to the curb, and then dropped it and sat down.

"I just do stuff, Aleah."

She followed me over to the curb, put her kickstand down on her Walmart mountain bike, and then sat down next to me.

"Can't you change your schedule a little?" she asked. "I want to see you more."

"I can't. It wouldn't be right."

"Why? Do you need to drive around with your football friends?"

"I don't. I don't do that during the day."

"What do you do?"

"I practice."

"With your football friends?"

"No. Alone. I practice running, I guess. Or maybe it's more just moving?"

"Oh my God. You're so weird, Felton. You practice moving?

"Yes." I looked down between my knees because it did sound dumb.

"Why?"

"I don't know. You know…Why do you practice?"

"I know if I'm good at piano, I can play in front of a thousand people who'll light up like Chinese New Year. They'll shout and scream, and there will be all kinds of fireworks blowing up every-where. Practicing for that makes sense!"

"Yeah." I clearly didn't practice running up a hill so crowds would clap for me—although I liked it when hikers were astounded by my running. I moved because I liked to move, I guess. "But is that why you play piano, Aleah? Because of Chinese New Year?"

"I guess. So I can perform for big…" She thought for a moment. "Also…Also because I know everything when I'm playing. Everything makes sense."

"That's it!" It hit me. While running on the Mound, I knew everything I needed to know. I knew everything. And whereas hippy crystals never helped me nor whispering Gus's name in fourth grade, knowing all I needed to know completely helped. "Me too, Aleah. Everything makes sense. So I have to move in the afternoon."

"You're so weird, Felton Reinstein. It completely stuns me. I mean, 'move'? How weird."

"I know. Don't tell anyone."

"You're weirder than me," she sort of whispered, staring.

"Shhhh." I gestured with my hand.

"It hurts my heart. I just love you." She shook her head.

I nodded.

Then we kissed for about twenty-five years, I think.

CHAPTER 32:
THE MOUND AGAIN

I bought an iPod with my paper route money, and I started carrying my school backpack filled with fruit from Kwik Trip and protein shakes and water bottles, and I'd go up there—and being up there became the best home I ever had. When the weather was good, I'd stay forever. I'd run myself totally out of energy, and I'd sweat and sweat (thankfully, Jerri had purchased a giant jug of laundry detergent in May, so I could clean the pee-stinker clothes) and then drink water and eat and take naps and listen to rap Cody gave me. I'd just relax, breathing, growing my body hair, running like the Road Runner, getting largely muscled (weights helped too), thinking about life and whatnot, but mostly not thinking at all. All the while, I'd look over all three states, Wisconsin, Iowa, and Illinois, far below me.

You're an adult, and this is what you do. Meep meep.

Aleah did take some nights off practicing. She even drove around with me, Cody, and Karpinski a couple times. Karpinski thought she was really hot, which wasn't surprising. What was surprising? Aleah liked Karpinski. That stunned me.

"Oh my God, he's funny!" she said.

"Really?"

CHAPTER 33:
MUSCLEY BARBARIAN

Oh my God. It's 5 a.m. There's every possibility that Grandma is going to wake up and find me awake and then give me the business about not going to sleep. Like I'm trying to stay awake. I'm not!

I'm very muscley.

Very bruised but very muscley.

I worked so freaking hard!

Because if I wasn't running the big M, I ran pass patterns with Cody. If I wasn't running pass patterns or running the big M, I lifted weights, getting closer and closer to the school record maxes that jerk Ken Johnson set for all backs and receivers. My shirts got super tight. My stomach muscles got ripply. Extremely muscley, like a barbarian.

Toward the end of the second week of July, Coach Johnson said, "Reinstein, you're putting on weight. Not fat, son. Don't worry about that. You've got no fat. You're carrying a lot more muscle though. Let's get you on the scale."

Cody, Karpinski, and I all followed Coach down the stairs from the weight room to the locker room. Down there, I pulled off my shoes and T-shirt and got on the scale. Coach adjusted the measures, sliding the stuff around. When it all balanced, the little arrow pointed at 182.

"Yes, sir!" Coach said. "What that's? Fifteen pounds in a month? Fourteen pounds? Big."

"You're going to be 185 by your birthday party," Cody said.

Then Karpinski said, "Too bad your…"

"Not in my locker room, Karpinski," Coach said.

"Is so tiny and useless," Karpinski whispered.

"Shut up, FishButt," I said like Arnold Schwarzenegger, "or I'll break you in half."

Barbarian!

CHAPTER 34:
I HAD TO BE A BARBARIAN

Or a warrior, seriously. I lived with Andrew. I lived with Jerri. I tried, but I couldn't just run away.

As the month wore on, Andrew worked to drag me into his Jerri battles. I had to fight him off. Once, he woke me up in the middle of the night, his little head hovering over me in the dark.

"She's a liar, Felton. She's a crazy old lady liar. You have to help me."

"What?" I was scared, didn't know what was happening.

"She won't tell me why you freak her out, Felton."

"Who?"

"You. You do. Help me. You have to ask her, Felton. You have to."

I woke up enough to know what was going on.

"No. I won't ask her anything."

"Why won't anybody help me?" Andrew whimpered.

Jerri didn't leave her room. Andrew wanted to fight her. He wanted me to fight alongside him. I wanted nothing to do with it.

"Get out of here," I told him.

CHAPTER 35:
DID I SAY BARBARIAN?

Because Andrew wasn't the only one I had to fight.

Ken Johnson.

He was just a couple of weeks from leaving for the University of Iowa, for the big time really. Why did he bother with me? Why was he such a pecker? He worked out half the time at the college and half the time with us at the high school.

When he was with us at weights, he'd do his best to make me look stupid. Usually, he'd just make bad jokes, which fewer and fewer of the honkies laughed at. He'd say crap like "Don't pop your squirrel nut" when I was squatting. Sometimes, he'd get close to me while I stretched, separated from my classmates, and he'd say, "Team's so screwed to be depending on a squirrel nut. There's going to be a lot of disappointment around here come fall."

"Guess we'll see," I'd say.

On one hand, I figured he was right. I didn't really know how to play football. It's possible I might fumble every time someone tackled me. At night, when I was half asleep and the barbarian wasn't in control of my emotions, I'd actually hear Ken's asshole voice in my head: "There's going to be a lot of disappointment around here come fall."

I could see the headlines in the sports page: BLUFFTON BLOWS AS REINSTEIN'S FUMBLES/BUMBLES FUEL ANOTHER LOSS.

This fact, the fact of my total lack of football experience, scared me. My heart pumped too hard. My mouth was dry. I had to fight.

REINSTEIN CATCHES FUMBLE-ITIS, BLUFFTON DISEASED AGAIN!

Ken Johnson.

CHAPTER 36:
DON'T GET THE WRONG IDEA...

These weeks in July were the best ever, sort of. They were. Even with Ken Johnson, etc.

I had lots of friends. Not just Cody and Karpinski but Abby Sauter and Jess Withrow too. I'd get texts from them all day long, and I'd write funny things back, which made them call me hilarious. I also had a girlfriend who was separate from anything Ken knew. She was even more big league than him. She wasn't one in like a million soon-to-be college athletes. She was *the* one in a million. She was *the* best. And she was fearless. And she loved me because I was gentle and weird. And I knew something else: I could tell from looking at him. Not only was I nearly as big as Ken, but I was faster. He's squat and really explosive. I'm explosive but longer. I could stretch and beat his ass. I knew it. I could beat his ass. *Felton the Barbarian.*

At night, when the barbarian was asleep, Ken scared me, Andrew scared me, Jerri scared me.

In the daytime? Felton the Barbarian did really well.

CHAPTER 37:
BARBARIAN NOT ALWAYS
GOOD

On the Tuesday of the third week of July, Andrew locked himself in the downstairs bathroom for like three hours, seriously, doing nothing at all (no bathroom-type noise). My running shorts were in there on the floor. To hit the Mound, I needed my shorts. I waited for a while, then knocked and asked him to throw my shorts out. In response, he sang (I wouldn't call it singing) some kind of terrible song (literally, I do not kid, he sang, over and over, *soup is good food, makes a great meal*). I waited for him to stop. But he didn't stop.

Then I went vaguely ape shit and pounded on the door. I shouted loud, "Let me the hell in there!"

Even though I knew she could hear me, Jerri was upstairs in bed with the TV on, so she could do nothing.

Andrew fell totally quiet and didn't let me in. So I went to my bedroom and got on my computer and sent emails to Abby, Jess, Cody, Reese, Karpinski, even Gus (who I had sort of stopped communicating with because he really let me down or so I thought. He thought I let him down. A week before, he'd emailed a long letter about how I'd abandoned him, which seemed like bull since I'd tried to tell him about Jerri earlier in the summer and he hadn't even given a crap at all). I tried to relax while emailing, tried to be funny (ha ha) about my brother (ha ha) who was locked in the bathroom.

Another hour passed, and he didn't come out, an hour when I could've been biking out to the Mound or running up it. Released from this hellhole. So I pounded again. This time, Andrew said, "Go away, Felton. I'm busy."

"You're going to tear your butt sitting on the toilet, Andrew."

"I'm not sitting on the toilet, jerkwad!"

"Then let me in."

"Never. Go away."

"Let me in!"

"No."

"Then throw my shorts out."

"Your shorts are not my responsibility."

"Goddamn it, Andrew. Let me in!"

"I. Am. Busy."

Blood pounded in my veins. Barbarian blood. This acid started burning up my throat.

"Let. Me. In. Now!"

"No."

"Now, you ass. Now! Or I'm going to *kill you*," I screamed.

Andrew shouted, "Shut the hell up, Felton. I'm working."

I bent down, breathing hard, trying to get hold of myself. *Not now, Barbarian.* But I couldn't hold it in. I stood up, leaned back, and kicked the door frame as hard as I could. The kick shook the house. The kick broke the door frame in two (luckily not the door because I might have gone in there and actually killed Andrew).

The reverberations knocked a picture off the wall upstairs, and glass shattered on the wood floor. Andrew screamed, "You broke the light! You broke the light!"

I scared myself. I stood back and breathed, then leaned in toward the door.

"I'm sorry," I whispered fast. "I'm sorry, Andrew."

"It's completely dark in here, you asshole," he shouted.

"Please just let me in."

"No," he sobbed. "Go the fuck away."

I didn't know what to do. What was I supposed to do? Why wasn't Jerri stopping this? I turned and ran up the stairs. In the kitchen, the goofy caricature of me, Andrew, and Jerri that was done at the Strawberry Festival last summer, right after we got back from camping at Wyalusing, was broken on the floor. There was glass everywhere. I stepped over it and walked down the hall to Jerri's bedroom. Unlike Andrew, I didn't want answers about Jerri's zombie life. I just wanted a mother to help me not kill my brother.

But I didn't go in. Why? I could hear Jerri in there crying. I couldn't go in. She was totally sobbing.

This was another moment when maybe I should've called Grandma Berba, whether she hated us or not.

Instead, I turned and ran back through the kitchen and down the stairs and out the garage and to my Schwinn Varsity, and I biked to the Mound wearing the pajama bottoms I pulled on after the route. Once at the Mound, I stripped down to my boxers, and I ran and ran and ran, crying "Shit. Shit. Shit. Shit," and, thank God, no visitors showed up. Because I might have killed them or something because who knows about barbarians and what they're capable of?

When I got back home, late in the day, Andrew was nowhere to be found. The light didn't work in the bathroom. The trim or whatever from the door frame was lying on the floor. Upstairs, most of the glass had been kicked into the corner of the kitchen (but little pieces were scattered around, catching light from the window). The Strawberry Festival picture was stuffed in the trash. I could hear the TV mumbling in Jerri's room.

What am I going to do, I wondered? *Run away. Run away.* I seriously considered running away, but I didn't want to lose Aleah. I didn't want to lose Cody. So I kept on fighting to keep my life.

I needed the Barbarian.

CHAPTER 38:
KEN JOHNSON

On the Wednesday of that third week of July, all us honky backs and receivers were out at the baseball field running routes when Ken showed up with a couple of even older guys who used to play for Bluffton and now play football at some of the small D-III colleges in Wisconsin. They wanted to coach us and tell us we were doing things all wrong.

A couple of times, I made catches and ran a little, and the older guys would say, "Jesus, that's speed," or whatever. Then Ken would make a squirrel nut joke, and they'd laugh as if he were funny. The more the other dudes acknowledged I was good, though, the more sort of red in the face and jerky he became.

Then he decided he would cover me.

I got a huge adrenaline kick when Ken lined up across from me. Finally, I'd get my chance. I would beat his jerk ass with my improved giant speed.

But more importantly, Ken was bigger than me. Not taller, just bigger. Even with me at 180-something, he outweighed me by twenty pounds. He used what he had.

Cody said go, and I took a step, and Ken leveled me. He exploded into me with both arms and knocked my feet right off the ground, and I landed on the back of my head.

I totally cried out like a little injured animal, like I would've in fourth grade or sixth grade or eighth grade even. It was an accident. The hit didn't hurt that much, just surprised me, but I high-pitch monkey-squealed.

Ken stood over me and laughed. The older dudes fell all over themselves laughing.

"That's how a squirrel sounds when it gets run over by a truck," Ken said. Then because he's a gentleman and because he succeeded in making me look like a donkey, he pulled me up by my shirt. "Going to have to get past d-backs, squirrel nut. Can't pull that pussy stuff. Jay Landry is going to kill you next month if you pull that pussy stuff."

I wanted to say "Thanks Coach," but I didn't.

Then he lined up again because he hadn't gotten enough.

I looked at him, looked over at Cody, and Cody shrugged. I was completely enraged and trying to keep from just fighting him, especially because I figured he could still kill me. I didn't want to run another pattern. But Cody picked up a ball.

My next thought was to punch Ken in the nuts when Cody said go. (What would I do then? Run away?) Then I thought I'd just fight him off the line, just go at him—maybe I can get a punch in by accident, I thought. What's the worst that could happen? Ken might beat me dumb, I guess. So? Just fight.

But when Cody said go, something else happened. My body made a move to hit Ken. But then I sensed him coil so he could hit me. As he unwound, I slapped his right shoulder, pushed, then spun. In a flash, he was on the ground on his face, and I was ten yards downfield, the ball already delivered into my hands by Cody.

Everybody, including the older dudes, whooped.

I slowed, turned around, and jogged back toward them. As I did, Ken pushed himself off the ground, turned, and held up his hands like he wanted me to throw him the ball.

Because I'm a trusting soul or an idiot, I tossed it to him underhanded.

Before I'd taken another step, he reared back and threw the ball at my head as hard as he could. My right hand, without me even knowing it, reached up barbarian-style and caught the ball in front of my face. I held it up above me for a second, squeezing it, staring at Ken, and then I smashed it into the ground. The ball bounced away about twenty yards. Ken and I glared at each other. Everybody stood there totally silent for like two months; I guess waiting for us to fight (which I was ready to do at that point).

Cody wouldn't let it happen though. Cody said, "That's enough for today."

Ken looked over at the older guys.

I exhaled, turned, walked up to Karpinski, Dern, and Reese, quietly said "See you later," and then went over to my bike and left without another word. I rode directly to the Mound to do my running. Little bolts of lightning kept firing all over my body as I rode.

CHAPTER 39:
TIRED BARBARIAN

That evening, Cody picked me up, and we went out to the deli at Walmart to have sandwiches with all the backs and receivers. On the way out, Cody said, "You hanging in there, man?"

"Yeah. Ken Johnson just pisses me off. No big deal."

"No, I mean, you doing all right other than Ken Johnson? You haven't been saying much lately."

• • •

In the morning, on the paper route, Aleah had asked me sort of the same thing.

"What's wrong? You're so quiet. Are you mad? You didn't come over last night."

No, I wasn't mad at all. Not at her. I'd skipped going to watch her practice because I thought I should clean my house. I mean, I'd broken that picture and the door frame, and there was trash all over.

I'd actually put in an hour or two cleaning too. But there was no point. The job was too big, especially because Andrew could dirty everything so fast.

I'd picked up the living room upstairs and swept the glass in the kitchen and then started with the TV room in the basement. While I worked downstairs, Andrew, apparently quietly because

I didn't hear him, pulled a couple of boxes out of the attic and spread the contents across the living room floor. Jerri must've heard him because she came out of her room and began shouting, "What the hell are you doing? What the hell are you doing? Stay out of my stuff, you little goddamn prick. You prick! You shit! You little ass!"

I ran upstairs in time to hear Andrew drop the f-bomb on her and slam the front door on his way out. Jerri was scooping up crap from the floor and crying. So the upstairs actually looked worse after I cleaned. It was a losing battle, so I quit and went for a fast bike ride, all the weeds and trees blurring, but didn't go to Aleah's (I had too much on my mind that needed to drain out).

The following morning on the route, I suppose I was quiet; I didn't make jokes or anything, just delivered the papers. By the time we got to the nursing home, Aleah was staring at me.

"Are you okay, Felton?"

"Umm hmm," I said.

"You're quiet."

"Just tired this morning."

"You haven't really talked in a couple of days," she said.

"I have a lot to deal with because football is coming up," I told her. She nodded but seemed concerned.

• • •

"Aleah is leaving soon. I guess I'm bummed," I told Cody in the truck.

He knew she was going back to Chicago, so it was a good excuse.

"Sucks. Make sure she comes to your party," he said.

I couldn't believe anyone was throwing me a party. I couldn't believe it was only a week and a few days away. I honestly felt like I was turning into an old man, not just some young dude about to turn sixteen. Barbarian getting old…

• • •

You know, I don't even know exactly what I mean by barbarian. I just saw that Arnold Schwarzenegger movie once. Big muscley man who can beat everyone. He even punched out a camel.

• • •

But these were still good times.

Cody and I arrived at Walmart a little later than everyone else. When we walked into the deli aisle where there's seating, there were more than the backs and receivers, there were like twenty honkies waiting for me, including Abby and Jess.

"Hey, what's up?" I asked.

And, seriously, I was greeted as if I were the king of the whole wide Walmart world. Nobody liked Ken Johnson very much apparently. They actually whooped when they saw me. Karpinski said, "If Kennedy Johnson thought he could take you, he would've thrown a punch." Everybody shouted "Yeah!" "He's scared of you, Rein Stone!" Then he shouted, "Kennedy's scared of a squirrel nut!" And right away, everybody chanted "Kennedy's scared of a squirrel nut. Kennedy's scared of squirrel nut," over and over, which might have been insulting because none of those people ever called me squirrel nut anymore. But it wasn't. What's the problem with squirrel nut? Nothing, if Ken Johnson's scared of it.

But the Barbarian was getting tired.

I'm so, so, so tired.

CHAPTER 40:
5:15 A.M.

There are these weird times in life that you sort of experience as if they're memories while they're happening. For example, the summer before, after we got back from camping and hiking at Wyalusing, when Andrew, Jerri, and I went to the Strawberry Festival, which was at the city square downtown, I felt like I wasn't just there having a really good time with my funny little brother and my funny mom. I sort of felt like I was watching it happen too.

It was like there was an older me remembering playing the hoop toss while Jerri and Andrew cheered. It was like the older me watched while the three of us sat still on little stools, cracking jokes while the caricature artist laughed and drew us.

The caricature artist made my Jew-fro huge, which was funny. He made Andrew's glasses huge, which was funny. He made Jerri's smile huge, which it really was. And the evening sun draped orange on the green grass and green trees. And an older me watched it all and remembered. I was sad and happy at the same time.

In November, right when I started growing, Jerri stopped being that Jerri. I think I knew it was about to be over while at the Strawberry Festival. The older me was remembering.

That's how I felt on the Mound one night. Everything was really good, and my older self remembered.

It was Thursday night, the day after I'd nearly fought Ken Johnson. I ate dinner with Aleah and Ronald. Good food. Ravioli. Aleah was intent on practicing a new piece, so Cody picked me up, and me, Reese, Cody, and Karpinski drove out to the Mound—all smashed in the cab of the pickup—and climbed all the way to the top and watched the sun go down over Bluffton.

Bluffton didn't look like Suckville at all. It was rolling and green, and as the sun set, the town's tiny lights came on one by one and twinkled. Bluffton sort of looked like a place where elves would live.

We'd gone up there for a dumb reason, to see if Cody could throw a rock all the way down. We all tried.

And I was laughing, and an older me watched and smiled.

Karpinski threw a rock, and even though he can catch anything thrown at him (including rocks me and Reese threw pretty hard, even though he was only ten feet away from us), he totally can't throw. He looked so dorky throwing, and he tried so hard, and he screamed really loud, and me and Cody fell over laughing. I threw a rock, but it only went halfway down. I watched the rock bounce down one side of the big M, just like my leather pouch rocks and crystals did. It was like in slow motion. Then Reese threw a rock and lost his balance, and he almost fell down the Mound, which probably would've killed him or at least totally maimed him, but I reached out and grabbed the waistband of his shorts and pulled him back on top of me.

"Nice, Rein Stone. You gave me a snuggy," he smiled.

"Yeah? You squished the crap out of me."

He did too. Reese weighs 270 pounds. And then Cody stood and threw, and it was really like in slow motion: the rock exploded from his hand and up into the setting sun and then it arched down, taking like ten minutes, amazing, arching, falling, until it cracked against the hood of his truck in the parking lot below.

"Jesus, no!" he shouted.

"Holy shit," I said. "You hit your damn truck!"

"Damn, man, you got a cannon!" Karpinski said, spazzing.

Then we sat up there, the sun coloring everything orange like orange juice, and talked about girls and football, and I had to agree when they talked about how hot Abby Sauter is. She really is.

"She's turning into a freaking swimsuit model," Reese said.

The Bluffton poop air smelled fresh, like Aleah's idea of the country, and we laughed and laughed, and the sun set. It was so fun. It's good to be almost sixteen, I thought.

"It's good to be sixteen," said my older voice. *"It's good to be sixteen."*

I watched myself watching the sunset, and I was both happy and sad.

• • •

It sort of freaks me out.

CHAPTER 41:
THE INJURY

At home that night, I found Andrew in my bedroom, using my computer. I told him to get the hell out, which made him scream at me (*My charger is dead!*), which made Jerri cry out "Shut up! Please! Shut the hell up!" from her bedroom.

Which caused Andrew to scream "You shut up!" while looking at me.

Jerri didn't respond.

I looked at him. His lips were trembling. He was so dirty.

"Andrew," I said quietly. "I honestly can't take this anymore."

"What are you going to do, kick me in half?"

"No. I just can't take it."

"Take what?" he spat. "You're never here. You've abandoned me and Jerri."

"What?"

"You don't care about Dad."

"Please stop, Andrew. I really can't take it. And I might kill you accidentally."

Andrew turned and stomped out of my room, but not before he stuck his tongue out at me (still a little kid).

I didn't go to sleep. I passed out. That's how exhausting dealing with Andrew and Jerri had become. I woke up only once when there was stomping and crashing above. Jerri shouted at Andrew really loud, and Andrew cried out. I think she screamed "Stop torturing me."

Jesus. Really.

• • •

Then at weights in the morning, while I was bench-pressing, Cody not paying enough attention, Ken Johnson walked up and pressed down on the left end of the bar as I was pushing up.

It happened so fast that Cody really couldn't have stopped him.

My right arm over compensated, and I went way out of balance. In a heartbeat, my back twisted really hard, and I flipped left off the bench. All the weights went crashing onto the floor. The bar nearly hit me in the head.

I was hurt. I cried out because fire rose in my lower back. Cody started shouting, "What's wrong with you? What the hell's wrong with you?" He shoved Ken, who just stared at me on the floor, not answering or fighting Cody. Others joined in shouting at Ken while I tried not to die. (Reese tried to pull me up, but my back hurt too much.)

In about five seconds, Coach Johnson was up the stairs shouting, "What was that noise?" Cody told him what happened while Ken stood there dumb-faced.

Then Coach totally lost his mind. He screamed at Ken.

"Go home! Go home! Get out of here! Don't you even think about leaving that house!' He nearly pushed Ken down the stairs, he was tailing him so close as he shouted.

After Ken left, Coach came back. Cody and Reese did pull me off the floor and helped me sit down on the bench.

"You okay? Oh, no. You all right, Reinstein? Jesus H. Christ. Do you need to go to the emergency room?"

"I'm okay," I said, not really sure if I was.

"I'll call your mom. You shouldn't ride your bike home."

"No, you can't call her," I said.

"Reinstein rode with me anyway. I'll take him home," Cody said, looking at me.

"Jesus Christ. I can't believe this," Coach said.

Pain shot up my back, and I winced.

On the way home, I was quiet. Cody couldn't stop talking.

"Ken's not a team player. He doesn't give a shit about anybody but himself. He'd rather see you hurt than have you help our team be better. You okay? You still hurt? It's no time to get hurt. We've got your birthday next week—it's going to be awesome—and practice starts the week after. Baseball's done after Saturday. We're not going to make the playoffs. Coach Jones is an idiot. Can you believe he pitched Kelly at Iowa-Grant? So we can hang out more next week. You can't get hurt now."

I turned stiffly and looked at Cody.

"Ken Johnson tried to kill me," I nodded.

"Yeah, I think so," Cody said. "I should tell my dad to arrest him."

"No. That's okay." I didn't want any more Kennedy Johnson. Not even in a court of law.

I didn't want to go home either.

Pain shot up my back. I'd have to be in my home, which wasn't my home. All day? Several days? Weeks? What if this was a really serious injury? As Cody drove and talked, I imagined the dark and dank and smell and Andrew stomping around listening to some harsh punk music Dad liked or dragging spider-filled boxes out of the attic, looking for God-knows-what and Jerri screaming at him and Andrew screaming back and Jerri crying in her bed, me holed up in my room, not able to run, not able to do my paper route, not able to see Aleah, too broken to fight Jerri and Andrew off. Cody talked, and I began to panic.

"I don't know what to do," I broke in. "What am I going to do? I can't lie around all day."

"I don't think it's serious, Reinstein. Seriously. You walked away from there. You'll be back moving fine in a day or two. It could've been a lot worse, like if those weights had hit…"

"I can't sit in my house for two days!" I shouted.

"You want to come to my house?" he asked.

I wanted to go to Aleah's, but she'd be sleeping. I thought about going to Cody's but would have to answer questions there because Cody's dad would know something was wrong. I had to go home. I had to.

"No, no. I'll just go home. I'll be okay," I said, nodding, trying to hold it together.

"You sure, Reinstein?"

"Yeah."

Cody wanted to help me into the house when we got there, but I wouldn't let him. I couldn't let him see the rubble inside.

"I'm okay," I said. "Don't worry." I tried to sound reassuring. "I'll come up to the game tomorrow," I nodded.

"Put some ice on it," he told me.

"On what? On my back? Will that help?"

"I don't know. Everybody always says to put ice on it."

"Okay. I'll put ice on it."

I straight-leg zombie-walked into the garage, totally wincing the whole way. When I turned, Cody wasn't driving away. He was waiting until I entered the house (and into the care of Jerri, I suppose). I waved and went in.

CHAPTER 42:
FOOD FIGHT

ndrew wasn't home or at least wasn't inside. There was no banging or music. And I don't mean piano music. He never played piano anymore. Not forever. The house was so silent, except for Jerri's TV, terrible and dead. Jesus Christ, I missed his piano.

I sat down on the couch because it was the closest seat to the garage door. I stared at the spot on the TV table where the TV had been. I'd missed cleaning that spot. The table was filled with trash. My trash. My food wrappers. No TV. Dead wrappers. I sat for maybe five minutes, but it felt like a year. My lower back throbbed, and I groaned.

If old Andrew had been there, I'd have crawled upstairs and asked him to play me a song to take my mind off the pain.

What happened to him?

I knew what happened.

Andrew had made good on his promise not to take Jerri's behavior sitting down. Andrew stood up tall. He'd taken all the dark in this story and pushed it right out to the outside. He turned his clothes black. He'd turned his eyeballs black. He'd turned into a pirate. And I'm not talking about a funny movie pirate. *Give me a bottle of rum! Arrggh! Feed my parrot!* I'm talking about the kind that would board your ship and kill you for your hamburger.

Me? I ran away up a cliff and then fought to keep both him and Jerri away. Andrew turned all Black Night Bart and refused to disappear. What a kid. The real Barbarian. Not me. I ran away.

I wanted to be with my little brother.

Or I wanted to seriously run away.

My little brother was gone, and Ken had broken my back. I had no brother left—and no ability to run.

I moved my leg, and the pain took away my breath.

I seriously moaned.

I sat, trying not to freak, for another twenty minutes. But my head spun. *Get out. Get out. Get out.* I can't. I can't. I can't. I was totally freaking out.

Then I thought: Go upstairs. Get ice. Ice back. If the back is iced, it might feel better. And I was hungry. Goddamn it, so hungry. I'd lifted hard before Ken's attack. *Eat cheese and bread.* I'd put bread and cheese in the refrigerator the day before. I bought it at Kwik Trip so I wouldn't spend so much money.

I could hear that awful TV in Jerri's room. She was up there. But I wouldn't bother her. Only Andrew bothered her. She wouldn't come out of her room. I didn't want to see her and have her not care about my back. She wouldn't come out, I was convinced. *My bread and cheese. Then ice.*

So I got up. I moved across the basement as silently as possible. I hobbled up the stairs. As I climbed, my back muscles pinched, almost taking me down. I gasped but tried to hold it in so as not to make noise. *Should I crawl?* No. I kept moving.

At the top of the stairs, the floorboards creaked, and I stood still both from pain and worry. Claustrophobic. I released my muscles, my brain telling them to let go, and I worked my way into the kitchen, holding on to walls, propping myself up on tables, etc. The pain burned in my back. Hunger burned in my gut.

Then I stumbled up to the refrigerator.

First things first. Bread and cheese.

I opened the door and looked in. Where was my bread and cheese? I bent, although it pained me, and rifled through the mess of expired eggs and black and mushy vegetables—and found nothing. No, there was no Kwik Trip bread. There was no cheese. What? Adrenaline rushed. Did goddamn Andrew take my cheese? "Where the hell's my damn cheese?" I whispered. Heat rose in my face. No food? I was stuck, broken, in this house with no food? Adrenaline pumped in my veins. Okay, pirate. Okay, Black Night Bart. Tell me right now: "Where in the freaking hell is my goddamn Kwik Trip cheese?"

Just then Andrew came in through the front door. He was wearing his stupid black trousers and his black pirate T-shirt. His hair had grown back enough that you could tell he had regular hair, but it was no longer. His face was dirty, and his plastic nerd glasses sat crooked on his nose. He was carrying a really big zucchini.

"Look what I found in the yard," he said.

I stood straight, and my back killed. He wasn't my little brother. He was a pirate.

"Did you eat my bread and cheese, you jerk?"

"No," he said, tilting his head to the side. "I didn't eat your white man bread."

"It was white bread, not white man bread, jerk."

"Okay," Andrew said. "Hey. Listen. I'm hungry. How do you eat this thing? It's big." He held up the zucchini.

"Where. Is. My *bread!*" I shouted, not even thinking of Jerri.

"I don't know, Felton!" he shouted back.

"Jerri wouldn't eat that white man bread, Andrew. That's why I bought it. Now tell me, where the hell is my bread?"

Andrew's face fell. His pale skin heated up. He was almost crying.

"I didn't eat your stupid bread, you stupid jerk. Why are you such a stupid jerk?"

"I'm a jerk?"

"You're an assface jerk!"

Oh, that was it. I'd had it. I was done. Old Andrew was gone from my brain. Night Breed Bart was in front of me. I didn't care if he was my brother. I'd totally had it. I took a step toward Andrew so I could finally throttle him once and for all. Andrew's eyes got huge and teary. He gasped really hard, then raised the zucchini above his head so he could brain me with it. I took another step, ready to kill him, all the sweet thoughts and memories erased. Then my back knotted into a tight ball. Flames shot up to my neck. I spazzed and shouted. I crumpled onto the floor, screaming in pain.

Andrew dropped the zucchini.

"What's wrong? What's wrong?" he cried.

"I hurt my back," I tried to say. But it just crushed me. This pain just completely crushed. I could only cry out.

"Felton, what's wrong? I'm sorry!" Andrew shouted. "I'm sorry! I tried to save your cheese. I told her she shouldn't eat it."

"Owwwwww!" I moaned.

Then Jerri cried from her room, "I can't help you. I can't help you. I can't help you." I mean, she was crying.

I breathed: *Please release muscles. Release!* I rolled over to the wall and propped myself against it, breathing hard.

Jerri sobbed from the other room. I could hear her throwing things. Calling out "I can't" as she twisted in her sweaty sheets.

Something thunked loud against the wall.

"I think Jerri just threw your cheese," Andrew cried, tears pouring down his face.

In her room, Jerri kept sobbing.

"Oh my God," I moaned. "What the hell's going on? I was about to kill you, Andrew."

Andrew bent over me, his eyeballs bleeding, his lips trembling, his nose all snotty.

"I'm sorry, Felton. I told her not to eat it."

"Andrew," I said, breathing hard, "You know…" I gasped with pain. "I think…ahhhh…this…this thing with Jerri…it's really serious."

"What the crap, Felton. I know. I know," he cried.

"I believe she's gone totally and completely bat-nut crazy."

"I know. I know. She really has. It's my fault."

"No, I don't think she's…I don't think she's going to get better."

"Oh, no. Oh, no. Oh, no," Andrew cried.

"I think we need help."

"I burned all my clothes," Andrew sobbed.

"I know."

"I told Jerri I wished she were dead," he cried.

"It's okay. It's not you."

"Nobody cares about us," Andrew drooled.

"I know. I know."

"What are we going to do?" he cried.

Jerri continued her hissy fit.

"I have to think."

And then Andrew kneeled down and clung on to my neck and cried for like two minutes (which hurt my back a lot, but it was worth it). We both calmed down a little.

"Let's get away from Jerri," I said.

CHAPTER 43:
A PLAN

Andrew helped me into the basement. We sat on the couch to make a plan. But Andrew began fidgeting. Then he stood up.

"I can't sit in this house anymore, Felton. It's completely deadly."

"Yeah. Outside."

Andrew helped me into the garage. He pulled two lawn chairs out and set them up and then helped me sit down on one.

"Thank you."

Andrew faced his chair toward mine. He sniffled. Then straightened himself up, looked me in the eye, and said, "I want to be your brother, Felton."

It was a peculiar pronouncement. But I knew what he meant. I straightened myself up as best I could and then said, "Thank you. I was thinking the same thing before you came in with that zucchini."

"Oh, good. That's good," Andrew nodded.

Okay. I was ready. Andrew knew stuff I'd been avoiding. *Here it goes:* "Do you remember when Dad died?" I asked him.

"A little bit. Not much. I remember getting closed in a bedroom and you crying."

"I'd just found him," I said. "I imagine I was freaked."

"Yes. It's fine you were crying. It must be difficult to find your father hanging from the ceiling."

"Right." I looked down the drive, the same drive that our dad certainly looked down ten thousand times. "And I believe you've come to the conclusion that this Jerri trouble has something to do with Dad."

"Of course," Andrew said.

"I didn't want to deal with it. I've been confused, Andrew."

"I was very mad at you for that," Andrew nodded.

"What have you found out?"

"Not much. Jerri used to keep a diary, remember?"

"Yes."

"I've been looking for it."

"You haven't found it?"

"No. I did find out stuff though."

"Like what?"

"Jerri won't tell the truth. You ask her a question, and she'll go crazy."

"Why?"

"I don't know. She doesn't want us to know anything about Dad though."

"Why?"

"I think because she lied about him."

"Lied? About what?"

"That he was nice."

"Why do you say that?"

"I found a photo album from their wedding."

"With Dad in it?" I really hadn't seen a picture of Dad since Jerri's bonfire. I had an idea of what he looked like, vague memories. I imagined he looked like the comedian Paul Reiser but also knew that probably wasn't right. "You saw Dad?"

Andrew nodded at me. "Yes. He was in their wedding pictures."

"Makes sense."

"Yes. But"—Andrew squinted at me—"he looked like you."

"What? Before I got big?"

"No. Like you now."

"But he was short."

"Maybe, but his face looked like your face."

"My face?"

"Jerri might hate your face, Felton."

"Why? Why would Jerri hate my face?"

"I'm very sure Jerri hates Dad," Andrew said.

"No. No, she doesn't. He was a sweet, little Jewish dude. He was… He was just sad. Why would Jerri hate…?" I began to lose my train of thought, and my chin started trembling. "What, Andrew? What?"

"I don't think he was sweet," Andrew said. "He looked really mean in the pictures."

"At his wedding?"

"He wasn't smiling. He was…He looked really, really angry." Andrew started crying.

"Where's the album?"

Andrew said something like "uhhhff," he clamped his mouth shut, and then he said, "I only found it yesterday. It was above her clothes in her closet."

"Was she in there when you found it?"

"Uh huh. She was sleeping."

"Jesus, Andrew. You're crazy."

"I took it to my room and looked at it for a long time and then I wanted to Google Dad because I think I've Googled Steven W. Reinstein and seen actual pictures of him that I didn't know were him, but my computer won't charge, and you wouldn't let me use yours."

"Oh, shit. I'm sorry."

"Then, in the middle of the night, Jerri came barging into my room, screaming at me to stop stealing her stuff—to stop torturing her. She was completely psycho, Felton. She screamed and pushed me against my wall and then she burned the album in her shower."

"That was last night? I slept through that?"

"I don't care, Felton. I don't care about her stupid diary anymore. I just want this to end."

"Yeah," I nodded.

"I hid in the garden all morning eating tomatoes."

"You hate tomatoes."

"I'm hungry."

"I'm so sorry, Andrew. I'm so sorry." I gulped for air. My eyes burned.

"We're both crying like babies," Andrew said.

"I know," I nodded. "No dignity."

"It's been stolen." Andrew wasn't joking.

We stared out across our yard, tall thistles all over the place. We didn't say anything for several minutes. We both calmed down. Then something occurred to me.

"Grandma Berba knows what happened," I said.

"Why?"

"She was here after Dad died."

"She was? I don't remember."

"You were three."

"You know she hates us," Andrew whispered, looking over his nerd glasses.

"I think we have to call her, Andrew. I think she better come here. If she will…"

"Jerri is going to go out of her mind," he said. "I don't know, Felton."

"Jerri is already out of her mind," I said.

"Yes, but even more so." Then poor Andrew's lip started trembling again, and his face heated up again.

"I miss Jerri."

"I do too," I said.

"I hate Jerri," he whimpered.

"We have to call Grandma Berba. Or if not her, I guess the cops or something."

"Grandma," Andrew nodded.

We discussed what to do next. One thing was very obvious: we couldn't stay in the house anymore. After going through our immediate options (neighbor, Andrew's piano teacher, Cody Frederick—Andrew had no idea who he was), I suggested the Jenningses.

"You mean Aleah Jennings?" he asked. "Her dad thinks we're nuts. Jerri slept in front of their house."

"I've, uh…" I realized that Andrew and I had been so out of touch that he had no clue I'd been with her.

"What, Felton?"

"Aleah's my girlfriend."

"Oh my God," Andrew stared at me. "I forgot she liked you."

"I...I really like her."

"I'm so stupid," Andrew said.

"Do you like her too?"

"Like her?" he asked, tilting his head like he does.

"You know, want her to be your girlfriend," I said.

Andrew gasped, "No! I'm just embarrassed."

"Because..." I was confused. "You like her?"

"Because I haven't practiced piano in over a month," he mumbled. "I'll be rusty if I play."

"That's the least of our troubles."

And with that, we decided to go to the Jenningses. Mr. Jennings was kind, and I loved Aleah. I was used to that house, and I needed something steady, which would help me call Grandma Berba, and—maybe most important—the Jenningses weren't connected to the town, so they wouldn't tell people about our trouble. If we went to Cody's, the cops and everybody else would be involved from the start.

CHAPTER 44:
ESCAPE

Because it was the middle of the day, I assumed that Aleah would be asleep and Ronald would be at the college. There was nobody around to pick us up, so I'd have to ride the bike, even though that jerk Ken Johnson (sorry) had broken my back. I stayed out in the driveway and tried to stretch, in complete pain. Meanwhile, Andrew ran into the house and pulled a bunch of my sweats out and stuck them in a backpack. There was no reason to pack clothes for him because he only owned his pirate outfit. He did grab our toothbrushes and my deodorant. ("You smell sometimes," he said. "You smell like you haven't showered in a month," I said. "That's fair," he said.) He also grabbed Jerri's address book, which wasn't easy because it was in the desk drawer in her room. He snuck in. She rolled over while he was in there but stayed asleep.

"What in the world would I have said?" he asked. "Felton and I are running away. We'll send Grandma?"

"She would have strangled you," I said.

"With her sweaty sheet," Andrew said.

I laughed.

"It's not funny. It's true," Andrew said.

We began to ride down the drive. Then I stopped.

"Andrew," I said. "We need my phone charger."

"Why?"

"I don't know. I want to keep my life. It's really important to me. The charger's on my night stand."

Andrew was inside for a couple of minutes. When he came out, he was trying to hold it together. Jerri was behind him. My stomach dropped. Andrew stared at me as he moved forward. He was definitely shaking. Jerri was in her robe. Her hair was frizzed out, and there was no color in her face, and she was super skinny. She followed him through the garage and onto the drive, where she squinted in the summer light. She looked like she hadn't seen the sun in weeks, which was probably true.

"Felton," she said. "Andrew won't tell me what he's doing."

"Don't worry," I said. "We're going for a bike ride."

"You're what?" She shook her head.

"Just a bike ride, Jerri." She looked confused. She probably was confused. "Don't worry, Jerri. It's going to be okay," I said.

"Okay, Felton," she nodded. "You give me a call. Okay?"

Maybe she wasn't confused.

"Okay, Jerri," I said.

At the end of the driveway, I looked back. Jerri was still standing there outside the garage.

"Does she know what we're doing?" Andrew asked.

"I don't know," I said.

• • •

It was probably good for my back to be riding the Varsity. It hurt like crazy to go up the hill on the main road, but by the time

Andrew and me got to the top, I was sweating, and my back was looser. Because he's small and really isn't and will never be an athlete, Andrew rode incredibly slow. I could've biked circles around him. If my back didn't hurt, I probably would have. We only had one conversation as we rode. It was very short.

Going up the hill, I said, "Andrew, why did you burn your clothes?"

"I wanted to scare Jerri into talking to me."

"That backfired."

"Yes. She told me the only way to move forward is to destroy the past."

"I guess that makes sense," I said.

"It makes no sense," Andrew said.

"I mean, that explains her behavior."

"Her whole stupid life."

We didn't say anything else as we rode, just pedaled. But when we hit the edge of my paper route, Andrew stopped.

"I think we should call Grandma Berba now," he said.

"Why?" I really didn't want to call her.

"Because she's a terrible person and if she tells us...you know... tells us where to stick it, we'll have a different situation on our hands. You know what I mean, Felton?"

"No."

"I want to have our situation in hand before we go to the Jenningses so we can tell them what's going on truthfully and completely," he said.

"Oh, yeah. You're smart."

"Yes," Andrew said. He swung his backpack around and pulled out Jerri's address book. Then he handed it to me.

"You call," he said.

No. No. No. Grandma Berba has never liked us—me and Andrew knew it. She called on our birthdays, said happy birthday, and then hung up. At Christmas, she'd send cards to Andrew and me and always wrote "Happy Chanukah" in them because our father was Jewish, even though there was always a Christmas tree or a baby Jesus on the front. She'd also send ten dollars. She never came to visit. She never invited us to Arizona. She moved there right before I was born. I only remembered her at all because she was around right after Dad died. Before she went back to Arizona, she shouted at Jerri. I don't remember what it was about, but Jerri shouted back. Jerri freaked on her. She wasn't a very good grandma. Jerri wouldn't ever even talk about her. So I wasn't exactly excited to make the call. I found her number in the address book.

"Okay," I said to Andrew. "I'm calling."

I punched in the numbers real slow. My heart pounded. My back hurt. I pressed the Call button and then held my breath. All this fear expanded in my chest. My phone hand was shaking. In a second, the phone at Grandma Berba's was ringing. It rang three times. Then someone picked up.

"Hello," the voice said. But it seemed too young to be a grandma.

"Um, could I talk to Carol Berba?"

"Speaking."

"Grandma?" I said.

There was a long pause.

"Yes?"

"This is Felton. Felton Reinstein."

"I know who this is, child."

"We…Me and Andrew…"

"Tell me you're safe."

"I…I don't know…" And then I just started sobbing. I couldn't hold it in. I was totally sucking air. Gulp. Gulp. Gulp. Snot poured out my nose like in that football movie with the broken legs, and my eyes burned. I choked. Finally, I got out: "Grandma?"

"I've been expecting this call for ten years. What's your phone number? Is it the phone you just dialed from?"

"Yes."

"Felton. Please. Are you safe?"

"I think so."

"I'll call you back in ten minutes with my itinerary. You hold on, Felton."

I hung up the phone and looked at Andrew. He was bawling.

"She's not interested in us, huh?" he said.

"No. No. She's coming."

CHAPTER 45:
GRANDMA

It's 5:41 a.m. I think most of the time, Grandma is up by now. She's not this morning. I just went upstairs to take some of her iced coffee out of the fridge because I just want to stay awake. It was a long night, and Grandma is snoring in the guest bedroom. I'm sorer right now than I was riding the bike to Aleah's that day.

You can't think Grandma is mean any longer. I won't let you, okay?

Grandma sold insurance, and she made a lot of money, and Jerri told her she didn't want Grandma's money-grubbing values to affect us kids because Grandma wanted to go after Dad's parents for more support money after he died. Jerri capped our presents at no more than $10, so Grandma sent $10, and Jerri told her there was no reason for us to see Grandma's Arizona condo with the pool or Grandma's BMW because then we'd value money over...what? Not family, because Jerri kept us from our family. Maybe vegetables or nature. So Grandma backed off and waited, even though she knew it made me and Andrew think she didn't like us. She also said that maybe Jerri was right about some of her values because me and Andrew sure turned out to be sweet kids.

Okay.

Let's go.

CHAPTER 46:
BRAIN MASH: PART I

The next hour of my life had to be the weirdest on record. After the phone call, Andrew and I went directly to the Jenningses'. I had to ring the doorbell fifteen times before Aleah came to the door. Andrew kept saying "She's not here." I kept telling him she was. Finally, she opened up and was all groggy-eyed. At first, she was kind of pissed we were there. Then she locked in to how serious I was.

"Aleah," I said. "You know that I wouldn't mess with your sleep except in case of emergency. Andrew and I have been experiencing an emergency."

"What?" she asked.

"Our mother has gone crazy."

"Alcohol?" she asked.

"No. No. This has been coming for a long time, I think."

"You never said anything."

"I know…But, Aleah, this is serious."

"Okay. It's not like I didn't know you were losing it."

"Yes, I was. Is there any way we can stay with you for a day or two?"

"What?" Aleah shook her head, totally confused.

"Our grandmother is on her way," said Andrew, "But, honestly, we don't know what to expect from her. We don't know our grandma."

"Uh oh," Aleah said, squinting at me.

"Uh oh?"

"Yes," she nodded. "Uh. Oh. Would you like some iced tea?"

"Do you have any food?" Andrew replied.

"Come on in," she said.

"Thanks, Aleah. Thanks."

"You're a very weird family," Aleah said as I straight-leg zombie-walked past her (my back hurt).

Then, while Andrew and I sat on the couch and gulped down chips ("Beats tomatoes," he said) and that berry-tasting iced tea, I began to tell the whole long story of Jerri's complete collapse as a mother and a human being.

"You told me nothing. That's not good," Aleah said.

"I wanted you to like me and not be freaked."

"Hmm."

While I was telling her the sordid story, I began to get text message after text message about my back. Apparently, word was spreading around. Most of the texts were from honky football players or friends of football players asking me how I was. A couple were from honky girls who'd heard about my injury.

"From who?" Aleah asked. "That Abby?"

"Uh, just friends," I said.

A conversation with Cody went like this:

> Cody: talked to dad. he'll arrest ken if you want. says it was definitely assault.

Me: no. not hurt.

Cody: dad might anyway he's pissed.

Me: tell him thanks but it was more accident than assault. ok?

Cody: ok. but might be out of my hands.

On top of the messages, I received two phone calls. One was from Coach Johnson.

"How many people do you know?" Aleah asked as my phone buzzed.

"Yeah?" Andrew asked.

I held up my finger to let them know I was answering.

"How are you doing, Felton? Your back feeling better?" Coach asked.

"I'm feeling fine," I said, even though my back really hurt.

"Thank God. I nearly took Kennedy to the police station. For his own protection, not just because he's an idiot. Kid's getting dozens of hate texts. Could you ask the crew to call off the dogs, Felton? Kennedy's pretty broken up."

"Okay," I told him, but I didn't do anything. Not that I didn't feel for that jerk Ken Johnson (sorry). I just had other things on my mind. I did have presence of mind to tell Coach not to take his son to the police station because of Cody's dad.

I still had my normal life.

"I guess I know a lot of people," I told Aleah and Andrew after I hung up. "It's really weird to be talking to these…these friends about my back, which isn't even that big a deal if you compare it to this whole Jerri…" My phone buzzed again.

"Mr. Popular." Aleah raised her eyebrows at me.

"No. No. This is Grandma Berba, I think."

It was.

"I'll be in to Bluffton tonight very late. I had to book to Madison and then I'll drive a rental. Are you staying at the house tonight, Felton?"

"No."

"Good boy. Where will you be?"

I gave her Aleah's address.

"I'll be over in the morning," she said.

"Should I let Jerri know you're coming?"

"I've already spoken to her. She's well aware."

"Is she okay, Grandma?"

"No. She needs her mother. Took her to age thirty-five to figure it out."

When I got off the phone and relayed Grandma Berba's comments, Aleah's mouth dropped open.

"Your mom is thirty-five?" she said.

"I guess," I told her.

"Yes. Jerri turns thirty-six in October," Andrew said.

"But you turn sixteen next week, Felton."

"Yeah?"

"That means your mom was a teenager when she had you. She was just like a year out of high school."

"Whoa," I said. I'd never thought of it. I guess it hadn't meant anything to me before. But since I was turning sixteen, nineteen suddenly didn't seem that old.

"It's not like she was in eighth grade," Andrew said. "Nineteen is adult. Jerri has a good head on her shoulders too." Andrew trailed off as he realized what a dumb statement he was making relative to the current situation.

"She was a kid when she had me," I nodded. "Like I'm a kid right now."

"How old was your dad?" Aleah asked.

"He was thirty-four when he died," I said.

"You were five, right?"

"Yes."

"Hm," Aleah said. "He was way too old for your mom. That's a very bad power dynamic if you ask me. A thirty-year-old man with a teenager?"

"How is it a bad power dynamic?" Andrew asked, mouth full of chips.

"I'd like us to drop this conversation," I said. "I don't like it."

"Felton isn't interested in the truth," Andrew said to Aleah.

"That's not true," I said. "I'm afraid of the truth."

"Oh, that's much better," Aleah said.

The two of them moved on to another subject.

But I couldn't stop thinking of it. Jerri was a teenager when I was born. I imagined Abby Sauter pregnant with some thirty-year-old's baby. Messed up. Really, sincerely messed up.

Just then Ronald walked in from the garage.

"Looks like we got ourselves a house full of Reinstein!" he smiled.

"Andrew and Felton are going to stay with us," Aleah said.

The smile dropped right off his face. But after he found out Jerri was a teenager when she had me and she was crazy and Grandma Berba was on her way, he helped Andrew dig Gus's sleeping bags out of the crawl space above the hall (I couldn't help, as I'd cooled from the bike ride and was near paralyzed from Ken's assault).

It was a completely crazy hour with everything coming at me from every angle. Jerri, you understand, was a pregnant teenager with me in her belly. Meanwhile, the entire honky universe was buzzing, chattering, texting, calling. Jerri was almost the same age as these honkies when I was in her belly.

CHAPTER 47:
BRAIN MASH: PART II

Because it was Friday, Aleah didn't practice piano. She might as well have.

After dinner, Aleah, Andrew, and I sat in Gus's basement watching movies. Or not really movies. We watched Aleah's DVD recordings of the Metropolitan Opera, which I didn't get. But Aleah and Andrew completely get opera. They whooped and laughed and talked about orchestration and about Mozart and about singing in Italian and singing in German, and I sat there thinking about Jerri and her baby, who was me. Then Aleah kissed my cheek, told me to get some rest, turned off the light, and disappeared upstairs. After, Andrew said, "Aleah's really a wonderful person. You're very lucky." In like a minute, he began snoring. And I laid there, my eyeballs staring into the black night of the basement, thinking about Jerri and her baby, who was me.

Jerri wanted to be a civil rights lawyer when she was my age. That's what she told me. Clearly, I was the reason she wasn't a civil rights lawyer. Jerri was valedictorian of her high school class. I knew that from before. That's part of history she kept. Jerri stayed in Bluffton for college because her dad would only pay for it if she did. I knew this because once, freshman year, after taking it on the chin from the honkies all day, I asked her why in the name of squirrel nut hell did she decide to stay in Bluffton for college when she was so dang smart in high school?

"My father trapped me," she said. Now I knew this too: Jerri got pregnant with a professor's kid (me!) by like November of her first year of college. How the holy hell did that happen? How the holy hell did she meet, fall in love with, and marry a professor in just a couple of months? Then it dawned on me: Jerri wasn't married to Professor Reinstein at all. That's why she still had the last name Berba!

Even though my back hurt like freaking terror, I rolled over and shook Andrew awake.

"What?" he asked, sleepy.

"Jerri and Dad were never married," I whispered. "We're bastards. Do you understand?"

"No," Andrew said. "That's not true. I saw the wedding album, remember?"

"The wedding album had to be from something else. Jerri's last name is Berba."

"Yes. She kept her last name. But they were married."

"No, they weren't, Andrew. Stop kidding yourself."

"I saw the wedding announcement from the *Bluffton Journal* too. They had a spring wedding."

"Where did you get that?"

"Same place as the album. Way up in"—Andrew yawned— "Jerri's closet."

"Oh," I said and started doing math. "Wait. Spring? That means

Grandma Berba let Jerri marry a thirty-year-old when Jerri was still in high school. Grandma Berba must be totally crazy."

"No. I think you're wrong. The paper said Jerri was nineteen and Steven Reinstein was twenty-nine. She'd have been out of high school."

"But that's impossible, Andrew. That doesn't make sense. Unless...Oh my God."

"I'm so tired," Andrew said.

"Go to sleep," I told him. He was snoring again in seconds.

I laid there so awake. I'd figured it all out. It all made complete sense. The reason why I'm such a freak of nature—growing all this hair all over, running so fast, gaining all this weight—was so obvious. I was a super baby (yeah, right). It must have only taken me a few months to grow inside of Jerri (uh huh). I must have been full-sized in just a few months (oh my God).

It probably killed Jerri, me growing so fast inside of her. I was probably born with white shorts on, which is why she referred to me as a tennis player when she called me asshole. Maybe that's what killed Dad, having a freak of nature for a son. They got married, and right away, Jerri was pregnant, and I was huge in her belly. I bet I was terrifying, especially for a little, kind Jewish fellow who only liked poetry. A tennis-playing baby? Come on! If only he'd stuck around while I didn't grow all those years and became squirrel nuts. He would've breathed easy then. Professor Reinstein would've recognized squirrel nuts. Maybe he'd just be killing himself now because now I'm a super baby again. It probably took everything out of Jerri, having a super baby. She must've lost all will to be a lawyer. I'm a curse. Stupid super baby grows too fast. Poor Jerri.

Are you kidding? Are you even listening to yourself? Didn't you hear Andrew say he looked like you?

That's the last thing I remember thinking before I fell asleep.

My brain was completely mashed.

CHAPTER 48:
BRAIN MASH: PART III

Aleah shook me awake. Light was coming in from the high basement windows. It was morning.

"Felton. Felton. Wake up."

"Whuh?" I asked.

"You didn't set an alarm. We've got to do your paper route. It's past seven."

"Oh, shit!" I sat straight up. My back hurt but not that much. My back didn't really hurt. "Wow. I'm not paralyzed," I said to Aleah.

"That's good."

"It only makes sense," I said. "I'm a super baby. I must heal fast."

"What?"

From upstairs, I could hear piano playing. Andrew wasn't at my side.

"Is Andrew playing piano?"

"Yes. He's very good."

"Oh, that's good. That's really good."

"Paper route!" Aleah shouted.

"Oh, shit!"

I pushed my way out of the sleeping bag and ran upstairs, with Aleah right behind me. I'd slept in shorts and a shirt. I was decent.

I could go out that way. We ran into the living room. Ronald sat there reading a magazine ("Don't have my paper yet. Ha ha"). Andrew played piano. I bent over to pull on my shoes. "Owww." My back did hurt a bit.

Andrew swiveled around and looked at me.

"They were married, so we're not bastards," Andrew said.

"Duh. I know that," I said.

Then Aleah and I were out the door.

"Well, maybe you are," Andrew called after us.

Ha. Andrew. *He's funny.*

Aleah and I biked to the pickup station. My paper stack was the last one left. Then I realized I hadn't brought my paper bag from home.

"Oh, shit!" I shouted.

"What?"

"We've got nothing to carry the papers in."

"Oh, brother," Aleah said.

I handed a bunch of papers to Aleah and said, "Do all the papers from your house on. You know, the one's you know. I'll meet you at the nursing home in fifteen minutes."

"I have to bike with one hand?"

"Can you stick them in your pants?"

"I'll figure it out, Felton."

"Sounds great!"

I had like thirty papers to deliver while Aleah delivered her small batch. I biked as fast as I could. The dull ache in my back didn't hinder me from really moving. So good to pump it. With one hand, I held the papers. With the other, I steered. My legs pumped like mighty elephant legs. At each house, I just let the Varsity drop, and I ran up to the front door. At some, old men or old ladies waited to give me the business for being so late. I didn't wait for them to say what they wanted to say; I just handed them the paper, turned, and took off.

One called after me, "I sure miss that little Mexican boy." He was talking about Gus.

"He's not Mexican," I shouted back. "He's Venezuelan. Get your facts straight!"

I'm going to email Gus about being a super baby when I get back, I thought. *He'll be freaked!* Then I remembered I was going to Aleah's and not my place and my laptop was at home. Crap! Maybe I can swing by the house?

In about ten minutes, I'd delivered almost all the papers. I was on fire. My back was complaining a little, but I felt good otherwise. I felt free. The truth sets you free, is what I thought (super baby).

Then as I ran up the stoop to one of the last houses, a familiar face plastered itself against the picture window, eyeballs wide, mouth open. It was one of last year's seniors from the track team, John Spencer, a bony long distance runner. I dropped the paper in the door and turned and ran. Spencer was out the door behind me in a nanosecond.

"Hey, faker," he shouted. "I heard you might be out for the whole football season. I heard your neck might be broken. How can you run?"

I moved to get onto my bike, but Spencer grabbed the handlebars.

"You're a faker!" Spencer shouted.

"What are you talking about?" I shouted back.

"Where's your broken neck?" he spat.

"I never said my neck was broken, asshole."

"Tell that to Ken. Police were on his ass yesterday."

"Get your hands off my bike."

"Apologize to Ken."

"I said, get your hands off my bike, dick. Do you understand?"

I must've spoken in an extremely threatening way because Spencer gulped air, let go, and backed away ten feet. I pulled my bike around and rode away.

"Faker!" Spencer shouted behind me.

I biked more slowly toward the nursing home, very nervous, feeling sick to my stomach. It did look bad, didn't it? Me running around the day after I was supposedly injured.

Within a couple of minutes, I could feel the buzzing of my phone in my pocket. I didn't want to look. Stupid cell phones.

As I pulled up to the nursing home, Aleah was just getting there.

"You did all those papers that fast? You're so fast, Felton."

"Well, I didn't ask to be."

"Whoa. Cranky."

My phone buzzed in my pocket.

"Goddamn it." It buzzed again. "Goddamn cell phone!" I shouted.

"Are you okay?"

"Let's deliver these stupid papers."

I handed a couple to Aleah, held on to the rest, and entered the building. Immediately, there was screaming and pandemonium.

The younger crazy lady was standing in front of the door in the lobby. She saw me and went total ape shit. She screamed "Ghost! Ghost! Ghost! Leave me alone! Ahhhh! Ghost!" She pointed at me. Orderlies and nurses came running to her aid. I turned to Aleah, handed her the papers, and said, "Um, could you take care of these?"

"Yes. I'll see you out front, Felton."

I turned, punched in the dumb 1, 2, 3 security code, and left the building.

While I waited for Aleah, I looked at my jackass phone. There were five texts from five different honkies. All of them forwarded this message:

> squirrel nuts a faker saw him running this morning.
>
> what about? Jason Reese asked.
>
> faker? Jamie Dern asked.
>
> spencer a dick, said Cody.
>
> this going around, Abby Sauter let me know.
>
> squirrel nut faker! an anonymous texter wrote.

It was only eight in the morning too. Most of the jerks wouldn't even be awake yet. I felt so heavy. Really heavy. *You called yourself a super baby. Idiot.* I had a feeling about the truth. These people weren't my friends; they were about to turn.

As I closed my phone, Aleah exited the nursing home.

"That was weird," she said.

"What was?" I replied, so tired.

"That crazy woman thinks you're her lover and you're dead."

"It's probably true," I wheezed.

"Did you do something to her, Felton? Did you touch her?"

"Are you freaking kidding me, Aleah?"

"Okay, okay. It's just weird."

"I didn't do anything to her. I wouldn't hurt anyone. I'd never…" And the words left me because I was so heavy. So heavy. A crazy lady's lover…No freak baby…A crazy mother who doesn't leave her house for weeks and a dead dad who murdered himself and now the honkies are calling me names, and everything is so bad.

"Aleah," I said. "I'm really messed up." Then because I'm a dork, I cried.

"I'm sorry. I'm sorry, Felton," Aleah grabbed my hand.

• • •

As we biked home, I told Aleah all about my childhood as Squirrel Nuts and how, because I'm fast, it all seemed to have ended.

"Being fast doesn't seem like a reason someone would be your friend," she said.

"No. You're right. They don't really like me."

"That's not what I mean."

Then I told her how Ken Johnson had assaulted me and how his assault hurt my back and how Cody's dad, the cop, must've stopped by the Johnsons to scare Ken or to arrest him and how John Spencer had seen me running around with papers this morning and how (even as I was telling the story) the entire honky world was texting me.

"Did you say honky?" Aleah asked.

"That's what Gus and I call them," I responded. "They're town kids."

"Pretty gross," Aleah said.

"What?"

"Using inflammatory racial language to describe a bunch of your classmates," Aleah said.

"What do you mean?"

"My gosh." She stopped her bike. We were in front of her house. "You're an innocent child, aren't you?"

"I used to think I was retarded," I said. "I think...I think it's possible I am."

She stared at me and touched my cheek.

"Simple boy," she said.

I felt my heart tear (as if the other stuff weren't bad enough). My head dropped. I looked at the ground. Something drained away. Something big. I swallowed hard. *Aleah called me simple. I'm simple. I'm stupid. I'm me.* I looked back up to tell Aleah that she should break up with me, but she was looking away, toward her house, not paying attention to me.

"Who's giant SUV?" she asked.

It was blocking her entire driveway.

"Oh, crap," I whispered. "Grandma Berba."

CHAPTER 49:
BRAIN MASH: PART IV

As I walked toward the steps, my pocket continued to buzz. The honkies—or whatever they should be called—continued the text barrage. I was only vaguely aware of my buzzing pocket. Grandma Berba had gotten Aleah's address from me the afternoon before. I knew she was in the house. I paused outside the door and looked at Aleah.

"Do you mind going in first?" I asked.

"Will that help you?" Aleah said.

"I don't know," I told her.

Aleah opened the screen door and walked in. As she did, I peered around her and saw a woman who didn't look like a grandma hugging Andrew on the couch. She wasn't wearing old lady pants. She was wearing a business suit, and her hair was brown like Jerri's, and she was pretty, like Jerri would be if Jerri hadn't gone crazy. The woman let go of Andrew when Aleah was fully in. She stood up. She was ready for me. I pushed on the screen door and took a step in. Grandma Berba took a step toward me, opening her arms to hug me and then she stopped in her tracks. She stared at my face. She shook her head and said, "You've got to be kidding me. You've got to be…" She slapped herself on the forehead. She backed up a step and fell back on the couch and cupped her head, laughing. Andrew stared at her through his big nerd glasses—his mouth open. Then he looked at me, eyes wide behind his lenses.

"No," Grandma Berba looked up. "Really. You have got to be joking. No wonder. No wonder," she cupped her face with her hands and laughed.

"Wow," Aleah looked at me. "You're having a bad day."

"I don't know what to do," I said.

"Come here, Felton," Grandma Berba said. "Good lord, good lord. Really." She stood. I walked to her. She reached up and hugged me and laughed and sort of cried at the same time. She wiped her nose on my chest.

"I mean, no wonder," she said. "You're the spitting image."

CHAPTER 50:
I GUESS IT WAS ALL TOO MUCH

Even if you've been awake all night long (6 a.m.), you have to stay awake for this (if you haven't sort of figured it out already).

Grandma had a lot to get off her chest right away, which she's apologized for later because maybe there was a better way to do this, a better time. While my cell buzzed in my pocket, I heard:

Steven W. Reinstein, who's my dead dad, was an All-American, one-time national champion tennis player at Northwestern University. He played some pro tennis. He nearly qualified for major tournaments. He was six foot three inches tall. I, Felton Reinstein, have stretched and grown in such a fashion that I'm now an exact replica of Steven W. Reinstein. That's why Grandma Berba freaked when she saw me. (Andrew figured right.) Steven W. Reinstein got his student, Jerri, pregnant during her freshman year of college. Steven W. Reinstein married Jerri because Jerri pressured him. Grandma Berba told Jerri she should not—absolutely not—marry that man.

"He was just a brutal man," Grandma Berba said. Steven W. Reinstein's rich parents treated Jerri like dirt. Steven W. Reinstein didn't want to be married and continued to have girlfriends. Jerri tried to make a home. She bought our house with Steven W. Reinstein's money. Steven W. Reinstein would scream that Jerri trapped him. Jerri had Andrew to try to stabilize the situation (stupid, said Grandma). Steven W. Reinstein told Jerri flat out that he didn't have enough love, that he couldn't love. Steven W. Reinstein got another student pregnant. He got fired. Jerri hated him. *She hated him. She hated him. She hated him.* Jerri served him divorce papers when Andrew was three. He killed himself in our garage.

I only knew the last part—that he killed himself and where. I was fucking there to see it. I thought he was a small, kind Jewish fellow who only loved poetry. Jerri not only hid the truth, Jerri lied. *Andrew was right. Andrew was right. Andrew was right.*

My head spun.

As Grandma Berba spilled it all, inappropriately, right there in front of everybody, everybody in the room opened their mouth wider and wider. I was the only one who didn't. Instead, I stared at my long arms, clenched and unclenched my fists, pictured a tennis racquet in those hands. Of course. I sat tall and got red in the face and thought how I'd like to take a goddamn tennis racket and beat my stupid dad's face in (he apparently had the same idea). I also thought this: Jerri's a criminal. She's a terrible, despicable person. And then instead of listening any longer to Grandma Berba talk about Jerri's "unhealthy" reaction to these events—how Jerri decided to erase Steven W. Reinstein from her life by burning his stuff and by making up a story about who he was so Andrew and me would think we had a loving father—and listening to her talk about Jerri's silence in the face of Grandma Berba's repeated attempts to get her help; her repeated attempts to move us to Arizona; her repeated attempts to get more support money from the Reinstein grandparents; her repeated attempts to get Jerri to get ahold of her fucking life, I exploded out of my chair and out of that house.

I got on my dad's Schwinn Varsity and pumped it as hard as I could. I exploded around corners and up hills until I got to the main road that leads to my house, the house Jerri bought with Steven W. Reinstein's money. I exploded down the road past the golf course, flying by signs and light posts and cars and the blurry tall grass that grew in the ditch. I flew over the hill, pumping, and down toward our drive, boiling over and completely exploding. At the bottom of the hill, I turned the bike too hard and slid out trying to make the turn to my house. I fell and slid on my side on gravel, tearing up the skin on my legs and ass. I slid for probably thirty feet, but I didn't cry out. I picked up the bike, got back on, and exploded up the hill toward the house. In front of the garage, I got off my bike. I held it steady. Tilted it to the side. Stared at its blue paint and scratched up logo. *Schwinn Varsity. Schwinn Varsity. Schwinn Varsity.* Then I grabbed the bike with both hands, lifted it over my head, and threw it into the ground as hard as I could. The bike bounced up from its tires and hit me in the chest, hurting.

"Fuck you," I cried. I grabbed it again, and this time, I flung it—spinning out into the yard.

"Felton," Jerri yelled from the window.

"Don't ever talk to me, Jerri," I shouted.

I went into the garage and pulled out a shovel.

"Felton, stop," Jerri shouted.

Then I went nuts on it, on my Schwinn Varsity. I jumped up and down, bending its frame. I beat the mirror to pieces with the shovel. I stabbed the shovel's pointy end down on the spokes with all my might, breaking them. I hammered off the back gear shifter and bent the front. I stomped on the chain wheel. I stomped on the front fork until it bent and then broke. I was tearing off the brake levers, crying like crazy, when Jerri grabbed me.

"Felton, stop!"

"No," I said. "No, Jerri," I cried.

She pulled the bike's handlebars out of my hands and let what was left of it drop on the ground. Then she pulled me by the wrist to her and then she hugged me saying, "This isn't yours. You were right. You were right," and she sobbed. I cried, "I'm so mad at you. I'm so mad at you." And then we sort of fell over.

I guess we more crumpled over. We crumpled, and I bled all over from cuts on my hands and the scrape on my side, and I cried.

"He wasn't…" I said. "He wasn't kind."

"This isn't yours. It isn't," she cried. "I shouldn't have lied."

"I won't," I said.

"I should have told you who…"

"I won't, Jerri," I said.

"This is mine."

"I won't ever play asshole tennis, Jerri," I cried.

"It's my fault," Jerri told me, her hands on my face, totally sobbing.

Then we laid in the yard crying, the broken pieces of my Schwinn Varsity littering the ground around us.

CHAPTER 51:
ONE ALMOST NORMAL
CONVERSATION

Jerri and I were in the kitchen. With a hot washcloth, Jerri cleaned the gravel out of the skin on my leg and ass. I winced, trying not to cry out. Jerri was doing a mom thing, but she didn't seem like a mom. She was sort of jittery, and she was trying really hard, but I could see she was seeing ghosts or whatever.

"I told Grandma Berba to tell you everything," Jerri nodded too hard.

"Umm, mission accomplished," I said.

"I'm surprised she told you at the Jenningses'."

"Well, you wouldn't…"

"I couldn't do it, Felton. I couldn't tell you. I couldn't deal with it."

"Jerri, listen, I've decided not to be mad at you."

"Oh, thank you. Yeah. I don't know. I don't think that's something you can decide. But thank you." She kept nodding.

I didn't know if I should say it, but it was on my mind. *Dad had girlfriends.* I said it.

"I think one of Dad's girlfriends lives at the nursing home."

"Oh. Uh huh. Kelly Mayer," Jerri nodded. "She's been there for a long time."

"She recognizes me. She thinks I'm Dad's ghost."

"Oh God, oh God, oh God. I'm so sorry, Felton."

"She's completely nuts."

"Uh huh. Yeah. I'll say. Steve knew how to pick 'em. Kelly was already schizoid twelve years ago when your dad was…She'd call here all hours of the night. I wasn't much better. Steve went for the weak ones."

"You weren't weak, Jerri. You were smart."

"Yes, smart. Okay. But I was looking for the escape hatch. Right? Your dad…That's why hicks like me were so attracted to…He was from a different planet. I was weak."

"Are you…Are you better now?" I asked.

"Oh, no," Jerri said, shaking her head. "I need serious help."

We both giggled, which was weird.

"I'm going to get serious help, Felton," Jerri said seriously when we got done giggling.

• • •

Jerri went to get some tweezers from the bathroom. While she was gone, the phone rang. Neither of us made a move to answer.

The machine beeped. Cody's voice carried through the house.

"Uh. Hey. This is a message for Felton. I think his phone's off. Felton, don't worry about…Don't worry about faker or whatever. Nobody cares. Only the seniors from last year. They're jerks, you know? They're making a big deal out of it, but nobody else gives a damn. Call me, okay? You still coming up to the baseball game? You should. Give me a call."

"Oh my God. Everything," I said.

"What was that about?" Jerri asked, holding up the tweezers as she re-entered the kitchen.

"Bullshit," I said. And I meant it. I had no interest. There were serious issues in the world. Faker? What a bunch of crap. Jocks are total idiots, I thought, and they're assholes. My dad. If I could punch him.

I had turned my phone off. I wouldn't turn it back on. And I wasn't going to any game.

You know, later that day, Cody left another message on our home phone:

"Felton. Didn't see you at the game and your phone's off, man. Do I need to come over there and shake you out of bed? Give me a call!"

"Is that Cody threatening you?" Jerri mumbled.

"Probably," I said. I wanted to rip the phone off the wall. I would have if Grandma Berba hadn't been there in the kitchen cooking spaghetti. Grandma looked at me and smiled.

"Make sure you call him tomorrow so he knows you're all right," she said.

Yeah, right. Honky's out to get me, is what I thought.

Crazy. Crazy.

CHAPTER 52:
I CAN JUGGLE CLEAN
SOCK BALLS

Hey, check this out! Imagine some circus music! I have three pairs of clean white socks in my hands, balled up tight by Grandma Berba! I'm juggling them, baby! Three balls! Wooo! 6:12 a.m., and I'm juggling three balls! I can't juggle four balls. I'm juggling three balls!

Whoops. Shit!

I'm juggling two balls!

Sock balls!

CHAPTER 53:
FIRST THREE DAYS

You know, if I think about it, I was really upset. Why is it so hard to know why you're behaving the way you are when it's all going down? I don't know.

The following three days were hazy. Grandma Berba washed my sheets for the first time all summer (every morning because I bled on them), and for like three days, almost all I did was sleep in my clean bed.

I got up to eat (huge doses—there was good food in the house). I got up to hang with Jerri. I did the paper route.

Andrew, Grandma, and I went together. Grandma Berba drove. Andrew and I dropped off papers. (I was slow because on top of a slightly achy back, I had a gravel burn the size of a small child on my leg and ass.) We'd go super early in the morning so nobody could see us. Andrew and Grandma delivered the nursing home so I wouldn't have to see Dad's old girlfriend, Kelly Mayer. Everything else was dark on the route. So early.

All the lights were out in every house, including Aleah's. She changed her practice schedule, not so she could hang out with me but so she could help Andrew with piano. I guess that was nice of her. She biked over to our place each day, and they played and played and played. I didn't even watch but listened from my clean sheets below. I couldn't go upstairs.

Because.

I was so embarrassed and mortified. Aleah couldn't possibly be interested in me. I'd freaked out. I'd told her about squirrel nut. She'd called me a simple boy and an innocent child, and that's not good. You want a boyfriend who's simple and innocent? Date a baby? No thanks. My chest hurt.

One time, while I was downstairs listening to them play, I did turn on my phone to see if she'd called or texted, but there was such a blizzard of texts from honkies (I'm sorry, but I have to call them honkies) and voicemails from Cody and Coach Johnson asking me to contact him that I shut the phone back off. I couldn't deal.

Anyway, she didn't need to call. I was downstairs. And Aleah knew I was there while she was with Andrew. How could she not? Where would I go? She didn't ever come down to see me. That's all the information I needed. Aleah didn't come see me. And it made my chest so heavy, extremely heavy, because I didn't mean to have childish thoughts that popped out of my mouth. I couldn't take them back.

At least I had clean sheets.

• • •

I also got up to use my computer. I didn't check email. Google searches. That's all I did.

I had Googled "Steven W. Reinstein" before. I remembered the results, which I thought weren't about my dad. I redid those searches and knew they were about my dad. I saw pictures I'd seen before and archived articles I'd glanced at before. Tennis pictures. Tennis articles.

STEVEN REINSTEIN LEADS NORTHWESTERN PAST PURDUE.

COURT COVERAGE KEY FOR REINSTEIN.

REINSTEIN IS FORCE OF NATURE.

REINSTEIN BRINGS NCAA SINGLES TITLE TO NORTHWESTERN.

All of it was on the Northwestern website (except one small picture and paragraph on the NCAA website). He wasn't all over the Web or anything. (I suppose he played tennis before there was an Internet.)

I had for several years seen, over and over, a particular picture on the Northwestern website of a big Jew-fro dude in a purple T-shirt explosively hitting a tennis ball, a grimace on his face, sweat shooting up in the air everywhere. A dude who happened to have my dad's name, who really happened to be my dad.

I stared at that picture. I downloaded it to my computer. I blew it way up. Dad. There. Probably rode to the courts on our dead Schwinn Varsity. Steven W. Reinstein, while he was in college, looked exactly like I would if I were four years older. He was enormous and obviously hugely powerful. He was a force of nature.

It made me miss him, and even though I'd decided not to be mad at poor Jerri, missing Dad made me so mad at her. I had nice feelings about Dad pent up in my muscles because of years of lies (he's sweet and kind—wrong). But I should never be mad at Jerri. She was his victim, and the notion of me being so low and terrible that I could even fathom being angry at Jerri made me hate *me* and then I thought I better get the hell out of bed and go eat a sandwich, which Grandma Berba would prepare and which would taste much better than Kwik Trip white bread with a hunk of cheese on it. She bought some ham, which was good. Wheat bread.

Even when I ate, I boiled in my guts about everything.

Grandma Berba bought lots of stuff. For example, she bought me new clothes that fit.

"You can't go back to school in high waters. Here, try these." She threw me jeans. (I could only hope they fit in a month—they do, by the way.)

She bought Andrew a whole wardrobe full of little polos and blue jeans and tossed out his pirate wear. ("Thanks, Grandma," he beamed.)

She did lots of other stuff too. She cleaned up and threw out the Schwinn Varsity. She weeded the jungle garden. She mowed the lawn. She washed every corner of the house for hours on end.

"Why is all this junk pulled out of boxes?" she asked.

Andrew shrugged.

On the third day, she drove Jerri to Dubuque, Iowa, to see doctors and therapists.

I didn't like Jerri going to Dubuque. I didn't like her not being close by. I had a job. When I wasn't sleeping those three days or on the computer or delivering papers or eating, I'd be next to Jerri watching TV in her room, laughing too hard, to make everything normal. That's what I had to do. My job was to make Jerri know I think she's great and know she can count on me because I'm not like my dead dad, who I missed more and more every hour, which really pissed me off.

Very upset.

Grandma Berba came down to my room before they left for Dubuque, after I asked to go with, then pleaded, but was turned down.

"Felton," she said. "You can't fix your mom."

"I can help."

"It isn't your job. You're the kid, okay?"

"I want to help."

"Be a kid, Felton."

"I want to…"

"No. I'm here to take care of you. Your job is to be a kid."

Oh, man.

It was decided in Dubuque that day that Jerri would leave. She was put on serious medication, which made her sort of dull and retarded but resistant. To get better, to make sure she wouldn't hurt herself, she'd go away. She'd be checked into some kind of mental health facility in Arizona that Grandma knew about (it looked like a freaking vacation ranch with doctors—I checked it on the Web). Jerri was leaving.

"She can't leave!" I shouted at Grandma Berba.

"She needs to get better," Grandma said back.

The voice in my head said: *She's leaving you.*

And so, three days passed. Three days closer to Aleah leaving, which didn't seem to matter anymore. Three days closer to Gus coming home, giving me an opportunity to officially lose my only friend. Three days closer to school starting, which I didn't want to think about at all. In four days, Jerri would go, which made me cry. And it was three days closer to my sixteenth birthday, which happened to be in three days.

Who cares about birthdays? I didn't want to. I probably did care though. I know I did.

CHAPTER 54:
HONKIES DUMP TRASH

Do farmers sometimes dump on your property?" Grandma Berba asked.

I was sitting at the kitchen table with Jerri on Wednesday, two days before my birthday, eating lunch, a ham sandwich and some cold tomato soup and another sandwich and some broccoli with ranch sauce and another sandwich.

"Dump what?" I asked.

"Trash."

"Farmers? No."

"Somebody just dumped some trash." Grandma Berba stood at the picture window and pointed.

I wiped my mouth on my sleeve and pushed back from the table. I joined Grandma Berba at the window. There were a bunch of black trash bags down at the end of our drive and hundreds of loose pieces of white paper blowing around in the breeze.

"Farmers never dumped before. Jerri?"

Jerri was stirring her cold soup around, staring at it. As usual, she was about ten feet deep in the haze.

"What?" she asked.

"Farmers ever dump trash on our property?"

"Umm, no," Jerri said quietly, looking up from her soup. "I suppose I used to find beer bottles every now and then, just kids partying probably. Not farm waste."

"I saw a pickup truck out there. I didn't see anyone throw trash. It was just leaving when I looked. I assumed farmers."

"Pickup?" I asked.

Just then Aleah rolled down the hill on the main road up to the foot of our drive. She stopped and looked at the trash. She got off her bike and bent over, staring at something on the ground. She stood up and surveyed the trash. Then she bent down and picked up one of the pieces of paper. She got on her Walmart mountain bike and rode up the hill, carrying the paper.

"Andrew," Grandma called. "Your friend is here."

"I'll be right out," Andrew called. He was in the bathroom after showering, which was never his strong point, even before he became a pirate.

Aleah walked up the front sidewalk and entered directly into the living room without knocking. She looked at me for a moment, sort of stunned. We hadn't seen each other since the morning Grandma Berba showed up. She smiled big, but I didn't smile back.

"What's in your hand?" I asked.

"There's a whole bunch of beer bottles and papers on your driveway," she said.

"Yeah? So? Why did you pick that up?" I asked, pointing.

"Oh." She stared at me, squinting.

"Yeah?"

"All the paper down there has FAKER written on it. See?" She handed me the paper. "I thought you'd want a look."

"Faker?" Grandma asked.

"The trash is for me," I said, looking at FAKER scrawled big in black marker. "I'll go take care of it."

"What do you mean for you?" Grandma asked.

"Honkies," I said, staring at Aleah. She grimaced.

"Honkies?" Grandma said. "I'm beginning to miss Arizona."

• • •

I rolled Andrew's old plastic wagon down the drive. The wagon was Jerri's utility vehicle in the yard. The sun was really hot, and the beer bottles, even though they were mostly in bags, were incredibly stinky. They reminded me of how much I hated the smell at weights that first day. Pee and poison.

How could the honkies turn on me so fast? I couldn't return their stupid texts because my father was a giant, dead, sex maniac tennis player, and Jerri was crazy. I had a life outside their piddly assfaced circles. How could they turn on me like that? Didn't they know I was a kind guy who wanted to take care of his mother but wasn't allowed?

I'd be of no use to them without football. And, no, I wasn't going to play football. There was too much going on. Cody probably figured out I wasn't going to play since I hadn't gone to his game—hadn't been at weights or pass routes the last couple of days—so he must've joined Ken Johnson and the senior honkies in their total contempt for me. It was probably his pickup that Grandma Berba saw. He, Karpinski, and Reese probably emptied dumpsters behind bars and hauled the crap out here to throw on my yard. Abby Sauter and Jess Withrow probably spent hours writing FAKER on a thousand sheets of paper. Those assholes. *This how you're going to shake me out of bed, Cody?* I'd learned a lesson: never trust a honky. My stomach hurt at first. But then it didn't. It began to boil. *You're assholes.*

I had to make five trips to get the garbage up to our bins. There were no other messages other than FAKER. That was message enough. I was hot and stinky like a honky lifting weights. Disgusting, I thought.

I couldn't go back inside, not to Aleah and Jerri and Grandma Berba. I didn't want to explain myself. My family didn't need to take more hits. My family didn't need to know the gory details. *This is bullshit.*

I had too much energy. Probably from being mad.

I hopped up and down in place. While I did it, I wished my dad were alive and loved me enough to take these jerks down. I wished we were driving in his car, him with a baseball bat across his lap, looking for honkies. Looking so we could show these idiots they shouldn't mess with Reinsteins.

But my dad is dead. Even though I finally had a real picture of him in my head. Even though I could see his long arms in my arms and sense his wicked court speed in my legs.

I wanted to go to the big M. I wanted to run. I'd killed my dad's bike. *Oh, shit.* I took off running and ran up and down the hill on the main road for as long as I could. A couple of cars went by, kicking up dust that choked me. *Doesn't matter.* It wasn't the same as the Mound, but it felt good. The scab on my side cracked and bled. Sweat poured into my eyes.

Those honky bastards were very lucky they didn't happen upon my hill while I was out there. It would not have been pretty.

That's what I thought.

CHAPTER 55:
FAKER!

On Thursday morning, the day before my birthday, there was more trash piled at the end of the drive. I had to move it to the side so Grandma Berba could get her giant SUV past so we could do the paper route. I swore and kicked those stupid bags, which was dumb because there was old milk in one that sprayed all over me and made me nearly throw up. Sour milk smells like Andrew's baby poop.

When I got back in, Andrew plugged his nose and complained. Grandma didn't complain. She said, "Are you going to tell me what's going on here?"

"What?" I asked, even though I knew what she was talking about.

"Somebody has it in for you. Does this have something to do with you being in sports? Are your rivals coming after you?"

"I'm not in sports."

"Yes, you are," Andrew said.

"I'm just a guy."

"No," Grandma said. "I've heard you've become quite an athlete. In part, that is why your mother had troubles."

"Great. Exactly. I'm just a guy, okay?"

"No," Andrew said. "I know for a fact you've been running up the big M all summer. Aleah said. No regular guy would do that. I can't even make it up walking."

"That's because you're a turd," I hissed.

Andrew gasped. He looked like I slapped him.

"Sorry. I'm just mad."

"Because your rivals are dumping garbage on your lawn?" Grandma asked.

"Sure. Let's leave it at that."

"We should notify the police," Grandma said.

"That won't help. They are the police."

"What do you mean?"

"The police's kid," I said.

"I hate this town," Grandma said.

"Maybe we should contact Homeland Security," Andrew said. "They have jurisdiction over terrorism."

Grandma Berba giggled.

"What?" Andrew asked.

"I'll clean it up," I told them.

After the route, I did clean it up. It took me over an hour, and it was totally gross and smelly. Then I ran up and down the hill on the main road. It didn't help my urge to destroy. *You all better watch out.*

• • •

That afternoon, while I was lying downstairs and considering all kinds of ways that I'd have my revenge, the phone rang. Grandma Berba answered it. She shouted down the stairs, "Felton, your football coach is on the line."

"Tell him to stuff it in his ass!" I shouted.

"Felton can't come to the phone right now. Yes, he's all right. Really? I'll have him check his phone. Oh, no, he seems fine to me. Oh, well, that's nice. I'll let him know. Good-bye."

Grandma Berba came downstairs and found me in my room.

"First things first," she said. "Don't you ever tell me to have a caller stuff something in his"—she swallowed and pursed her lips—"ass. That's disrespectful to me and completely inappropriate."

I breathed. I swallowed. Looked down. *Such a jerk, Felton.*

"Second, your football coach informs me that someone from the school will be videotaping you doing drills next Wednesday because of a recruiting website? Is that what he said?"

"Maybe."

"He'd like to put your profile on a recruiting website."

"Recruiting for what? I'm not playing football. I don't know how to play football."

"Third, during practice on Thursday, he's invited a couple of gentlemen from the university in Madison to meet you."

"Wisconsin?" I sat up. "For football? Oh God, no! I want out of this!"

"Felton," Grandma glared at me. "Why aren't you returning messages from your cell phone? What are you doing?"

"How do you know?"

"Your football coach told me."

"I don't want to speak to him."

"Andrew's little friend said the same thing yesterday. You're not returning her calls, either."

"Aleah?"

"What are you doing? What's wrong with you?" Grandma Berba was pressuring me, and that made me hot.

"Is Jerri staring at the wall upstairs?" I asked.

"She isn't going to recover overnight, Felton."

"Did my dad have girlfriends all over town and then kill himself in my garage?"

"Yes," Grandma whispered.

"That's a lot to absorb, Grandma Berba! That's pretty big, don't you think?"

"I don't appreciate your tone," she said.

"Well, maybe I don't appreciate being responsible for Jerri cracking up. Maybe I don't appreciate that I look just like my asshole dad. Maybe, huh?"

"I'm sorry, Felton. I understand how upset you are, but you can't speak to your grandmother that way." Grandma Berba turned and left my room.

I was such a jerk.

When I found my phone after digging around for it, I saw that others shared that opinion: Felton Reinstein, Jerk. There were a dozen FAKER texts from numbers I didn't recognize.

The last text before my inbox got full three days earlier was from Cody Frederick. It said:

cant believe i plan a party for six weeks and you wont call me back!

Yeah, I can't believe you trash my house because I won't go to a stupid party.

I erased the entire inbox and then erased my voicemail, which was also full. If Aleah wanted to get hold of me, all she had to do was come downstairs.

It did occur to me that neither she nor Andrew were at the house at that point. They weren't playing piano anyway.

I looked at my phone. It was still on. Then I did it. I called her cell, breathing really shallow, but she didn't pick up. I left a message and then left the phone on, waiting for her to call back.

CHAPTER 56:
CELL PHONE

My phone was like a ticking bomb that could go off at any minute. Maybe I wanted it to ring? Maybe. Maybe it would be Aleah, and she'd call me *hers*, and she'd bike over, and we could hold hands on the couch.

It didn't ring. I looked at it.

But what if it did ring and it was Cody Frederick telling me how they were all coming after me because I was a jerk, because I wasn't a jock and I ruined his party? I looked at the phone.

Did it light up?

No, that was a reflection from the overhead light. I hoped it would ring. I was terrified it would ring. I paced back and forth. I growled and jumped in place. It didn't ring.

Andrew wasn't at home for dinner. Grandma Berba made lasagna, which I hate, except this was delicious because it contained no turnips or radishes or zucchini or spinach or whatever else Jerri always used to throw in there. It was made with meat and cheese, and my leg bounced up and down. My phone was in my pocket. I ate and ate and ate. Grandma Berba told me to slow down. Jerri stared at me, watery-eyed from her medication. My leg bounced. My phone didn't ring.

"Where the hell's Andrew?" I asked.

"He stayed at his friend's for dinner," said Grandma Berba. "They weren't done practicing."

"Great!" I stuffed a whole piece in my mouth.

"Slow down, Felton," Grandma Berba said.

• • •

And my phone didn't ring.

After dinner, I tried sitting on Jerri's bed, tried watching TV, but I couldn't sit still.

"You're bouncing the bed," Jerri said.

"I'm going to run." I got up.

"Run?" Jerri asked. "Like go running?"

"Yes."

I left the room carrying my stupid phone. *Asshole phone.* In the garage, I grabbed a hammer and smashed the stupid thing to pieces. Then I took off.

It was getting dark, and it was hard to see. Down on the main road, because we're just outside of town, there are no lights, and the footing got terrible. I couldn't really run.

I needed to find a lighted place, like the track by the college. How the hell would I get there? *My bike. Oh, no.*

Oh, no. Oh, no. Oh, no.

The Bluffton air smelled like poop-stinker. It closed in on me. I just wanted to bolt on my bike and break it all up. I couldn't.

Out on the road in the dark, I stepped in a hole and then stopped because I'd break my ankle if I tried to run there, so I turned around and jogged back toward the house.

Would Grandma Berba drive me to a track?

I had to run.

By the house, I turned right and began to circle. The house was all lit up, light in every window, so much cheerier than before Grandma arrived. Because of all that light, I could see where I was going, and I gunned it. One lap around the house at top speed. One lap around the house slow to catch my breath. Then again and again and again. I spent easily the next hour doing that until I could run no more. My body stopped its twitching.

I showered to rinse blood off my leg and the pee smell off my body. Then I went to bed. Andrew still wasn't home. My phone couldn't ring because it was smashed in the garbage.

That's fine, I thought. *Really. Fine.*

Oh, no.

CHAPTER 57:
SWEET SIXTEEN

My alarm didn't wake me. There was much stirring around the house. Hammering. Music playing. I looked over at my clock. It was only 4:15. *What?* I climbed out of bed and sleepily made my way upstairs to where the noise was. Jerri and Grandma Berba were hanging a big banner above the fireplace. I rubbed my eyes. It said "Sweet Sixteen."

"Oh, yeah. It's my birthday," I said.

Jerri and Grandma, who was asking Jerri to lift up her side so the banner would be level, swiveled and looked at me.

"There he is!" Grandma Berba shouted.

"Happy birthday, Felton," Jerri said. She looked tired.

"Sweet sixteen and never been kissed!" Grandma cried out.

"I've been kissed," I said.

"Oh?" Grandma said. She scrunched her eyes at me. Then smiled. "Well, happy birthday anyway!"

"Okay. Thanks. Should we do the route now? Is Andrew sleeping?"

"He didn't come home!" Grandma Berba said. "He called and asked to stay at his friend's house because they were working on a four-hand piece!"

I was getting a little sick of the false cheeriness.

"Aleah?"

"Yes!"

"Let's go," I said.

"Umm, I'm coming too, Felton!" Jerri said with a terrible false cheeriness.

The three of us loaded into Grandma Berba's giant rental SUV, me in the passenger seat and Jerri in back, and rolled down the drive. At the bottom, our way was blocked by trash. Grandma Berba put on the brakes.

"Not more of this mumbo jumbo." She put on the high beams because it was still dark. Somebody had gone to the trouble of writing out HAPPY BDAY FAKER!!! in trash down about fifty feet of the drive. The H was closest to us; the exclamation points went out to the road. "Enough of this crap," Grandma said. She gunned the engine, and we flew right over the top of the trash, scattering it behind us.

"Whoa!" I shouted.

"Terrible people," Grandma said.

"That probably took them a long time to make," I chuckled.

"Idiot kids can't spell," Grandma said.

Grandma Berba was funny, but the trash still hurt my feelings, which immediately turned to boiling in my gut. Did Cody decide to put all his organizing skills into vandalism? Cody is the one who'd remember my birthday. It had to be him. *Asshole.*

We rode through the route really slow. Jerri sort of meandered around. She'd get out of the SUV and walk a few steps and then stand and look at the sky.

"Get a move on, sweetie," Grandma would call to her. "We've got places to be."

"What places?" I asked.

"Oh, you know. Home," Grandma said.

But she was lying. I knew that for a fact when we arrived at Gus/Aleah's. For the first time in a week, the house was all lit up. Andrew and Aleah were staring out the window. When the three of us got out of the car, they ran away.

"Just two peas in a pod!" I said with false cheeriness.

"Let's stop at this lovely house for a moment," Grandma smiled.

"Oh, God," I said, but I followed her up the stoop and in, staring at my feet the whole way.

Immediately upon entering, Aleah and Andrew began to play happy birthday on the piano. Just the standard happy birthday. Aleah went first. Then Andrew followed. Then Aleah made up stuff that sort of sounded like happy birthday. Then Andrew did the same. Then Aleah went completely out of this planet, playing something that sounded like happy birthday a little but had so many notes. Her hands went up and down the keyboard, striking keys, pounding for emphasis, nearly knocking Andrew off the bench. I remembered the first time I saw her in her white nightie pounding the keys like that, how I was mesmerized and couldn't not watch, even though I hadn't learned to talk yet, and how that wave just built and crashed over me. I remembered her spinning around on the bench and staring at me. I remembered talking and walking through the night holding hands and biking double on the Schwinn and kissing in the garage and snuggling in the basement while watching dumb movies. Aleah stopped, turned, and smiled. Jerri and Grandma clapped and shouted bravo. Ronald leaned in from the kitchen, whooping. I swallowed hard. My nose was sort of running.

"Oh, man," I said. "That was so good. You're so good."

Andrew jumped off the bench and ran up and hugged me around the stomach. I was like a foot and a half taller than him.

"We worked on it all night!" he shouted.

"Happy birthday, Felton," Aleah said.

"Thank you," I nodded. "Thanks."

"Now get going, little girl," Ronald called from the kitchen. "Chocolate chip pancakes coming up."

Aleah jumped up and headed for the door.

"You ready, Mrs. Berba?" she asked.

"Aleah and I are going to finish your paper route, young man!" Grandma shouted.

"I'm going too!" Andrew followed.

"And it won't take long because I'm going to run as fast as Felton Reinstein," Aleah said, running out the door.

"You two make yourselves comfortable," Ronald called to Jerri and me from the kitchen. "I've got some cooking to do."

I stood there with my mouth hanging open.

"Ah. Cat got your tongue, Felton?" Jerri smiled. She was sort of teary.

"I think I'm experiencing happy?" I said.

"That girl. She can really play piano." Jerri sat down on the couch in the sort of awkward, slow way she did everything. "Just amazing."

"Oh, man," I said.

"Hey, Felton?" Jerri said.

"Yeah?"

"Sit by me?"

I moved and sat down on the couch next to her.

"You know what?" Jerri said. "I watched you running around the house last night."

"You did?"

"Umm." Jerri nodded slow. She looked like a little girl. "I watched the whole time. I couldn't take my eyes off you, Felton."

"Oh."

"You run like Aleah plays piano. It's beautiful."

"Really?" I never thought about how I looked.

"No offense to Andrew," Jerri said, "but you run like Aleah plays piano. Not like Andrew. Do you know what I mean?"

"I think so."

"I hope this thing, this trouble I'm having, won't stop you from running."

"No. Your trouble isn't it why I don't want to. I just don't see the value in…"

"You're not going to play sports?" Jerri blinked.

"No. I can't. Look what those asshole jocks did to me with the trash last night, Jerri. I don't want to be like them—like Dad."

Jerri's eyes focused. She squinted and looked really serious. Then for the first time in months, an "old Jerri" thing came out of her mouth. She spoke really quiet.

"Listen, Felton, your father was compelled to make different choices. Lots of them were bad. But this is the truth: playing sports was one of the good ones. He was at peace. He was sincerely happy when he was on a tennis court. Nowhere else maybe. But playing? Movement made him happy."

"Moving?"

"He was beautiful when he ran."

"But look what those jocks did to our yard," I said.

"Those people—those jocks—they really don't matter."

"I don't know."

"Of course, I'm crazy," Jerri said, staring out the window, the sun beginning to light the trees around the house. "I don't even know if I make sense."

"Yeah," I laughed.

Jerri didn't laugh.

"Thanks, Jerri," I said.

"I love you," she said.

. . .

Bacon sizzled in the kitchen. Ronald hummed along to classical music. Jerri stared out the picture window. And I got up to use the bathroom and noticed the masks had been removed from the living room and replaced by Gus's parents' mountain photos. There were boxes in the hall—and half-packed suitcases too.

. . .

After Grandma, Aleah, and Andrew got back, we ate. I stared at Aleah the whole time. She looked at me and nodded like Jerri, like a little girl. Breakfast was delicious and—I'm not kidding—cheery. Then we all moved to the living room and talked like nothing at all was wrong in the world. But I couldn't get the idea out of my brain that I might never see Aleah again.

Before we left, Aleah grabbed my arm and pulled me down the hall. She put her hands on my shoulders and stared at me. Then she said, "I didn't know what to do, Felton. You know, when you didn't return my calls? I didn't know what to do. Daddy told me to give you space."

"I thought…"

"Andrew said you were acting all weird, so I decided to give you space."

"You didn't want to…I was acting weird?" Duh.

"I had the greatest summer," Aleah said. "I…I loved every second."

"But I thought…"

"Last spring, I wrote out a list about the only kind of person I'd want for a boyfriend. I met him, exactly."

"Me?"

"Yeah, Felton. Duh."

"Exactly?"

"Funny, gentle, passionate."

"Passionate?"

"About football."

"Oh."

"You ask me questions and tell me stories and…"

"But I don't understand opera. And I'm sort of a chucklehead. And my family is a disaster. And I say honky because I don't know what it means. And I freak out like a little kid."

"You think I want to date an old man? I want to be with another kid."

"Oh."

"I'd like you to listen to opera though."

"I'll try, Aleah. I'm not sure if Andrew has any CDs."

"Please, Felton. We're leaving as soon as Daddy's grades are in. Please."

"When?"

"This afternoon, late morning if Daddy can get done."

"Oh, crap."

She spoke quickly.

"Please. Please. Can we stay together? I feel like I'm going to die without you," she said. "Please?"

"Oh." I paused and thought. "I'm so sorry," I said.

Aleah stared at me. She swallowed hard.

"It's okay. I know you're having a hard time right now. I know. I know."

"What? No. That's not what I'm saying."

"It isn't?"

"No, no, no. I want to be together."

"Oh!"

"I'm just sorry I'm so weird."

"Shut up, Felton. You know I like that," Aleah said.

Then we hugged for approximately six years. Then we kissed.

Then we said good-bye and kissed some more.

Then we went into the living room, and I said good-bye to Mr. Jennings. Jerri, Grandma, Andrew, and me all shook hands with him, etc. Then my family left for home, with Andrew's bike jammed in the back of the SUV. I turned and watched Aleah's house disappear. How would it ever be Gus's again?

"Wow, Aleah is the greatest," Andrew said, smiling at me.

CHAPTER 58: BIRTHDAY

We spent the afternoon of my birthday in the big city! Dubuque, Iowa. We went out for lunch at a brew pub (I ate a Reuben) and then went bicycle shopping for me. That was Grandma Berba's present.

"Since I'm not getting you a car, we can spend a lot of money," she said.

"I'm so sorry I was a jerk about your permit," Jerri said.

"I don't want a car," I told her. And I didn't.

In the end, we did spend a lot of money. Well, $800 anyway, a lot more than the old $10 limit, on a road bike. I took it for a test spin and raced cars up Dubuque's big hill. It rides much easier than the Varsity, which I'll always love but am glad is gone. This bike is super fast and thus matches me. Then Jerri bought me a new cell phone, which I appreciated, as I had just bashed mine to bits, much like I bashed my poor Schwinn to bits. Then we went to a movie. I sort of wanted to see a teen flick but didn't want to bawl about Aleah, so we ended up going to a serious Meryl Streep movie that was just depressing.

Andrew loved it: "Ooooh. Ohhhhh."

Grandma and I didn't: "Blah blah blah."

Jerri stared at her shoes through it. What else would she have done? She was leaving for Arizona the next morning.

On the way home from Dubuque, I got that weird feeling again, sort of a light feeling. I believe I was feeling happy. I looked over at Andrew, who was sleeping because he'd been up all night practicing piano with Aleah, and smiled. Good kid.

Back home, I charged my phone and watched TV with Jerri in Jerri's room while Grandma Berba cleaned the trash from the drive (she insisted she do it, and I was grateful for that).

Around 8 p.m., my phone connected to the network. Within minutes, I received my first text. It was from Aleah. It said:

> See Chicago skyline. Very sad. I'm serious about you.
> me too, I replied.
> You replied! YAY! :)
> new phone!!!

We continued to text until Aleah arrived at her Chicago apartment. She called.

"I'm here. I miss you."

"I miss you."

"Talk tomorrow, Felton. Okay?"

I didn't have a chance to say okay back. I could hear Ronald telling her to get moving in the background. She hung up.

Then I knew it was time to run because I had ten thousand square inches of adrenaline jangling in my legs. It was nearly 9:30, but I knew I wouldn't sleep unless I ran some of this energy off.

CHAPTER 59: GRAVEL ASSAULT

was outside running my laps around the house for maybe a half hour when a car peaked the hill on the main road and began to roll down toward our drive. It was pretty rare for cars to drive out this way, especially after dark. I had a feeling I knew who it was.

I stopped in my tracks, hands on my hips. I was breathing hard, loose-muscled, really pumped. Oh, yeah, I thought. *Just do it, jerks. Just trash me.*

I slid through the dark, down the side of the drive as fast and smooth as I could. It was a minivan. Come to Papa, I thought. *It's go time.* I reached down and grabbed two handfuls of gravel from the driveway and bent into a crouch in the shadows of the ditch. They would pay, these honky trashers of my yard. *That's right.* The van slowed to a crawl. I could see the windows were open in front. An easy target.

The van made a turn into our drive. *It's them!* I leaped out of the ditch and blackness, screaming like hell. I threw both handfuls of gravel at the passenger window as hard as I could, shouting yahhhh! Because I don't throw that well, most of the gravel hit the side of the van, but some went in because there was an immediate scream. The van skidded to a halt. Someone cried "I have dirt my eye!" I recognized the voice. Karpinski. *That jerk! Gonna shake me out of bed?* Girls screamed. I bent and picked up another handful of gravel and reared back ready to let them have it point blank and then I heard Cody's voice shout "Reinstein, stop! What are you doing?"

I paused.

A girl voice said, "Is Reinstein attacking us?"

"Yeah, he is! I've got a piece of gravel in my damn eyeball," I heard Karpinski say.

I walked up closer and looked in the window. Karpinski sat there barely lit by my house. I could see there was a bunch of dirt on his face (my dirt). He was rubbing his right eye. Cody drove the van across from Karpinski.

"What are you guys doing here?" I asked still mad, but less sure.

"Why are you throwing rocks at my dad's van, man?" Cody shouted.

"I…I thought you were someone else," I said.

"Oh, John Spencer and those guys, huh?" Karpinski said, still rubbing his eye.

"Yeah," I nodded, although I didn't exactly know what I was nodding about.

"What a bunch of assholes. They even came to your party. Cody had to tell them to get the hell out. Total assholes."

"Reinstein," Cody barked. "Get in the damn van."

"Um, okay," I said. *Am I the jerk?*

The side door slid open, and I stepped in. In the back sat chuckleheaded Jason Reese ("Hey, Rein Stone. How's it going, man?") and Abby Sauter and Jess Withrow ("Reinsteeeeeeiiinnnn!"). It was the whole honky all-star crew from my grade.

I sat down on a bench next to Reese.

"Oh, yeah," he said. "We heard about what Spencer was doing. You should totally kick his ass."

"Were you going to kill him with your gravel, Reinstein?" Abby asked.

"Yes, I was," I said very soberly. *Oh, no. I'm the jerk.*

Cody backed up and began to drive up the main road.

"Why didn't you come to your party, Rein Stone?" Karpinski turned and said.

"Um." I thought fast, embarrassed. "I had to protect my property from Spencer. Plus, my phone broke or I would've called. My mom has been really sick."

"Oh, we were wondering why you weren't getting your messages. Sucks," Jess said. "Is she okay?"

"Better," I nodded. "A little."

"Well, you don't have to protect your property anymore," Reese said. "When Cody was kicking Spencer out, Ken Johnson found out what he was doing to you and totally went off. He said he'd beat all those guys stupid if they ever dropped trash even near your place again."

"Ken Johnson?" I asked. The surprise in my voice wasn't hidden.

"He feels terrible, man," Karpinski said. "He came to your party to apologize."

"Yeah, man," Cody said, "He told me to say he's sorry about what he did in the weight room. He freaked himself out, I think. He leaves for Iowa City in the morning or he'd have come with us."

"Ken Johnson?" I said again.

"Are you deaf?" Karpinski said. "Ken Johnson!"

"And now we bring your party to you!" Abby said.

"Rocky Crotch," Cody nodded. "I mean…Can you leave your mom?"

"Yeah, yeah. My grandma's here."

We rolled past the baseball fields and then the schools and the practice fields and then further east, toward the Mound. Abby and Jess and Reese all laughed. Karpinski and Cody were quiet. I sat there with that feeling I'd had a couple times before during the day. I was also thinking this: Felton Reinstein is seriously paranoid. He jumps to conclusions and is quick to turn on people close to him (such as Peter Yang, Gus, Cody, even Aleah). And also this: Felton Reinstein can't listen to the voice in his head anymore because it's most often dead wrong. Talk all you want, voice. I'm not listening.

We pulled up in front of the Mound and parked. Karpinski jumped out of the van and shouted "Rocky Crotch!" Then he slid open the sliding door, letting the four of us out of the back. Cody opened the hatch and pulled out a box. He showed it to me under the light. It was a cake in the shape of a football.

"Kind of looks like a turd," he said. The message on it was HAPPY 16 REIN STONE.

We climbed halfway up the big M and then crossed over to the middle where the M comes together in a point. The honky all-stars called this the Rocky Crotch because there are big rocks right at the M's crotch. We sat on those rocks, ate cake, made jokes, talked about nothing, and looked out over the twinkling nighttime lights of Bluffton and the farms around it. Elf land.

It was perfect and great to be with these honkies. It occurred to me that my older self might have been remembering this night the last time I was on the mound. I didn't say anything about that, of course.

As we were finishing up, Cody said, "Hey, Reinstein, listen." He paused. He was sort of shaky.

"Okay."

"You know, we all know about your dad. I guess we've always known, you know?"

"Yeah?" I said really quiet.

"I can't believe I was so mean to you," Abby said.

"We've been talking about it all summer," Cody said. "We're so sorry."

"Yeah, yeah," Karpinski nodded. Reese nodded too. Jess stared down at her hands.

"We suck, Rein Stone," Karpinski said.

And then I almost cried like a baby. Almost went donkey. I held it together, but my eyes were really wet. I said, "Thanks. It's been kind of bad. Not because of you guys. I had a tough childhood."

"Yeah," Cody said, quietly.

"And I'm really weird. Seriously," I said.

"Yeah, you are," Jess said. She was smiling. "Remember your shiny jewel pouch?"

"Your brother is really, really weird," Karpinski said.

"He's a good kid," I laughed.

"Remember when he was sitting upside down in your driveway?" Karpinski asked, like I wouldn't remember.

"Yeah," I laughed. "But you'd like him if you knew him. He's a good kid!"

"I already like him," Karpinski said. "He's your brother."

"I'm not going to be mean to anybody ever again," Reese nodded.

"My dad said because he's a cop and he sees weird stuff all the time that everybody's weird," Cody said.

"I'm not," Abby said.

"What are you talking about, Sauter? Everything that comes out of your mouth is weird," Cody said.

"You mean psycho," said Karpinski.

"Shut up!" Abby said.

"No, really. You're psycho," Cody laughed.

"I have to go home," Reese said. "Dad is waiting up for me so he can smell my breath."

"That's disgusting," Jess said.

"See, he's weird too," Abby said.

We walked down from Rocky Crotch, laughing and pushing, and then drove back to town.

When Cody dropped me off, he made me take the rest of the cake. All the lights were on in the house. Instead of going in through the garage, I climbed up the steps and went in the front door into the living room. Grandma Berba and Jerri were up and waiting for me. Grandma stood as I entered.

"Where have you been, Felton Reinstein?" she shouted.

"We almost called the police, Felton" Jerri said. She looked shaky.

I tilted the box so they could see the half-eaten cake.

"Um, my friends threw me a surprise party," I said.

"Oh," Grandma tilted her head. "That's sweet."

"Is Gus back?" Jerri asked. "Did Peter pick you up?"

"Cody Frederick, Karpinski, Reese, Jess Withrow, and Abby Sauter," I said.

"Abby Sauter?" Jerri's mouth hung open.

"Stop, Jerri. I liked her in middle school. We're just friends."

"Middle school was only two years ago. How am I supposed to keep track?" Jerri said.

I went downstairs and washed my face. Then before I went to bed, I climbed back upstairs. Grandma was brushing her teeth and standing in front of Jerri. Jerri was talking, and Grandma was nodding. I interrupted, and they both looked at me.

"Couple things. One, there won't be any more trash. Ken Johnson told the guys who were doing it he'd kill them if they didn't stop."

"You don't like Ken Johnson," Jerri said.

"He's all right."

"Well, that's a blessing," Grandma said.

"Second, I'll go on the route on my bike tomorrow morning. I have to exercise because football starts next week. So sleep in, Grandma."

"Another blessing!" Grandma said. "We'll go to the airport to drop off your mother after you get back."

Jerri looked down at the floor. It was so strange to think she was going away.

"Okay. " I nodded. "Just one other thing. I just want to say it's been a bad week and everything, but that was the best birthday I've ever had. Thank you."

Grandma nodded at me. Jerri looked up, smiling across her whole face like she was at the Strawberry Festival.

When I think of her now, that's the picture I have in my head.

CHAPTER 60:
GOOD-BYE, JERRI

After my route the next morning, which I biked so fast and amazing on my new bike (especially fast past Aleah's), Grandma, me, Andrew, and Jerri drove to Madison to drop Jerri off at the airport. On the way, Jerri didn't say much. Grandma did.

"Your mother just needs time to get her thoughts together. She's not going to a hospital, you understand. It's much more of a resort."

"Mom, come on," Jerri mumbled.

"It's a beautiful place. She'll get a lot of help from psychologists, but it isn't really a hospital."

"Mom," Jerri said.

"It isn't! She's going because she wants to get better. She's free to leave whenever she feels ready. There are no locks on the doors, except at night, and there are hiking trails, and she can call home whenever, and she'll have Internet. She's going to have a wonderful time."

"It's a mental healthcare center," Jerri said.

"Yes," said Grandma. "It has a swimming pool."

"Can I go?" Andrew asked.

"Do you need mental healthcare?" Jerri asked.

"I'm pretty sure," Andrew replied.

"No, Andrew, you can't," Grandma said.

I was sitting in the front seat because I'm so tall. I turned to look at Jerri and Andrew. They were smiling at each other, holding hands.

We dropped Jerri off in front of the airport. I pulled her suitcase out of the back of the SUV and put it on the sidewalk. Then we hugged. Then she hugged Andrew and Grandma. She turned, walked five steps away, then turned back.

"Make sure you look on my bed, okay? Sorry I kept it hidden."

"What?" I asked.

"Andrew knows," Jerri smiled.

And then she was gone through the doors.

When we got back in the SUV, I turned around, looked at Andrew, and asked, "What did she keep hidden?"

Andrew was staring out the window.

"I bet it's her goddamn diary."

"Oh. You boys should have your mouths washed out with soap," Grandma Berba said.

We drove the hour or so home in total silence. I missed the new Jerri, not just the old.

• • •

Of course, we both beelined for Jerri's bedroom after getting home.

And Andrew was right. Sitting in the middle of Jerri's made bed was the diary. Andrew and I stared at it.

"Jesus," I said. "You think that tells her whole story?"

"She used to carry it around with her all the time, remember? She was always scribbling in it, and she wouldn't let me touch it."

"Me either."

We walked over. Andrew picked up the diary. He opened it.

There wasn't a single word on any page, just a bunch of really bad sketches, most of which were cats.

"What in the crap?" Andrew said.

And then we started giggling and then laughing and then totally howling. We laughed so hard that we almost missed the picture stuffed in the back cover. It dropped out while we were laughing. I bent down and picked it up.

In the picture, my towering Jew-fro dad smiled huge, his arm around a really young and pretty Jerri. In the corner, overexposed because I was much closer to the camera, my Jew-fro toddler head smiled like the moon.

"He's smiling," Andrew said.

"Yeah" was all I could get out.

On the back of the picture, Jerri had written: *Your father wasn't as terrible as Grandma says.*

CHAPTER 61:
GRANDMA'S AWAKE!

Shhh. 6:47 a.m. She's sneezing upstairs. Shhh.
Must end this dark, dark tale!

You like breakfast?

CHAPTER 62:
SWEETNESS

You know what? Football is a very tough game. You use every muscle in your whole body. Of course, that's good stuff for a squirrel nut who is twitchy in every muscle of his whole body.

You also get beat to hell, which is why I'm so sore now.

We started practice doing two-a-days. That means we'd practice for a couple of hours in the morning, break for lunch (and to sleep), and then practice again in the afternoon. The first week was without pads, only our helmets. We did tons of conditioning work. Everybody sucked air except for me. I could go and go and go. Run and run. I could hit the blocking dummies and the sleds with the same squirrel nut power every time. I heard Coach Johnson say to another coach, "He's as advertised. Motor doesn't quit." But biking back and forth from practice, even on my new, fast bike, almost killed me. I was exhausted. By the end of the week, Cody was driving me.

I loved practice at first. It was almost as good as running up the big M. But I wanted be sort of straight with myself about it. It wasn't clear at all that I could play football, even though my motor wouldn't quit. I met with Coach early in the week after afternoon practice and asked him to cancel videotaping for

Rivals.com and asked him to cancel the meeting with the University of Wisconsin people.

"I don't really know how to play football, Coach," I said. "I'd like to make sure I'm good and I like it before anybody makes a big deal out of me."

"I can respect that," Coach said. "If this thing works out the way I expect it will, there will be plenty of time to talk recruiting later."

I asked him how Ken was doing at Iowa.

"Kid got his ass handed to him all day long yesterday," Coach said. "That's good. High school comes too easy for good athletes sometimes."

"Oh," I nodded.

"You know, he really appreciates that you didn't come after him after the stunt he pulled, Reinstein. I appreciate it too. You're a class act."

"Uh huh," I said.

• • •

Football is also confusing. That first week, even though I'd looked at the playbook a lot over the summer, most of the time I had no idea where to go. I sort of ran around.

"Study your plays, Reinstein. Got to get them down."

I was embarrassed, so I didn't tell Coach I'd already studied the plays.

The only time I knew where to go was when I got the ball, but that wasn't always good either. Cody would hand it to me or toss it to me, and within two steps, I was past the linemen, and they hadn't even started pretending to block yet (we didn't have pads on, so there was no real contact).

"Be patient, Reinstein. Run under control until you see your hole."

I wasn't exactly sure what my hole was.

In the second week, though, after I looked at the playbook every night for like three hours (Andrew couldn't believe I'd sit there staring at it so long), and after we got pads on, things began to make more sense. With a defense in the way, the linemen could plow guys to the side and make holes that I could run through. I could understand that. I found my hole! Sometimes! If I got lucky, there would be a hole, and I'd run through it very fast. But if I didn't get the ball, I still got lost, and I'd end up sort of wandering around. Sometimes, Coach Johnson would yell at me to get my head out of my butt. It didn't make me mad when he yelled that. I agreed. I didn't enjoy having my head in my butt.

Everything was so quiet at home during these weeks. It was sort of rhythmic and automatic. I'd get home from practice beat. Grandma Berba made big meals that I ate like I was starving. While Grandma cleaned up, Andrew played piano, and I looked at the playbook. Then, around 8:00, Jerri called and told us about horseback riding or the pool or walking in the mountains, whatever she did for fun that day (none of the other stuff). Then I called Aleah to talk to her before she started practicing. Then I'd go to bed. In a blink, it was time to get up for Gus's paper route. I was so exhausted, I barely noticed I was sleeping.

The only thing that changed was the amount of time I talked to Aleah. Every night, it seemed, the call got longer. Aleah was very sad to be back in Chicago. Everything there reminded her of her mom. Her apartment felt really empty, and she missed Bluffton's poop smell. She missed me, and she missed the paper route, and she missed riding her bike wherever she wanted. In the second week of football, though, she got sort of exciting news. The college really loved Ronald. They were going to try to bring him back. "Daddy says it's a good possibility!" Aleah shouted. The idea got me so excited I actually didn't sleep one night (almost all the rest, I slept like a rock).

The third week of practice, two-a-days were done, and we did less conditioning and more plays. Play after play after play. I got really confused. Seriously. I fumbled a bunch and went the wrong direction and ran into people and dropped passes and missed blocks. On Friday, Cody, Karpinski, Reese, and I went out for pizza.

"Don't worry about it. It will come, man. We've all been playing forever, so it all makes sense. You'll figure it out," they told me. But I could tell they weren't sure I'd figure it out.

I had a very nervous night after that because the next morning, just six days before we were to play our first game against that Jay Landry bone-breaker dude and St. Mary's Springs, which is a big school near Milwaukee that made the state semifinals the year before and had—I heard this again and again—most of their players back, we had our first full scrimmage.

Apparently, a scrimmage is like a game but doesn't count for anything. Our first team offense played against the second team and vice versa.

And I was totally lost. Things were really fast, and when I tried to go as fast, I'd get ahead of my line and get tackled without going anywhere. It wasn't easy to tackle me, I mean. It took the whole defense really. I wouldn't go down without fighting, but it just felt like I was running through mud all the time. There were always defensive players on top of me. "Slow down, Reinstein," Coach kept shouting. But I couldn't. Everything was too fast.

The starting offense couldn't do anything against the second team defense. Even Cody and Karpinski were misfiring. It was terrible. Everybody was demoralized. Coach Johnson's face was completely red.

I told Aleah on the phone that night that I just didn't get football.

"Maybe I should stick to track. You don't have to think in track. You just run. Football is too complicated."

"Keep practicing," she said. "I can't play hard pieces at first. My fingers feel dumb. But after I practice, I don't even know the music is hard anymore."

"Yeah," I said, but I wasn't sure. Practice had been fun, especially the conditioning. But actually playing didn't seem fun at all (unless you like running in mud until a whole bunch of pee-smelling guys knock you down and lie on top of you).

On Monday, before we hit the practice field, Coach told all the lineman that they had to move faster to keep up with me. They all looked at the ground. Reese said, "We're trying."

"Try harder," Coach shouted.

During practice, though, the same stuff happened. I tripped all over the line and couldn't go anywhere.

"Goddamn it all!" Coach shouted.

After practice, Coach called me into his office. He handed me a DVD.

"Watch this tonight, Reinstein. It's Walter Payton, maybe the greatest running back ever. Watch how patient he is. Pay attention to his footwork. He's why I gave you number 34. I want you to be great."

After dinner, even though I'd sort of had my fill of football, I popped the DVD in and watched...and watched...and watched... and watched...and, quite startlingly, I seemed to figure something out. Walter Payton played for the Chicago Bears mostly in the 1980s when my dad was in Chicago. He had a big fro and wore a headband and seemed to smile a lot. The DVD was titled *Sweetness*, maybe because he smiled so much. He died for some reason in 1999. "Sweetness," 1954–1999. The DVD was mostly filled with high-lights of him running the ball. And, most important, this hit me really big: Walter Payton ran with a football like Aleah plays piano. He was totally under control when he got a handoff. He took small steps to go slow, even occasionally reached out and put his hand on his lineman's back to make sure he stayed behind his blocker. Sort of like Aleah when she played the simple birthday song for me, quiet and controlled. Then when the hole opened, the opportunity came, and, just like Aleah, he exploded forward. It was almost like he was falling, barely under control at all, and he was ferocious and unforgiving, and he crushed anybody who got in his way. There was no talking on the DVD, only bad music. I turned off the sound so it was completely silent. I'd watch a play in normal speed and then watch it in slow motion. It was so beautiful. Walter Payton running was so beautiful. Number 34. I couldn't take my eyes off him. It was like watching Aleah, and seriously, I figured something out.

The next day in practice, when Cody handed me the ball, I took short steps and ran low and slow. If I got close to my lineman, I'd slow way down and wait. If it was a toss, I'd barely run until I saw where my tackle (Reese) was. Then when a hole opened, the opportunity, I uncoiled and exploded through.

"Holy cats!" Coach yelled. "That's what I'm talking about!" He clapped his hands.

Reese looked much happier.

"Thanks, Rein Stone," he said in the huddle.

• • •

I told Aleah about Walter Payton that night.

"I know who he is," she said. "I'm from Chicago, you know."

"He played football like you play piano."

Aleah shouted to Ronald that I compared her piano playing to Walter Payton running.

"I love that kid!" Ronald yelled in the background.

On Wednesday, everything seemed slower. I remembered my blocking assignments. I ran my routes. I took small steps and then exploded. "We're getting there!" Coach yelled. We practiced against a scout defense that included a guy wearing a red jersey. He was supposed to be Jay Landry.

"This kid is a killer. You have to know where he is at all times, Cody. You got it?"

"Yeah, Coach," Cody said.

That killer thing made me a little nervous. But the scout team Jay Landry couldn't come close to me.

"Real Jay Landry is going to be a lot faster," Coach yelled.

On Thursday, we barely practiced. We just walked through plays so we wouldn't be tired for the game. I knew the plays. Then we watched video of St. Mary's Springs. Oh my God. Jay Landry wasn't the only killer.

At home, Grandma Berba made her lasagna.

"You need to carbo-load, Felton," she said.

"What's that mean?" I asked.

"I like Jerri's lasagna better," Andrew said, playing with a noodle.

"No offense to Jerri, but no way," I said.

"Eat," Grandma said, "You'll need your energy tomorrow!"

"I miss Jerri," Andrew moaned. Then as if they were psychically connected, the phone rang. We put it on speaker and ate and talked. Jerri climbed a big red rock that day using rock-climbing gear.

"I want to visit," Andrew moaned.

"Soon enough," Grandma said.

I felt sort of weird after Jerri's call. She wished me good luck for the game. It was weird she wouldn't be there, and it was hard to believe I'd be playing in an actual game against a really good team in 24 hours and that there would be people in the stands and that the other team would try to knock me down and break my legs. Weird. I was a little wound up.

I went out through the garage, pulled a lawn chair out into the driveway, and stared out down the drive and across the road. I breathed deep to relax. I could hear the drunk golfer dads whacking golf balls up on the course. I could hear a tractor driving in the distance. Someone squealed their tires around a corner (the Randles?). Just then a figure crested the hill on a bike. I stood up and took a couple of steps forward. The person coasted down to our drive and then turned and pedaled up toward the house.

"Holy…Gus! Gus! Hey!" I shouted.

Gus pulled up in front of me.

"Hello, my long lost friend. What up with you?"

His hair wad was gone. I could see his eyes.

"They made you cut the wad."

"Yeah, it drove Grandma psycho, man. So Mom made me cut it."

"That sucks!"

"You know, I kind of like being able to see."

He got off his bike and walked over to me. Then stopped, stood there, stunned, shaking his head.

"Jesus Christ, Felton. You're huge,"

"I know."

"What the…? You got huge!"

"I know. Weird, huh?"

"I mean, you're enormous!"

"I know."

"What the hell did you do?"

"Well." I took a deep breath. This was sort of hard to say to him. "I'm the starting tailback on the football team."

"Oh, man," Gus said. He plopped down on my lawn chair, covered his eyes with his hands. "I should never have left."

"Did your grandma die?"

"No. She's fine." He looked up at me, and we both laughed. I grabbed another lawn chair from the garage.

We sat out in the driveway until the sun went down. We had a good time. He told me about Caracas (no friends, no fun, bad food—he really liked it though). I told him about Jerri and Aleah and my dad. He was appropriately dumbstruck about Jerri (even though I wrote him—he didn't know I was serious).

He apologized.

"I'm dumb. I got jealous because of your Aleah email and then the jock stuff. If I'd known Jerri really was going crazy, I wouldn't have been such an ass. I think I wouldn't have been. Maybe I would've been. I'm an ass, Felton."

"You're an ass? No. I'm an ass."

"Yeah. No shit, Felton. That's true."

Then Gus said something sort of weird.

"I always knew your dad was huge. I remember him. You should have asked me."

"Asked you what?"

"If he looked like you."

"Did he?"

"I don't know. Probably," he laughed. "He was your dad after all. I guess I remember he was a lot bigger than my dad. Really big."

"He was big."

Gus wasn't exactly happy about all my new friends.

"They're not bad, man. Seriously."

"I'll deal," he said.

"You can always hang out with Peter Yang and the debaters."

"I guess I'll take my chances with the honkies."

Before he left, he promised to come to the game, even though he thought it was ridiculous. And I got some very good news out of him.

"Mom says I have to take my paper route back."

"You mean tomorrow?" I asked.

"Do I have a choice?"

"No, you don't." I stood and raised my hands over my head "I'm done! *I'm done!*" I'd been staring at my dad's crazy lover in a nursing home all summer. She'd been screaming at me all summer. "*I'm done!*" Then I thought about Aleah in her tiger-striped bike helmet and wished I could do the route with her forever.

"You done celebrating?" Gus asked.

"Yes."

"I'm out," he said and biked away.

I got even better news later in the evening. I called Aleah, and before she even said hello, she shouted, "Daddy and I are driving up to your game!"

"What?"

"We're leaving at noon! We're staying all weekend!"

I was totally dumbstruck, overcome like an emotional donkey.

"Tell Ronald thanks," I swallowed hard. "Really. Seriously, Aleah. Tell him thanks."

"I can't wait!" she shouted.

I'll be honest. I had a hard time going to bed. I'm jumpy. Have I said? And there was a game, and Gus was home, and Aleah would be here, and Jerri did rock climbing, and Andrew played piano again. I really couldn't sleep. But I couldn't run, you know? I had to conserve energy. I had a game to play. There was a killer! A killer!

On that team! Jay Landry, *killer!* I seriously couldn't sleep. Not at all. Then I thought about Jerri and just repeated, "Om shanti shanti shanti shanti."

I fell asleep and slept until beautiful noon this morning (I mean, yesterday morning).

CHAPTER 63:
LAST NIGHT'S GAME

It's 7:06 a.m., and I can smell Grandma's coffee. Andrew just got up. Now he's plinking the piano. Okay. Grandma will start cooking soon.

I spotted Aleah in the stands right away (she's still in town, and I didn't sleep all night—aahh!). She waved and jumped up and down. I waved back. I wanted to go up there, but you can't go into the stands before games. I asked Karpinski. "Are you kidding me, Rein Stone? No." I completely would have otherwise. I waved. Ronald waved too.

Bluffton High School plays games at the college stadium. It's pretty big. But as it got closer to the kickoff, the stands got totally packed, completely packed. Football is apparently a big deal in Bluffton. I had no clue. I'd never even been to a game before.

While we did pregame stuff, ran pass routes, stretched, ran a few plays, I made sure I spotted Grandma and Andrew too. They were sitting near the front. They waved and smiled. Andrew brought this little pendant thing from his room that says BEETHOVEN! on it. He waved that. He's gutsy. I also found Gus. He was with Peter Yang and the debaters in the student section. He spread his arms and nodded and smiled. He really looked better with the hair wad.

Poor guy. I pointed at Aleah, but I don't think Gus got the message. Then I thought, better concentrate. Warm up.

I breathed deep. The moon was up. Those big stadium lights were on. So bright. The field was so green too. The air smelled really good. It was Bluffton air, but different.

"Can you smell the food stand?" I asked Cody.

"You freak, Reinstein," he smiled. "I don't know."

As the St. Mary's Springs players ran out on the field, they said a bunch of jerky stuff, told us to get ready for an ass-whipping, etc. They were big for sure. Jay Landry, number 18, was easily my size. I watched him. He looked around, scanning our side of the field. He locked in on me. He wouldn't take his eyes off me. He pointed. "You ready for this, 34?" he shouted. 34? My number. Donkey adrenaline surged in my veins.

In the locker room before kickoff, Coach said, "Don't back down. They'll try to intimidate you. Don't back down." I had to jump up and down. "Don't back down."

We won the toss. We elected to receive. Cody, our captain, ran to the sideline after the toss, pissed off. "These guys think they're going to run over us."

"Run it back, Rein Stone. Let's show 'em right away," Karpinski said.

I was deep for the kickoff, but the ball went to the right to Jamie Dern. He caught it, ran five yards, and was totally creamed. Their guys piled on. Jay Landry pointed at me. "You're next," he said. Squirrel nut donkey adrenaline.

We huddled up. Cody ran from the sideline with the play. "Toss left, Reinstein."

We jogged into formation. Cody began calling the signal. From across the line, Jay Landry pointed at me. "Watch toss to 34," he shouted. "Watch toss to 34."

Cody took the snap. I stepped left. Cody swiveled and tossed me the ball underhanded. I caught it and tucked it under my left arm. I took small steps, under control. The defensive end reached for me, but I bent around him. Karpinski fought the cornerback. I slid by. I looked for my tackle. I looked for Reese. I found Reese. He cracked the linebacker. The sea of green opened. I exploded with all my donkey speed. Jay Landry accelerated toward me. One stride. Two strides. Jay Landry dove at air. I was gone.

I'd like to say I thought of Jerri on a mountain or Andrew in the stands with Grandma or Aleah pounding on piano keys or my force of nature dad pounding a tennis ball, but there was no thought, just this field in slow motion, teammates and fans like the blurry grass waving in the main road ditch as I ride my Schwinn Varsity faster and faster in silence except for the wind whistling, down the hill so fast, down the field so fast, that I'm surprised to find the end so soon.

I slow, stop, all is silence. I look into the stands, and it all explodes like Chinese New Year.

Listen. I'm stupid fast. Seriously.

ACKNOWLEDGMENTS

As always, I am in debt to a big wad of people and places. First, thanks to Jim McCarthy, my agent, for caring about good books. Thanks to Dan Ehrenhaft for caring about this book. Thanks to the effervescent Leah Hultenschmidt for her excellent shepherding. That goes for the whole Sourcebooks crew too. (Thank you!) My mom, Donna, actually copyedited the manuscript before I turned it in (apparently copyeditors don't like ellipses as much as I do…still, thanks, Mom—I love you). A big thanks to Platteville High School in the great state of Wisconsin. I can't believe the opportunities this school afforded me: sports, music, theater, serious academics. Thanks to my whole hometown, Platteville, come to think of it. Thanks to the fantastic English Department at Minnesota State, Mankato. Thanks to the Class of 2k11. Thanks to Dustin Luke Nelson for encouragement and support. Thanks to my pal Sam Osterhout for writing so funny he makes me want to write. To Stephanie Wilbur Ash, whoa, so, so, so much for a thousand things. Finally, to my dad, Max Herbach, for warmth, for enthusiasm, for curiosity, for action, and for the fantastic sense of the absurd that ripples through my sense of humor. Thank you. I love you.

ABOUT THE AUTHOR

Geoff Herbach writes novels, hosts funny and sad radio shows, collaborates on indie rock musicals that may or may not be produced, and teaches in the creative writing program at Minnesota State University, Mankato. He is the father of two great kids, Leo and Mira. He is partnered to a very tall girl from Iowa named Steph. He loves big cities but feels most comfortable on dark quiet streets in the rural Midwest. He grew up in Platteville, Wisconsin, where he was both a dork and a jock.